double dare

Double Dare

saskia walker

heat | new york

THE BERKLEY PUBLISHING GROUP
Published by the Penguin Group
Penguin Group (USA) Inc.
375 Hudson Street, New York, New York 10014, USA
Penguin Group (Canada), 90 Eglinton Avenue East, Suite 700, Toronto, Ontario M4P 2Y3, Canada
(a division of Pearson Penguin Canada Inc.)
Penguin Books Ltd., 80 Strand, London WC2R 0RL, England
Penguin Group Ireland, 25 St. Stephen's Green, Dublin 2, Ireland (a division of Penguin Books Ltd.)
Penguin Group (Australia), 250 Camberwell Road, Camberwell, Victoria 3124, Australia
(a division of Pearson Australia Group Pty. Ltd.)
Penguin Books India Pvt. Ltd., 11 Community Centre, Panchsheel Park, New Delhi—110 017, India
Penguin Group (NZ), Cnr. Airborne and Rosedale Roads, Albany, Auckland 1310, New Zealand
(a division of Pearson New Zealand Ltd.)
Penguin Books (South Africa) (Pty.) Ltd., 24 Sturdee Avenue, Rosebank, Johannesburg 2196,
South Africa

Penguin Books Ltd., Registered Offices: 80 Strand, London, WC2R 0RL, England

This is an original publication of The Berkley Publishing Group.

This is a work of fiction. Names, characters, places, and incidents either are the product of the author's imagination or are used fictitiously, and any resemblance to actual persons, living or dead, business establishments, events, or locales is entirely coincidental. The publisher does not have any control over and does not assume any responsibility for author or third-party websites or their content.

Library of Congress Cataloging-in-Publication Data

Walker, Saskia.
   Double dare / Saskia Walker.—1st ed.
       p. cm.
   ISBN 0-425-21297-1
   1. Investment advisors—Fiction.   2. Nightclubs—Fiction.   3. Businesspeople—Fiction.
I. Title.
   PS3623.A35956D68   2006
   813'.6—dc22

                                                                        2006015921

PRINTED IN THE UNITED STATES OF AMERICA

10   9   8   7   6   5   4   3   2   1

For Barbara,

who taught me so much,

and for my real life hero,

Mark,

who dared me to live my dream

and is right there with me every step of the way.

one | ɘno

"Coming through, hold the doors." Abigail Douglas clutched her take-out lunch packages to her chest and made a dash for the elevator.

An arm shot out, one strong hand halting the movement of the stainless steel doors. She ducked under it, noting as she did the rolled-up white linen shirtsleeve and the muscular male forearm.

She quickly counted three occupants: a couple, and the man who'd halted the doors for her. "Thanks," she breathed, turning on her heel quickly as the heavy doors shut behind her.

Bright blue eyes met hers, a wolfish smile. "Anytime."

She looked him over, and her body switched all systems to red alert. She'd already been on amber alert—it was a sweltering August day, and heat did bad things to her. Men weren't safe from her scrutiny. Especially gorgeous ones with wolfish smiles. Tall and lean, with black hair and startling azure eyes, he was incredibly handsome. A document dispatch package rested easily in one of his hands.

As the elevator moved, she picked a napkin out of the lunch bags and fluttered it in her hand in a futile attempt to stir the air.

Reflected in the shiny surface of the doors, she could make out the couple at her side, wobbly but distinct. A suited man, flirting with a bubbly blonde. He was running his fingers over her back while whispering in her ear. The blonde giggled in response and shuffled on her kitten heels, pinning him up against the wall of the elevator.

Abby glanced at the guy by the door. He caught her eye. He was half smiling to himself.

She looked away, then back.

He didn't falter under her stare but nodded toward the couple to her right.

The blonde was leaning in against her man, nuzzling his ear with her mouth. He was gone on it, his face contorted with pleasure. His hands clutched at her bottom, riding her dress up. He had a handful of it in his greedy paws as he fondled her behind. As a result, the tops of her lacy stockings were on display, her buttocks peeping out below the hemline, too.

Abby stifled a laugh, then looked back at the wolf smile on the guy's face. His eyes were narrowed while he watched her watching them. Curiosity stirred inside her, and arousal. They shared the silent joke. He'd made an intimate connection with her. More than that, there was a contained sexuality about him that aroused a deep response. A pulse charged through her body and began a slow throbbing between her thighs. It was a direct response, a need: she wanted him.

She barely registered the ping of the elevator doors. It was her floor. She gathered herself, shoving the napkin back in the bag.

He rose up to his full height and nodded as she passed.

What a hunk. Dangerous looking, too. Wouldn't some sexy leisure time with him be something? She shook her head as she walked across the plushly carpeted landing and through the heavy glass door of the Robertson Corporation offices.

As she waited to hear the familiar sound of the door whooshing shut behind her, the hairs on the back of her neck rose, awareness darting over her body. She turned around just in time to see the doors close behind another body. The guy from the elevator was standing directly behind her.

Up close, he was devastating. She was tall, but he was taller still. Those startling bright blue eyes of his contrasted with his darker looks, long black hair tied back, and lashes to die for. His nose was a little overlong, not entirely straight, and his lips were firm, passionate. Hooded eyes measured her reaction, his brow drawn down as he looked at her—an urban predator, his presence sending all of her senses into overdrive as he stalked in her wake.

He's a man, and you're horny. Get over it. She took a deep breath and gave him a professional smile. "Can I help?"

"Documents for Tom Robertson." He gestured with the package in his hand.

"Right, of course, come in." Glancing over at the front desk she saw that Suzanne, the receptionist, was busy on the phone. She stepped behind the desk, set down the lunch bags, and put out her hand.

He passed her the package.

She noticed his poise. Even dressed casually in faded jeans and a soft, white linen shirt, he made an impact. The shirt fell open around his neck, revealing the elegant line of his lean throat and collarbone, the taut muscle of his upper chest. His hair was knotted at his nape. She wondered what it would look like loose.

"You'll need a signature," she managed.

His eyes lit. "Yes. Indeed." He felt around in his back pocket and pulled out a piece of paper, glancing at it.

She scrabbled on the desk for a pen. Suzanne put one in her hand without breaking her conversation. Glancing down at her, Abby could see Suzanne watched with amusement.

He put the piece of paper on the desk, pointing. "Just sign over that one: the last client signed in the wrong place." His voice had a deep, resonant timbre, as if he were suggesting an illicit rendezvous rather than asking for a signature. It ran over her body like silk over naked skin, making her prickle with awareness. She could collect packages from him all day long.

She signed and passed it back.

"Anything I can help you two with?" Suzanne turned to give them her full attention, her call over.

"Thanks, Suz, we're fine." She smiled apologetically at the guy. "She's training me in."

Suzanne chuckled at the comment but didn't contradict it. "Got anything else for us, or is that it?"

"That's it, no . . . wait." He dipped his hand into his back pocket again.

Abby watched, suddenly aware of her fingers and how they might feel dipping into that pocket for him.

He put a couple of business cards down on the desk, black, with a silver hologram image of an eye. "New venue, over in Camden. I recommend it."

Abby picked up one of the cards, passing the other to Suzanne. She felt as if she'd been given a calling card by a magician. When she moved it, the hologram eye winked.

THE HUB : THEATER : GALLERY : MUSIC : HAPPENINGS

Location details, contacts, and Web addresses were scrolled beneath.

Suzanne grinned and popped the card into the pocket on her shirt. "Thanks, personal recommendations for party time are always welcome."

The courier saluted, pocketed his receipt, and with one last glance at Abby sauntered out onto the landing. After he hit the elevator call button he stood to one side, where he glanced back at them from under those hooded eyes of his.

Sex on a stick.

Abby pulled herself together and gestured at Suzanne, pointing at her lunch bag, trying to regain some semblance of normality.

"Thanks," Suzanne mumbled, reaching into the bag for the food, not moving her eyes from the view.

"No problem," Abby replied, also unable to force her gaze away.

"Now I know why you're always smiling, Suz," she whispered. "Being out here on reception duty is so entertaining."

Suzanne shook her head. "They're not all like him, believe me."

"Shame."

The elevator doors opened. He saluted them one last time before stepping inside.

"He was interested in you."

Abby smiled. "You think?"

"Absolutely."

"I wouldn't turn down the chance to check him out." She watched as the doors slid shut and the numbers on the overhead panel began to descend. "But guys like that always do a runner when they find out what I do for a living. Most men can't cope with a woman who's an investment advisor, unless they're already in the high finance business themselves."

"I can see how that might happen." Suzanne nodded, ruffling her curly hair in her hands. It immediately fell back into place.

Abby smiled. If she'd done that, her hair would be a tangled mess, and she'd look like the Wicked Witch of the West.

"Is that why you let him think you were a receptionist?" Suzanne added.

Abby shrugged. "It just kind of happened, but I have been known to tell the odd white lie when I'm on the prowl."

Suzanne glanced up as she unwrapped her stuffed ciabatta. "You know, I think that shows a human side."

Abby quirked a brow. "Why?"

"You don't get caught up in the image of all this like the rest of them." Suzanne gestured around the plush offices. "You're the only one who offers to get me some lunch when you go for yours. Did you know that?"

Abby shook her head. It hadn't even occurred to her. "It's easy to get caught up in it. Working in finance at this level can become all-consuming. I love the buzz, but I don't want it to be the be-all, you know." She winked and looked back at the shiny elevator doors. "I wonder if he rides a motorcycle."

Suzanne's eyes rounded. "You mean does he have a big, throbbing engine between his legs?"

"Oh please." Abby shut her eyes for a moment, savoring the image that leapt to mind. She laughed and snatched up her lunch bag. "You are so bad."

Suzanne grinned as Abby set off down the corridor, gesticulating with the stuffed ciabatta, her bubbly blonde hair bouncing. "He wanted you; he'll be thinking about you while he's riding his big, throbbing engine."

Abby couldn't help laughing.

Inside her office she propped the calling card against her monitor. Opening her take-out bag, she set her lunch down on her desk, then stepped behind it and looked out the window. The view never failed to inspire her—the beautiful facade of the City of London: pristine glass towers that cloaked the interior mechanisms of power and wealth, toil, and corruption. A tremor of excitement passed over her, part business, and part pleasure.

She sat down and glanced at the array of computer screens lined up on her desk, stabbing her fork at her pasta salad. The words and figures flitted across the screen, unseen. She was as restless and alert as a prowling lioness during the mating season. The August heat always hit her this way, and either some action or a cold shower was in order.

She picked up her coffee and blew across the swirling black liquid. It made her think about black satin sheets being rumpled across a bed. She smiled. She saw sex everywhere, but that was no revelation. It was everywhere, and besides she did think about it a lot; she wasn't about to deny that. Especially right then. She wanted to know what Wolf Smile looked like with his hair loose, preferably trailing over her naked body while they had hot, dirty sex.

She pushed the lunch debris away and crossed her legs high on the thigh—an attempt to crush the insistent pulse point that was pounding there, which didn't help—returning her attention to her work. She checked the latest FTSE index feed and the BBC twenty-four-hour news channel. That was her anchor, even more so than the FTSE. Her tactic was to watch the news as closely as the FTSE index. Share prices were led by world events. She made many a quick maneuver, salvaging potential losses and earning quick, successive gains, on the basis of world events. As she scanned updating news, an instant message popped up on her laptop. It was from her teammate, Ed.

ED: e-mail from Tom. What do you think?

Abby scanned her mail and saw the message. It announced an urgent team meeting the next morning to discuss project control. In the investment broker business imminent change was regular, expected, and greeted with enthusiasm. They worked in a fast-paced environment, one that looked for winners to back and took no passengers for the ride to the prize.

AB: And?
ED: Rumor is I'm going over to the Pascal account.
AB: You'd like that.

If he was right about the change, it was something Ed had been working toward. A big, meaty project, international. He and Abby had been functioning as a team for the past few months, taking up new projects, start-ups, and the management of established portfolios.

ED: You are the obvious person to take over the Ashburn portfolio.

She nodded as she contemplated the thought. If he were right, it would be a good chance for her to flex her business muscles.

AB: We'll find out tomorrow. Meanwhile, can you help me out with something personal? In here . . .
ED: something . . . personal, as in something . . . physical?

Abby smiled. Ed was so reliable.

AB: Why don't you get in here and find out?

"One, two, three," she pushed her chair back, "four, five, six . . ."

The door sprang open. She stood up, glancing over at his shoulders as he strode toward her. Ed was built; he'd rowed for his team at college. She often imagined herself the cox, shouting orders to them while watching their strong, supple bodies heaving over the oars.

He shook his head at her. "It's a miracle Tom Robertson's making any bloody money with you on site." He was as keen as a drawn bow.

She looked up at his brown eyes and neatly cropped hair. Smart. Sophisticated. Stud. She leaned over her desk and pressed the button that illuminated the In Conference sign outside the office, the sign that indicated international videoconferencing was taking place.

"Distracting a male member of the team. Misuse of office equipment."

She lifted one eyebrow. "Are you keeping a list of my bad behavior?"

"You never know. I might need to blackmail you one day."

She gave a breathy laugh and beckoned him closer with one finger, her other hand slowly unbuttoning her electric-blue shirt. Two buttons later he was helping to ease her breasts up from her bra, squeezing her nipples out over the edge of the sheer, silver gauze.

"Oh, Abby." His breathing was already speeding. There was nothing like exposing a bit of nipple to get Ed going. She glanced down. A bulge was showing in his finely cut Armani pants. He was easily provoked—the proverbial city-boy stud—pure testosterone, be it in the office, on the rugby pitch, or between the sheets.

"Whatever is the matter?" she quizzed, tweaking her exposed nipples between her thumb and fingers.

He groaned and began to lick her nipples reverently, moving from one breast to the other as he held them firmly in his hands, massaging them deeply at the same time.

A flame ran the length of her, from clit to throat, melting everywhere in between. He knew how to handle breasts; that was for sure. She bit her lip and wondered vaguely if anyone could see them from the many windows opposite hers—her breasts on display, the man avidly sucking at them. The idea of someone watching excited her immensely; she couldn't deny it. She thought about the couple in the elevator, the shared sexy joke with the courier.

She pulled at Ed's head; she was more than ready.

He didn't need any further encouragement. His hands yanked her close-fitting, short black skirt up around her hips as he moved her back toward her swivel chair.

"Ed . . . remember, I don't have long." She used her most controlled tone, trying not to chuckle, knowing the suggestion of time limitation would send him into overdrive. She gasped when he put his thumbs over the edge of her G-string and pushed it down. Her bare buttocks met the chair. He stripped the G-string down the length of her legs.

Kneeling, he opened her legs and bent to taste her pussy, sending wild spasms through her overaroused clit.

"Oh God, you are so wet," he muttered.

She heard his zipper. He ripped a condom open with his teeth, holding the thick, hard shaft of his cock in his hand while he rolled it on. She smiled down in approval, an eyebrow raised in appreciation. She lifted one leg, draping it over his shoulder, stacked heel and all.

He teased her hot, moist hole with the swollen head of his cock, edging a little farther, until he finally lunged deep inside her.

Her hands gripped the arms of the chair, taking it, taking it all. She groaned with pleasure, her head thrown back by the force. Boy, did she need this. His thrusts became deep, regular. She ground her hips against his to pull him in to the hilt.

He rested his large hands behind her hips, pulling her uptilted hips to the very edge of the chair, wedging his cock deep. His expression was strained from effort, his neck corded with tense muscle.

She latched one hand over her clit, anchoring the riotous feelings there, crushing it hard inside her hand. That did it. Her advancing climax took over. Her whole body arched, levering the contractions at her core. Ed swore softly, his hips jerking in release as if he'd had trouble holding on for her. She closed her eyes, her breathing erratic, her body swamped.

She felt his hand on her breast and opened her eyes. There was amusement in his expression. She'd been so absorbed she'd almost been unaware of his climax.

"You're the horniest woman I've ever met, Abby Douglas." He pushed stray hairs back from her face and then disengaged, lowering her feet safely to the floor.

She stood, pulling on her G-string, straightening her skirt, and buttoning up her shirt.

He watched her as he redid his tie. "You know, Abby, I'd give up all the other women I'm shagging, just for you."

She smiled at his remark. He was baiting her. "No need. We agreed. We have sex because we want to. You said it yourself." She stroked his cheek fondly before ushering him to the door. It was familiar territory. He'd told her that if she ever wanted a good shag, he was there for her. He called himself her willing "fuck-buddy," but he occasionally asked for more, all the same.

As she returned to her current market report, a doubt niggled at her. Some women would kill to get a man like Ed suggesting a proper relationship, but she loved him as a friend, no more. Was she too demanding of life—a life that was already full? She hoped not, she tried not to be, but she often doubted herself at moments like this. She had so much: a fabulous career in London, her own home, friends, and lovers. It was a good life, but she craved something else. Mystery, something wild and dangerous. Something that challenged her in a different way. She'd give it all up—career, money, the lot— for that: a walk on the wild side.

She reached over to where she'd perched the business card from the courier. The hologram winked, like an eye watching her, beckoning. At the back of her mind a little voice began to chant.

I dare you, Abby. I dare you.

Zachary Bordino eased his Mercedes SLR down a gear and took the next exit off the London circular. He'd passed into Surrey, where the commuter belt merged with the countryside. It was green and calm, the August heat mellowing out in the more tranquil setting. The city had been uncomfortably hot, the pavement sizzling.

Sizzling.

The word ran back and forth through his thoughts, returning him to the image of the sexy redhead he'd had the lucky chance to encounter earlier that day at the Robertson Corporation. The way her eyes had sidled over to him as she walked into the elevator had brought out all his hunting instincts. She was intriguing. He'd sensed a wild streak in her, just beneath the surface, and it caught his interest immediately. She was attractive, too, in an unusual, bohemian way. Pale skin and amber eyes, hair that needed to be tamed. Her body was curvy but lithe, blatantly sexy in the way she walked and moved. She'd taken the business card for The Hub. He wondered if she'd find her way over.

Who'd have guessed the chore would turn out to be so interesting? At first he'd been perplexed when his mother requested he deliver papers on her behalf, but he soon forgot that, thanks to the receptionist he'd had the pleasure to deliver them to. Her direct gaze had been filled with blatant appraisal, as if she was scoring him on his potential sexual performance when she looked him over, and that alone made his blood roar. She was one hot woman.

He pulled the car onto the gravel driveway of his parents' home and took off his shades, dropping them on the passenger seat as he climbed out of the car. Instead of going to the front door, he walked farther down the driveway. Reaching over the fence, he unlatched the gate and stepped inside, catching sight of his mother on the patio as he did so.

She was carrying a tray of refreshments over to a table in the shady corner of the patio, beneath the trellis laden with trailing honeysuckle and bougainvillea plants. Hearing the dogs' friendly barking, she squinted over and lifted her glasses in one hand, peering through them without actually putting them on.

"Vain as ever," he murmured to himself as he returned her wave. Strolling over, the hounds at his heels, he put his hands out to embrace her.

She hugged him, petite and fair against him, although they shared the same blue eyes and inquisitive minds.

"Mother, you look more beautiful than ever." He rested a kiss on her forehead.

She dismissed his remark with a wave of her hand but beamed, nevertheless. Smoothing down her perfectly smooth, silver-gray bob, she gestured at the seat next to her own.

"You're the perfect English gentlemen, despite the dash of Greek blood you have inherited from Dimitri."

"Just a dash?" He gave her a quizzical glance as he took his seat. "You're after something. When you don't need me, you tell me I'm his offspring." He already knew she was after something when he'd had to play courier on her behalf.

"Nonsense, I wanted to see you. Boredom is making me crazy. This early retirement business can drive a person mad."

He tutted, reached over, and held her by one slim shoulder as he looked her over. "The rest is doing you good. You look stronger than you have in a long while."

She shrugged from his grasp, drawing his attention to the refreshments. Zac eyed her watchfully. She hated to admit she wasn't as strong as she used to be, but he was relieved to see her with more color in her cheeks than she'd had this past year. She'd been a fit woman all her life, until the previous year, when she'd had a mild stroke and her lifestyle had come under severe scrutiny.

"Did you manage to deliver that little package for me?"

"I did. And I hope you have a good reason for sending me with documents the courier could have taken directly himself."

"What did you think of the place?" She sipped her drink, feigning nonchalance.

"The Robertson Corporation?"

"Yes."

"They have a very attractive receptionist."

"Zachary!"

He rested back in his chair and chuckled. "I assume it's the company you've hired to oversee the Ashburn investments?"

She nodded.

"I checked them out online before I went over. They have an impeccable reputation. I'm sure you knew that when you hired them. Just relax."

"I'd be able to relax if you helped me with my work." The way she spoke about the company as if she was still at the helm was such a giveaway.

Zac sipped his drink, making her wait. "I'm well aware that you plan to carry on by hook, crook, or subterfuge." He smiled at her benevolently.

Adrianna let out a dismissive grunt and then rested her perfectly manicured hands together in a contemplative pose. "You are more observant than your father, I'll give you that."

"And less easy to influence?"

"Yes." She rolled her eyes. "I suppose it's an admirable quality, even if does make my life more difficult." She shuffled forward in her chair. "Zachary, darling, I realize I made a mistake not encouraging you to get involved in the family business earlier, but I thought your father was right, and you should establish your own interests first."

"And I agreed with that."

She nodded impatiently. "You've created a little niche of your own in the property business now, but it takes up more time than it should."

"Time you could use elsewhere, I suppose?"

"Why you have to get so involved with each and every aspect of it is beyond me. Why can't you maintain some distance?"

Zac chuckled. His mother portrayed herself as the ultimate business paragon. He'd learned from her example but had gone his own way. He liked to be out there in the thick of it. He also blamed his father, a Greek restaurateur who could never keep himself out of the kitchen, despite the fact he was supposed to be managing his chain of restaurants from a distance.

"I like to work that way; I enjoy seeing things grow and flourish." He lazed back in his chair, breathing the heady aroma of the flowers on the overhead trellis.

Adrianna pouted.

He shrugged, opening his hands in a sign of surrender. "You're going to have to come completely clean with me if you want my help."

She gave a regretful sigh. "I'm in trouble with your father." She looked at him sheepishly. "When I got the managers set up with the portfolio, I insisted the team leader send me a daily report, not just when they needed approvals. I wanted to monitor and approve their every move." She paused. "I had George write it into the contract . . . but only so that I could check what they were up to."

"Poor old George, I suppose you sweet-talked him into doing it?" George was the family solicitor and like putty in Adrianna's hands. He'd had a crush on her for nearly thirty years.

Adrianna carried on regardless, as if eager to get the confession over with. "Your father caught me going through the e-mails. He was furious. Threatened to leave. You know what he's like."

He thought they'd managed to convince her to outsource the development side of the Ashburn Foundation, her company. But apparently she hadn't let it go. She'd begged Zac to take over from the outset, but he'd recently got his own business onto steady ground, and the time wasn't right. Besides, she had to learn to trust others outside the family. It wasn't easy; God knows, he knew that himself. He'd had his fingers burned in the past. But these were professional money managers they were talking about. "It was only a matter of time until you were found out, naughty Adrianna."

"Please, Zac. I know you're busy with your . . . thing." She waved her hand. She'd never thought the art world was worthy of his attention. "They do have a good reputation, but I'm not happy with them. They've just announced a change in personnel. The man I've been in contact with is going elsewhere. What sort of impression is that supposed to give a soul? I'd much rather they were working closely with one of us, but your father won't let me." She gave him an imperious glance. "It is your inheritance, Zachary."

"Ah, so we're playing the inheritance card now, are we?"

She glared at him.

He adopted a more serious expression. "In another few months I can look at the entire situation again; right now my commitments wouldn't allow me to do it justice. In the meantime, do you want me to deal with these daily reports for you, keep an eye on the Robertson people?" Robertson people, attractive receptionist—now why did that sound so interesting?

Adrianna broke into a relieved smile, leaned forward, and rested her hand over his. "Would you, darling? I'd be so glad."

"If you promise to rest."

She didn't answer. Instead she rustled about under the table, pulling out a glossy, bound file. "You'll need this."

He fought back another laugh and took it from her hand. It was the dossier of the Robertson team, a standard business pack presented to clients.

"I've arranged an end-of-month meeting, they've got the contract till then."

"That's not very long."

"I wanted a get-out if I didn't like them."

"Or you decided to take over again," he murmured. She was incorrigible. He leafed through the folder while sipping on his iced tea. Stats and recommendations lined up against publicity shots. It all looked pretty solid, but one could never tell. He was about to snap the file shut when something caught his eye. Red hair.

Adrianna was still verbalizing her concerns in the background, but her voice faded away. He flipped the pages back. There she was, the receptionist. His blood heated immediately.

He scrutinized the group shot. She was dressed impeccably and standing between the head of the organization and another suited man. He scanned the names. *Abigail Douglas, investment advisor.* He did a double take.

What do you know? He flicked through the résumés at the back of the file. According to the suggested Ashburn team list, she was heavily involved in running his mother's affairs. *How amusing.* "Well, well." He glanced up.

"What is it, have you found something already?"

"Don't get carried away with your wishful thinking." He closed the file. "Trust me. I'll do all that I can to watch over your interests."

"And you won't tell your father?"

"I won't tell," he assured her, smiling. He was happy to take it on. Especially if it meant he had access to the lovely Abigail Douglas.

two | owt

Abby closed the boardroom door behind her and joined the meeting. Tom Robertson, the executive director, watched as the team arranged themselves. It was a fairly small, select group that had been summoned for the project control meeting, and they gathered at one end of the large, polished mahogany table.

Aside from herself and Ed, Penny Conroy had been asked to attend. Penny had been working as an assistant to Abby and Ed for the past eighteen months. She sat poised at the edge of her seat, her ash-blonde hair scraped back into a tight swirl, speared at the nape of her neck with a carved wooden creation akin to a spear. She had strange gray eyes and looked as if she never needed to rest.

Caroline Bradshaw, the legal representative of their company, was also present. She was the one who kept them all on their metaphoric toes. Quiet and observant, her personal characteristics reflected her role as shadow to the team's work.

"Thank you for gathering so promptly," Tom began, rising to his feet and pacing, as was his way. "I want to discuss some reorganization of project control, with changes taking effect immediately. If anyone has any problems with my suggestions, please voice them." He was, as ever, leading the group but giving an appearance of shared control and responsibility.

"I'd like to begin by stating that I don't normally advise shifting project control about like this, and you may be wondering why I am taking this route now." A murmur of acknowledgment ran round the assembled group. "The situation is, I've been asked to personally manage a prestige account, so the asset management of the Pascal portfolio is going to have to leave my hands. This has an inevitable knock-on effect on the team workload, but I've already informed all the affected clients, so we can move forward."

"Pascal has been a complicated client portfolio because they wanted analysis of previous investments as well as onward management. I'm only midway with the analysis, so that's the first priority." He rested his hands on the table and looked round at them. "It's a two-person job, so you're all going to be affected."

As the meeting rolled on, it turned out to be just as Ed had suggested. Tom was handing over to Ed, who would lead the team for Pascal. Penny would also go over to the project full-time. Abby wondered how Ed had found out so much beforehand, and then she noticed that Penny anticipated every word from Tom's mouth with a self-satisfied gleam in her eye. Abby began to wonder what the purpose of the meeting was, if everybody already knew what was going to be said. Where was the fun and the mystery in that? She smiled inwardly, amused at her own background thoughts. It was one of the reasons why she didn't socialize with her colleagues as much as she used to—they all took themselves far too seriously.

Tom turned to Abby. "And briefly, in conclusion, the matter of the Ashburn portfolio. That I am going to place in your hands, Abigail. I am confident that you'll be able to continue with that project and see it through to a long renewal." He smiled graciously, his sharp eyes affectionate, as if he knew she'd be pleased about it.

Abby felt the rush of adrenaline that came from a welcome challenge. It was indeed a good opportunity. "I'll be glad to take it on, Tom," she replied, and her smile was genuine. Next to the thrill of an orgasm, this was the sort of thrill she enjoyed most of all.

"I'm sure the new arrangements will benefit the clients involved and exhibit our dedication to success. We always have 'the best interests of the customer's account at heart.'" He smiled while he quoted the company motto.

When the meeting dispersed, Tom targeted Abby and took her to one side. "Are you happy with the additional responsibility?" He had a quality about him that was both charming and disarming, a skill that had undoubtedly established him in life. His presentation was immaculate. He never had a silvering hair out of place.

She gave him a confident nod. "I'm sure things will go smoothly; the project has less than three weeks until the contract renewal date."

Tom nodded but remained thoughtful. "Adrianna Ashburn is a formidable lady."

Abby smiled. "So I understand."

Tom returned the smile, but briefly. "She's also rather eccentric and liable to move her account after the trial period."

Ed had hinted as much, but Abby hadn't realized Tom was anxious about it.

"It's her baby, and handing it over clearly hasn't been easy." He paused for emphasis. "I'd really like to secure this portfolio for permanent management by our team."

Abby nodded. He was concerned that she'd thought she was

getting the easy part of the bargain, and he was telling her privately that she hadn't; far from it. She knew that. "If I keep the turnover levels up and complete new developments to the client's satisfaction during that time—and I am sure I can—then there shouldn't be anything to worry about."

She was aware that Tom considered her a bit of a law unto herself. She didn't exactly play by the rules when it came to business, but her track record had proven her a risk worth taking. She was also aware of his watchful eye over her work. To be left alone in charge of such a major account was quite a step forward and no small acknowledgment of her ability.

"I don't doubt you can, Abby. But if you need any help, don't hesitate to come to me. At any time." He gave her a lingering look edged with sexual references.

Abby was surprised. She'd heard about his many affairs but hadn't previously felt his attention focusing on her. It was flattering, but Abby didn't reciprocate his interest. In their high-flying corporate world it was far too easy to have sex for all the wrong reasons, and if she thought on it too long, she knew she was already doing that with Ed.

She thanked him for his confidence in her, then looked over his shoulder and saw that Ed and Penny were engrossed in conversation as they left the room. Caroline had already gone.

"I should grab Ed's files and get on with the job." She nodded at Tom, picked up her notes, and left.

In the ladies' restroom she peered at her reflection analytically. She didn't look like a high-flying investment manager, never had. Her mop of red hair didn't help. Different light brought out different shades of color. In here it was a patchwork of reds and browns.

The door opened behind her. "Hi, Abby." Caroline's oval reflection appeared next to her own in the mirror. "Grabbing a minute to yourself?"

"Yes, before the onslaught." Abby glanced down into her bag to find her comb.

"It's going to be tough, but you'll be fine. Call on me if you need any support." She patted Abby's arm.

"Sure thing."

"Still on for the gym next week?"

Abby raked the comb through her hair. "Absolutely, at least their air-conditioning works."

Caroline chuckled. "You're right, and it's just as well." She plucked the top off her lip liner. "I expect you'll be glad you don't have to work with Penny anymore." The words popped from her mouth as if they could no longer be retained, despite the fact she was assaulting herself with the lip liner at the time.

Abby looked up, surprised. She usually avoided office allegiances and gossip as far as possible, but Caroline's comment triggered her curiosity.

"Penny's a very good assistant. I always felt I could rely on her." She watched Caroline's face in the mirror. "I'll be sorry to lose her contribution to the team, but she'll be valued on the Pascal account, I'm sure."

Caroline gave a sad, knowing smile. "She wanted your job, you know. It won't be long until she's after Ed's . . . she's always had an eye for the main chance."

"Ah, well, ambition is a quality both valued and scorned. It all depends how you go about these things." Abby winked.

"You're so right." Caroline paused. "But watch out for her, and don't let misplaced trust be your downfall."

Caroline's words followed Abby as she returned to her office. *Misplaced trust?*

They were indeed a driven, ambitious lot, and that showed itself in many colors, good and bad. She'd always tried to maintain a life outside of work, to keep her feet on the ground. To keep her balance.

A life outside of this.

She slid open her drawer and lifted the card the wolf-smile man had given her. She'd wanted him as soon as she'd seen him. She wondered what his name was. Aside from hanging out by reception hoping he'd call by again, there was only one thing to do: hunt him down. And he'd left her bait. She was going to take it. But first, some research.

She picked up the phone and tapped in the number for her friend, Marcy, who also happened to be up on what went on in London at any given moment.

The answering machine clicked on after two rings. "I'm either out enjoying myself, asleep, or in the bathroom. Please leave your message now." Marcy's indolent tone rang out.

Abby started leaving a message and was interrupted by a lazy hello and a long yawn. "Sorry, honey, didn't make it out of bed in time. Heavy night. How you doing?"

"Doing good, but I'm straining at the leash. How about you?"

"That's what I like to hear. Can't have you getting all stuffy in that high-tech business world of yours."

"Not going to happen, and you know it. Listen, I was wondering if you'd heard anything about a new alternative arts venue on the north side. It's called The Hub."

Abby could make out the sound of coffee being poured at the other end of the line.

"Doesn't ring any bells with me."

"And there was me thinking with your connections . . ."

"Ha. Would you be referring to my connections as a photographer and media pundit, or my *other* connections?"

Abby spun her chair to look out the window. "Don't be coy, Marcy. It doesn't suit you."

"You're right there. So you're getting used to the idea that I walk on the dark side?"

"What a sense of humor. It took a little time, but yes. It's not every day your best friend of fifteen years announces she's bisexual."

"At least you didn't assume I was gonna pounce in your undies." Marcy's tone was rueful. Some of her friends hadn't been so understanding.

"I'm heartbroken that you didn't try, Marcy."

"Don't tease. If I thought you were interested in women that way, I could show you plenty of ways to loosen up after all that *brokerage*." She stressed the word. Marcy hated anything to do with figures, claimed it gave her a headache.

"I bet you could." Abby chuckled. Somehow teasing each other about Marcy's recent revelation had made it OK. Odd, but true.

A yawn echoed down the phone. "What did you say this place is called?"

"The Hub, Camden Town."

"Actually . . . I think it might be the venue where The Candy Shock Tarts are performing."

"Shock Tarts?" Abby's eyebrows lifted.

"They're a small theater troupe from Denmark; they specialize in spoofing musicals. Apparently they named themselves after some candy that explodes in your mouth and melts on your tongue." Marcy moaned with mock pleasure.

"OK, OK." Abby chuckled. "I get the picture."

"Why the sudden interest?" Marcy was waking up.

"I saw something that caught my eye." *Or someone*. She turned the business card in her fingers, watching the hologram wink at her.

"Shall I try to get tickets for the show? I think they're doing *Cabaret* this go round; it's on Saturday."

"If you can, I'll love you forever."

"Leave it to me."

When she put the phone down, Abby stood up and strolled down the corridor to Suzanne's desk. "Are you free on Saturday? I might be going over to that venue, you know, the one the courier recommended?"

Suzanne looked at her, impressed. "Go, Abby!"

"If we get tickets, can you come?"

"I'd love to, but I'm babysitting." She shot out a hand to grab Abby's. "I want to hear all about it though." She winked.

Abby rolled her eyes. "He might not even be there, but if he is, I'll tell all."

It was hard work with long hours, but by Friday Abby had a confident overview of the aspects of the Ashburn portfolio that were previously handled by Ed. She wanted to develop the property investments he'd been handling and perhaps action something unique to mark her period in charge. If she wanted to make a significant difference to the account—and that was her personal and professional goal—time was limited, because the contract renewal date was looming on the calendar.

She also had to push up the short-term stock turnover, enlarging her previous responsibility. She and Penny had done useful research on upcoming opportunities in the franchise market. Abby was determined to keep that side ticking over, alongside developing Ed's work.

She'd been with the Robertson Corporation for three years. Her experience had been varied, and she'd taken on a lot of responsibility, enough for her to consider going freelance. She'd made private investments that had been successful, and she certainly had the initiative to put her profits to good use. If the Ashburn portfolio did well, she would take it as the sign to go it alone.

The low pulse tone of the phone interrupted her thought trail. It was Ed, calling from Heathrow.

"I'm catching the eleven o'clock flight to Geneva to meet with Pascal. It's primarily to negotiate working parameters. I'll be back Sunday morning, early." He paused. "If you meet me at Heathrow . . . I'll buy you breakfast."

"OK, Ed. *Bien sur, au revoir.*"

He was still trying. He'd been trying for nearly a year now. Something about him made her fidget. He was more than efficient in the sex department, but when he got all cozy on her, she felt the urge to run naked through the streets—in the opposite direction. Actually, she mused, she felt the urge to run through the streets naked more each day. Perhaps it was the heat. Restless, she tapped her fingers against the desk.

She stopped tapping her fingers when she noticed an e-mail from Marcy that made her light up.

Success! It was no easy task, but I got us front row tix for the
Shock Tart show!

• • •

"'Delivering all the outrageous fun of a bawdy sex comedy, The Candy Shock Tarts manage to capture the pathos and ingenuity of the original, while bringing new life to this performance of *Cabaret*. An outstanding interpretation of one of the classic musicals of our time.'" Marcy read the quote aloud from the poster outside the venue, while they moved slowly past it in the queue. She had her camera slung over one shoulder, looking relaxed yet sophisticated in a black mandarin suit, her dark hair sleeked back in a topknot.

Abby nodded and looked at the glass entrance vestibule with interest. A doorman was taking tickets. She craned her neck, trying to get a closer look, but, alas, it wasn't Wolf Smile. He took their tickets and directed them to the corridor's end, where a buzz of voices emerged from double doors.

Is he in there? she wondered.

As they walked, she noticed a gallery to their immediate right, several sculptures showing in stark relief. What looked like a good-sized function room was on their left. Her eye for interesting property was curious and quietly impressed. The place had the feel of an old cinema—a conversion, perhaps.

The auditorium was packed, the atmosphere humming. A bar at the back of the space was five deep, tables closer to the stage full.

"We better hurry," Marcy urged. "The show's about to start. Our table is reserved." She winked.

Abby followed the direction she pointed out, to where one table was vacant.

"How did you get such a good spot?"

Marcy lifted the camera on her shoulder. "Press pass. It's an event. I immortalize events." She gave a naughty grin and hurried Abby along.

Muddling through the crush of people, Abby scanned for the

courier. While they settled at their table, she barely had time to glance over the crowd before the lights went down. Tension and expectation were high in the atmosphere, not least in her, but she hadn't homed in on that one particular onlooker she'd hoped to find.

A single spotlight on the stage lit a figure dressed in a black suit and bowler hat, poised in front of a large vaudeville sign painted in lurid neon colors announcing: Cabaret. The mistress of ceremonies bowed. Beneath her suit jacket she wore only a bow tie, her breasts visible as she moved to one corner of the stage, followed by the spotlight.

"*Willkommen!* It is so nice to be able to see such a fine-looking audience," she extended her hand around the venue, and the spotlight followed her lead, picking up smiles and the laughter of surprise on its passage across the audience. "We are The Candy Shock Tarts, and we hope you enjoy the show. Tonight the girls are beautiful; oh but the girls are beautiful." She growled seductively, drawing more appreciative laugher. "On with the show. Allow me to introduce the Fraulein."

In true cabaret style, the Fraulein was dressed in stockings and suspenders, a bowler hat and bow tie, satin shorts and a corset that molded itself beneath her breasts. She was a vivacious brunette, her makeup emphasizing her big brown eyes and delectable pouting mouth.

She sang her lament, which told the audience of her many lovers in the past, summing each up with a witty phrase and a physical gesture that was part dance and part display. She cavorted her way back and forth across the stage to the sound track, periodically posing against a bentwood chair to focus the audience on her body in an exotic pose. The theater troupe had taken the play and stripped it down to the bare essentials, physically and literally, and the audience was on the edge of their seats to take in every delicious detail. The music paused occasionally, and the mistress of ceremonies would interject the performance with a trumpet blast or a comment.

Marcy loved it, taking candid shots every now and then. She turned to Abby, winking. Abby covered Marcy's hand with hers, squeezing her fingers in response. She looked around at the spectators, now as interested in their reactions to the show as to finding that one familiar face. Almost. The onlookers were titillated by the decadent show; it was fun, campy, and outrageous, and the audience loved it. Still no sign of Wolf Smile, but her skin burned up with the notion that he was there. Maybe he'd spotted her. The idea made her heart tick that much faster.

Onstage, two female suitors courted the Fraulein. The innocent suitor was a demure redhead, dressed in a sheer white net smock and ballet slippers, her virginal body on display through the light gauze. A strong blonde punk acted the part of the Playboy suitor, her rubber Nazi uniform so skintight that each line of her athletic body was shown off to absolute perfection. She wore a commandant's hat and toted a riding crop that, by scene two, had already undertaken service on the redhead's perfectly formed and naked buttocks.

The adaptation was a marvelous spoof, giving the women every opportunity to show off their bodies and demonstrate how confident they were about doing so. Abby was already totally engaged with the eroticism of the performance, when in the final scene the punk woman stepped onto the stage wearing nothing but a pair of rubber khaki-colored shorts, storm trooper boots, and a massive strap-on penis.

A wave of horniness rushed over Abby. A handful of people in the audience clapped, while others murmured admiringly to one another. The punk threw a decadent smile out to them, one hand gliding up and down the scandalously large cock she wore. Her nipples were rouged and coned into peaks. The audience responded with more delighted laughter. The punk began to sing about her jealousy of the other suitor. The spotlight followed her as she clicked her boots over to the left-hand side of the stage, where the circle of the spotlight slowly enlarged to reveal the other two women. The Fraulein was hunched over, her breasts hanging free as she knelt between the virgin's thighs, stroking her body through the white gauze. The redhead lay on the floor with her face turned to the audience, her eyes wide, her mouth mimicking a comically shocked open-mouthed gasp.

Another ripple of delighted laughter ran over the audience, the erotic tension heavy in the atmosphere. Abby couldn't hide a kernel of desire to be up there with them, cavorting about and declaring herself as rampant and sexy as they were.

A hush fell over the audience while the crop fell, six times, across the plump, satin-covered behind of the Fraulein, who gasped and moaned and wriggled in delight. The punk then threw the crop to one side and knelt down behind the Fraulein. She grabbed her hips and led, as the three women began to simulate a chain-reaction interaction. The punk began to sing, "Come to the cabaret, old chum," while she thrust her cock at the Fraulein from behind. The Fraulein bent over the virgin's hips and made loud lapping sounds. The audience adored their outrageous love triangle and showed their appreciation by demanding three encores of the final bows.

Marcy was on her feet as soon as the lights went up. "Come on, honey, backstage passes."

Abby shook her head in amazement when Marcy waved the laminated badge at her, her camera ready in the other hand.

She felt flushed and light-headed—suddenly self-aware as the lights went up—following Marcy as she squeezed through a door stage right. They emerged into a hospitality room between the stage and the dressing room area. A bar ran the length of the room, with trays of champagne, Evian, and orange juice. People gathered in tight clusters, chatting and flirting, carrying with them the heady atmosphere of the show. She hadn't seen any sign of Wolf Smile. Was he even here? Her instinct said *yes*.

Marcy wandered when she saw someone she knew in the crowd. Abby picked up a glass of champagne and looked around expectantly. The champagne was good, and she let it fizz on her tongue while her gaze flickered over the crowd around her. She felt the urge to blend in, put the empty glass on the bar, and began to edge round, her eyes sucking in all there was to see. A journalist who was doing a piece on the show for a variety magazine asked for a moment of her time as she passed by. Abby gladly stopped and chatted; she was thrilled when he asked her reactions to the show and scribbled her appraisal down enthusiastically. He took her card and promised to send her a copy of the magazine. When he left, she couldn't see Marcy anywhere. Or the sexy courier.

"Come out and play, wherever you are," she murmured to herself, laughing quietly, moving through the crowd.

Zac stood with his arms folded across his jacket while he watched her on the closed-circuit televisions lined up in the security room. She was there. Was it coincidence? He gave a wry smile when she gave her card to the journalist. She smiled as she glanced around the place and then wandered deeper into the crowd, moving toward the backstage area and out of his view.

A hankering need to follow had him in its grip. He left the room and hurried after her. By the time he caught up with her, she'd disappeared into the corridor that led directly onto the stage. She was alone in the space, standing by a table of abandoned props. She looked fabulous, clothed in tight leather pants and a snakeskin top that left her midriff bare.

He paused, observing her appreciatively. As he did, she picked up an object from the table. His eyebrows rose. It was the strap-on cock from the play. He'd been about to announce his presence but instead stepped back and rested one shoulder against the wall, curious to see what would happen next.

She turned it in her hands, looking at it from all angles. She ran her finger over its head, tracing the ridges, the line of its crown.

He was quickly getting hard. When she put her hand around its girth as if to measure it, he couldn't stifle a quiet laugh. "That's quite a sight."

She turned, startled—caught red-handed—but her expression melted into pleasure when she saw who it was.

He straightened up. "I apologize; I made you jump."

"No. I was hoping I'd run into you." She smiled at him; it was rich with suggestion and humor.

He walked over to where she stood, the tip of the molded cock in her hand now idling against her chest.

"I take it from your examination of the objets d'art from the play that you enjoyed them and were taking a closer look?"

She purred audibly. "Absolutely, it was a great prop." She paused, a teasing smile hovering around her lovely mouth. "When I saw it lying there, I had to check it out firsthand." She eyed him up in a way that made his blood roar.

She was very aroused, her pupils dilated, her scent rich in the air. "Did its use in the show turn you on?"

"It would be impossible not to be turned on, wouldn't it? Weren't you?"

She had no trouble turning the question back on him, and he admired her mettle, chuckling in genuine amusement. "Oh yes, but . . . believe me, I had the best view in the house. From where I was watching I could appreciate the audience . . . as well as those on the stage." He inclined his head at her, eyeing her body, underlining the private message in his words. "And that was quite a pleasure in itself."

Color rose on her cheeks, but she didn't turn away. Her lips parted, but she did not reply. There was a palpable tension in her, similar to that emanating from him.

"Have you enjoyed your evening?"

"Yes, the show hit so many notes." She spoke slowly. "It made me think, and it made me hot. There was a directness about it; an unashamed attention to pleasure that was very refreshing."

"That's what the venue is all about. It's important for people to find places where they can enjoy a different kind of experience, something challenging."

She nodded, and her breath came quicker, her eyes flickering into his.

"The human character is a diverse thing," he continued, "people need many different stimuli to thrive."

"Such as exploring fantasies, like the play?"

Oh yes, she was interested.

"Such as exploring alternative realities." He touched her lips with his fingers, and she turned in to his touch, kissing his fingertip, her tongue darting out to taste it.

Hot. "That sort of behavior does very bad things to a man."

She smiled. "This?" She licked the end of his finger again, her eyes twinkling.

"That and the fact you're holding an erect cock between your breasts."

She laughed and glanced down in surprise. She turned away and put the strap-on back on the table where it belonged.

"Although I would much rather it was my cock in your hands."

When she turned back, she returned his stare with candor. "That's not beyond the realm of possibility." Her gaze dropped to the place where his cock was hard in his pants.

Any iota of self-control that might have been within his grasp vanished. He stepped against her, taking her face in his hands, his fingers sinking deep into her hair.

She looked up at him, her eyes sparkling with pleasure, her lips parted in anticipation. He bent to kiss her, running his tongue along her lower lip, tasting her.

She responded, her hands on his shoulders, her mouth opening. She was lush and supple, her body moving against his in the sexiest way. He moved one hand to press her closer still, resting it in the small of her back. They were body to body. His cock sensed warmth, softness. Willingness. It thudded insistently.

A cough issued behind them.

Drawing back, he glanced round and saw Nathan, his right-hand man, standing by.

"The journalist from the *Arts Bulletin* is here for you."

Reluctantly, Zac released her. "Bad timing," he explained. "I've agreed to give an interview about the venue and the autumn lineup." Maybe it was just as well. Their involvement was far from clear-cut.

She looked from him to Nathan and back.

Zac raised a hand. "Cheers, Nathan. Take him up to the office and offer him a drink. I'll be with you in two minutes."

Nathan nodded and departed, amusement apparent in his expression.

Surprise lit her face. "Are you the manager or something?"

It was a timely reminder of who they really were. "No title as such, but you could say that."

She gave a startled laugh. "And you moonlight as a courier?"

Coming from her, that comment tickled him no end. "It's always wise to have a backup plan when it comes to careers, don't you agree?"

She nodded.

"In fact, I bet you've got a few skills to fall back on, should your *receptionist work* come to an end." She had the decency to blush, he noticed, but she didn't correct him with her true job status. *Why?*

"A receptionist can always find work. As I suspect couriers can."

Her mouth was so very inviting. He wanted to kiss her again. *And the rest.*

"Tell me," she added, "do you rent the venue out for functions? I'm only a receptionist, but the company I work for might be interested."

"Anything is possible," he stated ambiguously.

What was she up to, playing the role over again? Why didn't she want him to know she was an investment expert? He couldn't resist the bait though—even if it did mean giving her his name and the possibility of her making the connection. He'd much rather that was avoided.

He slipped his hand into his inner jacket pocket and handed her his personal calling card.

She read it with interest. "Zachary Bordino?"

He nodded. "Call me Zac. And I don't believe you've actually told me your name."

"Abby. Abigail Douglas, but everyone calls me Abby."

"I'm sure we'll meet again, Abby."

"I do hope so." The invitation in her eyes almost made him forget the interview, but he needed the time to figure out why she was masquerading.

"I think we can bank on that." He pushed her loose hair back over one shoulder, his hands itching to hang on to her instead. "Call me or drop by, any time." What the hell—he wanted her. "Make it soon."

three|

The following morning Abby walked into the Heathrow European arrivals lounge seconds before Ed emerged, waving his folded newspaper at her, his suit carrier resting over one arm. He kissed her lightly and talked about the flight, the atrocious tea he'd had to drink.

It reminded her she was ravenous. "You promised me breakfast."

He laughed. "So I did. Let's go."

As they sat chatting over croissants and steaming black coffee, Abby found she could barely focus on what he was saying to her. She was looking beyond him, remembering her encounter with Zac the night before. She crossed and uncrossed her legs, trying to concentrate on what Ed was telling her about the problems with the Pascal account.

"It's a complete mess. There's so much paperwork that Tom hadn't been given access to in the early days. We only discovered it yesterday." He looked at her sheepishly. "I'm going to have to be in Geneva for at least a couple of days a week."

She restrained a smile and nodded, thinking that she really ought to stamp out his desire to be more than friends who had sex occasionally. "Have you organized a schedule yet?" She picked up her coffee cup.

"Yes, we plan to divide the time equally if at all possible. A few days in London, then back out, probably Thursday." She nodded. He seemed to take her silence as disappointment. He covered her hand with his.

"I'm sorry, Abby."

"Hey, you don't have to explain to me." She looked down at his hand. He seemed unreal, distant; she could barely feel him; she was still being touched by Zac.

She dropped him at his Islington terrace house, declining his invite to stay for lunch, and drove back to her own apartment, parking her mini for the week. Mostly she traveled by tube or taxi, but she loved having the car nonetheless.

She began to look at the files she had brought home from work. One of the criteria of the Ashburn account was to invest in property. Ed had already targeted a development of apartments around a large marina along the south coast. Abby was looking for something a bit more adventurous.

As she leafed through the upcoming auctions, her hands kept leading her back to a castle that was located in the west coast of Ireland. The photographs that accompanied the profile showed a gothic tower and ramparts that were architecturally outstanding but begging for restoration. It would be a real gamble investing in something like that on behalf of a client, but it was also a rare property opportunity, and Abby couldn't help being drawn to it. She smiled; she certainly liked the idea of being locked up in the tower with a dark prince who kept her there at his mercy, playing out some wild fantasy on a big white bed. *I wonder why?* When she closed the file, the castle remained on the top of the heap.

She worked on but turned to the window every so often to watch the curtains drifting on the warm breeze. As they were sucked out through the window into the heat of the afternoon, she felt herself being drawn out with them. Her restlessness was getting the better of her; she was being inextricably drawn toward the lure of the enigmatic Mr. Bordino.

He'd made her blatant; she couldn't resist flirting with him. And the things he'd said, about people needing diversity and challenge. It was if he'd been reading the words from her soul. Then there was the not so small fact that he was a total turn-on. She'd barely managed the taxi drive home from Marcy's the night before and had masturbated herself to sleep, bringing herself off four times, imagining herself captured in his arms again, his mouth on hers, his suggestive voice inviting her back. *Soon.*

She headed for the shower, gave herself up to it. Closing her eyes, she thought about the way his hands had felt on her body. Her skin wanted contact. She leaned her back up against the tiles and let the water pour down over her breasts. It pounded against her skin. She turned against the wall, letting the water slide down her back. Her breasts rode up against the wet tiles, but the cool, sleek surface couldn't respond to her warm, full flesh. She wanted contact desperately; her hands flickered restlessly over her body, but they were an insufficient panacea. She wanted him. She climbed out of the shower. She was going to take him up on his invitation, and she was going to do it now.

She dressed in knee-high suede boots and a black jersey minidress. After she'd ordered a taxi, she pulled on a long raincoat and left the apartment.

It was twilight by the time she got to the venue. Standing in front of the closed glass vestibule, her mind ticked over frantically. She hadn't even considered that the place might be shut, which put a bit of a kink in her resolve—but then she noticed a small illuminated bell on one side, set back and hidden from general view. She walked over and pressed it.

Seconds ticked by. *There may not be anyone here on a Sunday*, she told herself, but her body refused to believe it. Nerves were beginning to take hold of her when the interior doors flashed open, and a big, beefy man with short, spiked hair appeared. It was the man Zac had called Nathan, the night before. He looked at her with amusement, apparently his constant expression.

"Is Zac around?"

He swung the door wide, and she stepped inside. "There's a band rehearsing. He's in there." He gestured down the corridor and then he glanced down at her long coat. "Help yourself."

When she emerged into the auditorium, the place looked very different. It was more brightly lit, exposing its large and gaunt interior. The seating from the night before had been neatly stacked away at the back of the space. A handful of people drifted about, only glancing at her as they moved boxed equipment toward the stage at the far end.

Zac was working at a microphone stand, adjusting the height and rearranging its position. Her heart rate responded immediately. He was wearing a tight black T-shirt and jeans, his hair hanging down as he bent over. He was smiling and chatting to a woman in front of him. She was tall and elegant, her blue-black hair cut in a dramatic bob. She talked animatedly while fiddling with a guitar that hung across one very lean hip.

Of course, Abby thought, there would be a string of women in his life, she was no doubt one of many that he expressed interest in. Just as she began to wonder if she could escape unseen, Zac reached over to a mixing board on one side of the stage and flicked several switches. When he turned back, he glanced over and saw her.

His eyes flashed immediately. He said something to the woman in front of him, then jumped lithely from the stage, strolling over. "Abby, what a pleasant distraction." He looked her over with undisguised appraisal.

She smiled. "I thought I'd call over to find out some more details about hiring the venue for an office function." *How blatantly feeble an excuse was that?*

"Did you, indeed?" He gave her an indolent smile. "And this would be on behalf of your employer?"

Abby laughed. "Oh, absolutely."

He reached forward, put his hand inside her coat, and slid it open. His eyes fell to her boots, the flash of naked thigh between them and the hem of the dress. He lifted his head. His eyes glimmered, their irises crystal azure. "You look as if you're dressed for something entirely different."

"It's the weekend."

"It is, and I don't think you came here to discuss a business function at all, did you?"

She smiled and shook her head. Her heart was pounding in her ears.

"Seems like that would be above and beyond the call of even the most hardworking *receptionist*." He stepped closer still, resting his hand on her hip, inside the coat. His other hand slipped to the light jersey of her dress where it clung to her shoulder, and he lifted it lightly, tugging at her breasts with the movement. Her nipples were hard, and the movement of jersey across the taut surface aroused her even more.

"I think we both know what I'm here for." She breathed her response audibly, her body leaning into his, her lips parted.

He gave a dark chuckle. "I can't wait to see what you're going to say next." He glanced down at her nipples where they rucked against the smooth surface of the material.

Why did she feel as if he was teasing her? "We're adults, aren't we?"

"Yes, we are." He breathed in appreciatively. "And I can smell how aroused you are, just like I could last night."

His words thrilled her. His face was millimeters from hers. He wanted her, too.

"Yes," she whispered, "I am aroused. And so are you." Her lips parted with pleasure, the knowledge of reciprocated desire and anticipation of the event that could follow delighting her.

Capturing her hand, he led her to a door stage left, punched a sequence of numbers into the keypad, and pulled her through the doorway. It slammed shut behind them. He backed her up against the wall. Grabbing her wrists, he pinned them above her head, his hips pressed hard against hers.

They kissed, their hungry, open mouths locked together. Barely contained animal lust traveled between them, as palpable as electricity crackling across a stormy night sky.

He pulled her toward a door close by and into the room beyond. He fumbled in his pockets, drew out a ring of keys, and locked the door behind them.

She glanced around. A dressing table stood against one wall, mirrors over it and on the wall behind. A sink and clothing rails were fitted to the back wall. It was a dressing room.

Zac dropped the keys loudly on the floor and then walked over to where she stood. Music stirred through the walls from the auditorium. It was muted, but its dense throbbing sounds reached Abby at the very same time as Zac's hands pulled her body close to his. He took her coat off, letting it fall to the floor, and ran his hands very deliberately over her breasts.

She breathed out as the light jersey beneath his hands heightened the sensation of skin reaching for skin.

He kissed her neck, brushing the surface lightly. Sensation flew through her from the place where his lips moved on her bare skin. In one long, slow stroke he bent and moved his hands up from the top of her boots, under her dress, and around the back of her thighs. His hands traced the line of her G-string, pulling at the skimpy line of material.

She moved her hips, responding to the sounds that reached them through the walls. As a woman's voice flew up in a scream of song, Zac climbed his fingers into the humid spot inside her; her head fell back in ecstasy.

She looked into his eyes and moved her hips on his hand. She was burning; she was so hot for him.

"What is it that you really want, Abigail Douglas?" It was a whisper against her ear.

She couldn't reply, because the contact with him had taken away logical thoughts.

He drew back and looked into her eyes with a curious stare, his hot breath covering her face.

"I want you," she murmured, breathing his breath into her lungs. "I wanted you the moment I saw you." Her hips moved, begging for him to take control of them.

He nodded, smiling, and then turned her in his arms, pressing against her back, his cock hard and defined against her buttocks. The movement was so sudden and sexy, it knocked the breath from her lungs. Reflected in the mirror, she saw them molded together. He looked over her shoulder, admiring the image, too.

"I like these boots," he murmured. "They make you just the right height." He stroked his hand up the line of her spine and slowly but firmly pushed her over until she was bent at the hip. His cock was hard against her buttocks, her heels lifting her against him. She gasped, wriggling in his grasp, her sex clenching with need.

He lifted the hem of her dress and pushed it up to her waist, the bulge of his cock resting back between her arse cheeks as they were revealed to him. She glanced left, saw them reflected in the mirror, blatantly, provocatively. *Animal.*

He lifted her G-string to one side. She struggled against him, turning away from the image she saw in the mirror. It was hot, shocking. *Too much.*

"No, keep looking." His tone was demanding, making her quake with lust. "I want you to see how good you look while I'm fucking you."

A low moan escaped her lips, and she reached forward, her hands grappling for support. Her fingers met the cool porcelain of the sink; she gripped onto it and sent her hips back against him, looking at the mirror as she did.

His fingers plucked the G-string from his path, tightening it against her clit as he did so. The pull of the fabric on her clit made her throb, hot waves of pleasure condensing in her groin.

He stroked her swollen folds, and it was such sweet, sweet torment. Bent over like that, every part of her was on display to him, every quivering damp bit of skin and each lusting orifice. She whimpered quietly, desire and humiliation raging inside her. She whimpered again, louder, when he reached down and rocked one finger over her clit. She tossed her head back, her hair flying as she looked back at him. His eyes were dark, shining. His lips were pressed together, his mouth hard and determined.

"Zac, please," she whispered, her voice quiet and urgent.

"Hush, I intend to have you right now. I'm going to do what I should have done last night and bury my cock inside you."

"Dear God, yes," she uttered, her legs spreading wider, her sex pounding furiously at his words. She heard the merciful sound of his zipper, the rip of a condom pack. She watched in the mirror as he rolled it on, his fist anchoring it over the base of his cock in the sexiest way.

When he began to drive himself slowly into that oh-so-sensitive place, she groaned. He filled her completely. The fabric of her G-string was tight between her pussy lips, capturing her clit. She felt wild yet tethered. "Fuck me hard," she begged.

"Believe me, I intend to." He said the words through gritted teeth. He pulled her roughly into position on him and began to drive his cock in and out, his hands holding her hips.

She pressed back, meeting each thrust with a low cry from deep in her throat. She braced her arms against the sink.

"You're a wild creature, Abby, aren't you? I could see it the moment we met."

She drove back onto him, her feet spreading wide to hold her upright when she began to feel the heat of her climax building. "I'm going to come . . . I want to come." She was fevered, anxious. Her voice wavered up as she drew from him and then reached again.

Her fingers tightened on the porcelain; her head hung down, and her hips worked quickly against him. She felt him slide a hand up her throat and stroke her neck from her chin downwards, lifting her torso upright, taking her weight and crushing her entire body down onto his cock. Her toes barely scraped the floor. She screamed with pleasure. She felt his cock there, in her throat, beneath his hand. Hot, hard, ready to burst and flood. They both felt it.

He groaned deeply, and she felt his cock grow harder still, wedged against her cervix, then the leap and surge of flesh as he came. She wriggled and flexed, desperate for the release. A flash of divine heat traveled through her body. As the heat blossomed and spread outward, she gave a long, low moan, her body convulsing.

His hand stayed locked over her until she slowed her movements and finally stilled. She wavered. Her body felt weak. He pulled free, holding her until she fell against the wall for support. She watched, panting, as he removed the condom, knotting it. Her body gave a final shudder of release and she whimpered, her body sliding down against the wall.

He dropped the rubber in the wastebasket, pulled up his zipper, and then reached over. He kissed her mouth and stroked her body, calming her with his broad, warm touch, his gentle kisses. She met his mouth anxiously, realizing that this was a new sensation—his mouth on hers in intimate, gentle kisses. His lips were firm and sensual. His hands on her were possessive, giving their shared kisses the deepest intimacy.

"Alas, I've got to . . . move," he murmured. "I have an appointment." He pulled away from her slightly, a small frown gathering as he looked at her with curiosity. "But I'd like to entertain you again very soon, in better surroundings."

She moved her hands across his chest, touching his firm, leanly muscled chest through the soft material of his T-shirt. She wanted to see him naked; she wanted to see his fantastic cock again, taste it and ride it.

"Soon?" She looked at him, waiting to see his reaction.

He nodded. "Tomorrow. Come to my place. I'll give you the address or . . . I could collect you and we could go for a drink?"

She wondered vaguely why arranging to meet seemed to create a sense of awkwardness. Perhaps he didn't do dating? Perhaps that was all part of his elusive, mystery-man persona?

He arrested her in a tight grip and lifted her chin with his hand. "Do we have an arrangement?"

"Yes, tomorrow, please."

He straightened her G-string, and his hand closed over her mons. Heat surged up under his grip. She kissed his throat; she could taste the salt on his skin. She wanted him again already. She would have to go soon or never leave.

Mercifully, he took his hand from her, pulled down the material of her dress, and stroked it over her hips. He smiled down at her boots and bent to place a kiss on her bare thigh.

As they went through the door, she heard the music strike up again and turned to him, smiling suggestively.

He urged her on. "You'd better go before I decide to lock you in here with me and throw away the key."

"It sounds very tempting." Their eyes locked for an instant, and then he seemed to create a little distance between them; she felt it as clear and swift as a door opening on a cold winter's night.

"Did you drive?"

She shook her head.

"I'll get Nathan to give you a lift," he murmured, and she let her hand fall away from him.

She nodded. "Thanks."

"You've got my card. Call me whenever you're ready."

Nathan appeared and looked at the two of them, a suppressed smile obvious in his expression.

Zac tossed him a bunch of keys. "Take Abby wherever she wants to go."

She followed Nathan out to the street, turning to take another look at Zac as she went. He stood in the doorway, his posture that of a graceful but predatory animal. She felt the warm heat still glowing inside her from their joining. She still had the taste of him in her mouth and smiled back before they turned the corner.

Nathan led her to a silver two-seater Mercedes and held the door for her. He watched the swing of her hips, the slide of booted leg and bare thigh as she climbed into the car. She glanced at him as they sped off. He was smiling to himself. He could probably smell the sex on her. She didn't care; she didn't care who smelled it on her at that moment. She'd stepped away from her life, and she was having an affair with a mystery man.

She gave Nathan her address, then closed her eyes and savored every second over again.

Back at the venue, Zac once again entered the sequence of numbers into the keypad stage left and walked down the corridor, past the dressing rooms, and beyond. He ran nimbly up the narrow flight of stairs to the offices. Another key code entered him into his private sanctuary. The lights went on.

The room was his stronghold. Sparse yet comfortable, two long, leather chesterfields on opposite walls flanked a large glass desk mounted on ornate wrought-iron struts. He put his keys on the surface with a gentle chime and sat down, gazing at the expanse of heavy glass in front of him. He had intended to have her over the desk but hadn't been able to restrain himself long enough to get her up the stairs. *Maybe another time.*

He flicked on his PC. The computer whirred quickly, the screen flicking through directories. His eyes narrowed as he located the on-line Robertson dossier and Abby's corporate image filled the screen.

A knowing smile teased the corners of his mouth.

Her hair was swept up and clipped back, in line with her corporate image. She looked sophisticated, immaculate, but even in this official context he could see the wild side of Abby just beneath the beautiful surface, and within his grasp.

He scanned her credentials yet again, his eyes flickering quickly over the list of accounts she had worked on over the past two years, looking for a clue he might have missed. They were well-known corporations; she'd been given challenging contracts and successfully enhanced them.

"Well, well, Ms. Douglas," he whispered to the screen. "Are you truly the portal to all these good things, or are you playing some other game?"

She was intelligent. It wouldn't take much digging on her behalf to find out he was the Ashburn heir. Putting his name into Google would take care of that, a string of old news articles reporting what his mother called his "gallivanting years," the times when he concentrated on spending money instead of earning it. He was a regular in the gossip columns for a while back then, until he'd grown weary of that lifestyle.

If Abby already knew about the connection, why was she still pretending to be a receptionist? He could almost feel his mother's genes beating out their concern in his blood.

Abigail Douglas was now in charge of the account. She had enough confidence to take down a major corporation single-handedly, and with her sassy sex appeal thrown into the bargain she could be a powerful weapon. Could she have some nefarious purpose in tracking him down, commencing a sexual liaison with him? Something bound to her intentions for the Ashburn account? Could he take that risk?

He had to face that possibility; he already had. And things were getting more complicated by the moment. He'd had a taste of her, and he wanted more.

By the time Nathan returned to the office, he'd analyzed every possible scenario, and he'd become increasingly tense about the whole setup, because all he wanted to do was fuck her again.

He stood up, pacing the length of the room as he spoke. "Where does she live?"

"The southeast, an apartment, Greenwich Way."

Zac nodded, both cautious and thoughtful. "Alone?"

"It looked that way."

"I want you to find out for sure. I want to know everything we can about her. She works with Robertson; she's actually managing the Ashburn investments, and yet she's turned up pretending to be a little nobody out for a good time."

Nathan's eyebrows shot up. He gave a low, appreciative whistle.

"I've checked her out and, professionally, she's very good at what she does . . . although she's quite the risk-taker." Zac tapped his chin with one finger. What risk might she be running here, and was it on behalf of her boss, or was she acting alone? *Or am I as suspicious of everyone as my dear mama?*

He ignored the mocking voice in his head, reminding himself that he'd given her an invitation; that might be why she'd come. But why lie about her job?

"For some reason she isn't mentioning that she's a money manager, which is odd. I don't know for sure if she is aware of my relationship with the Ashburn Foundation, but it makes things . . . complicated."

Nathan nodded. Robertson was under their scrutiny anyway; it only made sense to keep a close eye on Abby.

"Any reason why you don't confront her, ask her why she's lying about her job?"

Zac shrugged. "I might do that, but I want to find out what she's up to first." He just had to keep his head long enough, and that might be the hard part.

"I'd like to know what else she's doing, if she's in league with anyone outside the Robertson Corporation, and if there is a reason for her little deception."

"No problem; I can handle that."

Zac looked at him meaningfully. "These are the family heirlooms she's playing with." *In more ways than one.*

four | ɹnoɟ

Suzanne popped her head round the doorway into Abby's office. "Let me know if there's anything you need sent out. I'll be heading home in an hour."

Abby glanced at the time display on her monitor. It was past five. "Thanks, Suz. Nothing for collection. You got a moment?" She gave her a grin and wink, indicating gossip.

Suzanne shut the door and barreled over. "Oh yes, you went man-hunting on Saturday night, didn't you? So, how did it go?"

"It was a great night. I wish you'd been there. The show was a lot of fun, very sexy."

"And did you find the guy?"

"Yes, his name is Zac. He works there, as well as the courier thing, and he was well worth hunting down."

Suzanne's eyes widened. "Come on, spill. What did you do, take him home?"

"He was working on Saturday night, but he asked me to call

again, so I went back on Sunday." She couldn't help chuckling. Relating the weekend to Suzanne made it feel so much more real. Zac's enigmatic nature made it feel as if she had a secret lover—that she was launching into the dangerous affair she'd dared herself to go after.

Suzanne clapped. "What a tenacious lady! I love it. And was he worth the effort?"

She nodded. "I'm seeing him again tonight."

"You go, girl." Suzanne beamed. "And don't forget to let me know if he has any single friends."

"Will do."

"Right. I better get on and do my last call on everyone else."

"Cheers, Suzanne. I'll be on my way out in about twenty minutes."

Suzanne waved and shot off to complete her scout for mail and do the evening head count.

Abby was about to switch off her monitor for the day when the New Mail icon flashed up.

"Well, what do you know?" She hadn't expected to hear back from Adrianna Ashburn until the next morning. She'd only just sent her latest report through, and here was the permission to go ahead with her latest recommendations. "The formidable Adrianna must have been waiting by her computer," she murmured to herself.

Her report included fast-track proposals, so she'd assumed the client would need time, maybe even some convincing. The Ashburn portfolio owned shares in an online domain company, and she felt sure the shares were going to peak soon. She'd requested permission to trade in before a possible downturn, stating her reasons and suggesting it was a good time to gain maximum return. It was a fast payback system, and she used it to underpin her other more unusual investments.

She hadn't expected the formidable Adrianna—as she'd forever be known—to agree so quickly, but she supposed you had to be able to act fast to get a reputation like hers. The mail confirmed that the release documents would be printed, signed, and returned to the Robertson offices by courier for her action first thing in the morning. Abby couldn't help wondering if Adrianna had noticed that the work pace had risen a notch since she'd taken charge.

She sent a swift acknowledgment and flicked off the monitor. Anything else could wait; she had her reward to collect. Standing, she lifted her mobile phone and Zac's business card. She'd left both items on her desk as her personal goal for the day. Smiling, she tapped the number into her mobile phone, adding it to the memory. As it rang, she set the card back on the desk, still looking down at it. It was unusual, she noticed: no title. Just his name and three numbers. The venue card had no names and one number. *How many cards did this guy have?*

The sound of his voice distracted her. "Zac Bordino."

"Hello, it's Abby . . . Have I called at a convenient moment?"

"Abby," he chuckled. "You know, I had a feeling you might call right about now."

She was gratified to hear the interest in his voice when he realized it was her. "Good. I thought I'd see if your offer to entertain me again was still on."

"Yes indeed."

The sound of his voice washed over her, warming her right through. She gave a breathless laugh, pacing her office as they spoke.

"Name a meeting point, and I'll be there," he added.

"Do you know The Bankers Draft? It's a pub on Carver Street, near the building you delivered documents to."

"I know it." There was humor in his voice.

Of course he knows it. He's a courier, they know where everything is. "I'll be there in about half an hour."

There was a distinct note of interest in his voice when he replied, and Abby smiled as she put down the phone, her pulse beating out a demanding rhythm.

She darted to the slim wooden locker that was neatly housed out of view behind the door. She always kept a couple of outfits and a makeup kit in there, in case an unexpected social occasion arose that she was obliged to attend with a new client or another member of the team. She had a choice: a sharp suit in midnight blue velvet that was a particularly flattering cut, black palazzo pants and a green shantung silk top, or a heavy black satin dress. She picked up the satin, letting it run through her fingers. The material was fluid and sensuous. She pulled it out and retrieved her makeup bag from the top shelf.

When she was done, she stopped at the reception post, but Suzanne wasn't there. Her laughter sounded down the corridor. Glancing at her watch, she realized she probably didn't have time to wait and say good night.

Outside, the sky was the color of melting honey, shimmering, marking the turn of a hot day in the city. She loved London more than ever when it was like this, when its fast-moving currents began to change on the ebb of the day. The city became sexier, vibrant in a different way, as if a dark spirit lover had invaded its character. Like her own dark lover, mysterious and seductive.

She'd had a good day, and it wasn't over yet. She was high on the excitement of living and had looked over the accounts with an eye for the daring, the risk that would pay off. It wasn't so much the financial gain that thrilled her, it was the ability to judge, the power to move in a certain way at the right moment. She smiled to herself; it was just like sex, and the pace of her activities in that arena were up a notch, too. Several notches, in fact. She'd had trouble keeping her steamy encounter with Zac out of her mind. Anticipation for more of the same had her blood racing.

Her body jolted to a halt. "Damn."

The heel of her shoe had caught in the pavement, and she dropped back to rescue it. As she did, a sudden sense of unease washed over her. She felt the scrutiny of an onlooker. The thinning crowd of pedestrians moved on around her. She glanced back over her shoulder, just as a car shot by with open windows pumping out a loud, bass-driven tune. The passenger whistled in her direction as the vehicle sped past.

Freeing her shoe, she shook off the notion and headed on.

On the opposite side of the street, Nathan stepped farther back into the alcove he'd been using as cover while he watched Abby's office building. For a split second, he thought she was going to look over and spot him in the shadows. It made him realize he didn't feel entirely comfortable with this task.

Life was never dull when he was working for Zac, that was for sure, but this assignment took the cake. Zac had never asked him to do anything quite as dodgy as digging the dirt on his current bit of fluff. He didn't mind hunting for information by asking questions or looking stuff up, but for a second there he wondered what the fuck he was doing. What excuse would he use if she saw him?

She wouldn't recognize him though. He'd made sure of that. He was wearing a black beanie hat and sunglasses, his oldest Motorhead T-shirt, and jeans. Even if she had seen him, he looked entirely different from when he'd driven her home the night before.

He watched as she headed down the street. She surely was a looker. Not his type, but he could see why Zac was so keen to give her one. She looked like a great shag, but you could maybe take her home to meet the family afterwards. A lot classier than the women Zac used to hang out with during his playboy years.

As Abby turned the corner and disappeared, he flipped open his mobile phone.

Zac answered as soon as it rang.

"She's on her way."

"Cheers. You've got that paperwork I gave you for cover?"

"Yes, no worries." The document dispatch package rested easily in his hand.

"Find out what you can."

"Anything I should be aware of?"

Zac took his time to reply. "The receptionist is a cute blonde."

Nathan laughed. "Heh. Nice one. I'm there already." He folded the phone into his pocket and made his way into the building.

The entrance vestibule was huge. Polished steel and mirrors, reflective surfaces everywhere. The uniformed security guard at the doorway frowned at him. Nathan saluted as he walked by, scanning for the elevators behind the cover of his sunglasses as he did so. A surge of people from a corridor to the left clued him in. They wore weary expressions and walked with a pace that showed him they were heading home at the end of a workday. He grinned to himself, popping a stick of chewing gum into his mouth as he strode round the corner and into the elevator.

During the ride up to the Robertson Corporation offices, a guy in a suit looked across at him with a wary expression. He was used to that. It was his build, mostly. The face didn't help. He had the sort of looks that invited trouble. *If you look like a thug, people will sure as hell treat you as one.* He had the scars to prove it.

That's how he and Zac had hitched up. He'd been minding his business in a nightclub when four men looking for trouble decided he would be a good test. They invited him outside for a kicking. He declined. Things had gone downhill from there. At least three of them had gone home with broken bones, but they had the advantage in numbers.

Zac had picked him up off the street where he'd been left for dead at the back of the nightclub. He'd looked after him, phoned for an ambulance, and stayed in the hospital while they stitched up his face and pumped him full of someone else's blood. When Zac had called by the next day to see how he was, he'd had the chance to say thanks. Zac had saved his life, but he shrugged it off as if it was nothing. They'd chatted. They'd got on. Zac had offered him a job.

The elevator doors pinged open, and Nathan stepped out onto the landing. Opposite him thick glass doors were emblazoned with the Robertson Corporation logo and several official looking affiliation insignias. He walked toward the door, scanning inside as he did so, quickly homing in on a moving figure. As he got closer, he found himself looking at a very shapely woman's rear end, tightly encased in shiny black pants.

He stopped at the door and observed the view through it. The figure moved, and the fabric of the pants glinted over her heart-shaped bottom. She was picking something up off the floor. He murmured approvingly under his breath, a drumming sensation at the base of his spine fast kicking in.

The figure straightened up, clutching a stack of envelopes to her chest. Dumping them on the countertop, she flipped her curly blonde hair and turned toward him. This had to be the receptionist. He gathered himself and pushed the door open.

She was tiny, barely over five feet, and Zac was right: she was cute. Nice and curvy, her breasts tightly packaged in a skinny-fit top that showed them off to perfection. The shiny pants made him want to grab her hips and guide them against his own.

"Oh my God," she declared when he walked in, eyes lighting up. "Give me a twirl."

He stared at her, baffled by her remark. "I'm sorry?"

"Your T-shirt. I want to see which tour it's from."

"You're a Motorhead fan?"

She nodded and then waved her hand, indicating he turn round. "Wow, you've been into them for years."

Nathan completed his turn, a bemused smile on his face. "That's right. You?"

"The first time I saw them play was the No Speak with Forked Tongue Tour."

"Heh. I was there."

"Well, imagine that." She stared at him, smiling invitingly. "I was only fourteen." She gave a naughty laugh. It was a great sound.

He took off his sunglasses and offered her the document dispatch package. "I've got some papers here for a Ms. Abigail Douglas."

She stared at him and then chuckled again, her eyes twinkling as she took it from him. "Damn it, another sexy courier. What are they doing, making you guys pass a sex rating before they give you the job?"

He wasn't quite sure what she meant, but it sure as hell sounded like she was giving him a come-on. "You like what you see, little lady?"

She put one hand on her hip, adopted a serious expression, and looked him up and down. She waved her free hand at his head. "Lose the hat."

Dutifully, he swiped the hat off, rubbing his spiky hair upright. It was bizarre, standing there, being examined by this tiny little fire-cracker, but what the hell.

She nodded. "I like. Are you on the market for a night on the town?"

For such a small lady, she sure as hell knew what she was about. "For a Motorhead fan as cute as you? Absolutely."

She smiled up at him. "Great. I'm Suzanne."

"Nathan." That drumming sensation at the base of his spine had started up again.

"OK, Nathan, give me two minutes to finish up here, and we'll hit the pub. Oh, and I'm buying the drinks for as long as you can keep me in good Motorhead gig stories."

He laughed. He couldn't help it. She surely was a firecracker. "You don't know what you're letting yourself in for, Suzanne."

Not missing a beat, she waggled her eyebrows at him. "Neither do you."

The Bankers Draft was a narrow, oak-paneled pub crushed between the City banking buildings. Decorated in dark colors, it harnessed the feeling of old money, the brass beer pumps gleaming in the lamplight. Despite the fact it was a hot summer's evening, the subdued lighting and old-world quality made it feel comfortable and inviting.

Zac leaned on the polished wood bar and glanced around, noting that the seating was all taken.

"Mr. Bordino?"

Turning, he saw a familiar face behind the bar. "Joseph, I didn't expect to see you here. You haven't left us have you?" Joseph was a cellar manager at his father's West End restaurant.

The barman chuckled, shaking his head. "No way. I'm just topping up with a couple of evening shifts here."

"My father isn't paying you well enough?"

"Very well indeed, but my wife is expecting our second child. Your father won't let me do any more hours for that reason. He's offered me an advance, but I'd rather just make a bit of extra hay while the sun shines."

Zac nodded, thoughtful. "Do you see much of my old man?"

"Not since he's retired, but I heard a rumor he's been looking at a new bistro somewhere out near home."

"Doesn't surprise me," Zac commented.

Joseph tipped his head at the bar. "What can I get you?"

"I'm expecting company . . . Do they stock any good champagne?"

Joseph leaned over the counter, scanning left and right as if he thought he might be overheard. "They keep Bollinger, but you might be interested in a couple of bottles of retsina, apparently ordered in for a party a few weeks back."

"Retsina it is then. Actually, that might be fun for my guest. I haven't told her about my Greek heritage yet."

"Is she beautiful?"

Zac smiled. "Very."

"I'll put the retsina on ice and bring it over." He nodded over at a booth, where the current occupants were making ready to leave.

"Thank you, Joseph. I appreciate it."

As he eased into the booth, Abby emerged through the heavy oak and brass-inlaid door. He waved, smiling when recognition lit her features.

She looked like a dream as she sauntered over, wearing a shiny black dress that hung heavily, like a pool of oil, from her shoulders. Occasional ripples in the fabric moved from the points where her breasts and hipbones disturbed the material. Her hair was pinned up, but bits of it spilled down onto her bare shoulders. He patted the seat alongside him, urging her to join him on the banquette.

"Am I late?"

"No." He rested a gentle kiss on her mouth, the touch of which was enough to make every part of his body pay attention. He breathed deep the scent from her warm skin, musky, floral, all woman.

"Mmm, are these part of your courier uniform?" she asked, her hand resting on his thigh, stroking his leather pants.

"Actually, I only did the courier job as a favor to someone."

"Does that mean I can't call on you if I need some documents de- livered?" The flirty look in her eyes was doing bad things to him.

"You can call on me anytime."

She gave a decadent chuckle. Twines of copper fell from her ears, echoing the colors of her hair, lips, and eyes. He wanted to commis- sion a portrait of her, looking just that way.

"Did anyone ever tell you that you smile like a wolf?"

He wasn't sure he felt comfortable being likened to a wolf. "No. Is it a bad thing?"

"Oh no, not so long as we're playing out the adult version of the fairy tale."

"Now that sounds good."

"Here you go." Joseph deposited an ice bucket and two glasses on the table. Zac folded several notes into his hand and winked, putting up his hand to indicate he didn't want any change.

"I hope you don't mind," he said, as Joseph left, "they had retsina, and it's not often you find it in London. I can order you something else."

"Greek wine, yes?

He smiled, nodding. "Yes. I'm half Greek."

"I'd love to try it." She watched with curiosity as he lifted the bottle out of the bucket. "Is that where you get your dark looks?"

"My father's side is Greek; my mother is English."

"Are you bilingual?"

"Yes, although I start in with the Greek when I get angry or emotional, without even noticing." He grinned. From past experience he'd found it was best to warn people of that little foible in advance.

"I'll keep that in mind." A teasing look passed over her expression. "Did you grow up here or there?"

"Here mostly. I went to school in London, but we spent a lot of time in Athens, too. My older sister is married and lives there."

"Tell me about her."

Something about her made him feel comfortable, relaxed, so he talked. That wasn't what he was expecting at all, nor to be talking about his own family, his sister Nanette, and her family life. He'd intended to learn more about Abby this evening; he wanted to find out what made the intriguing Abigail Douglas tick.

"And does the English blood account for your blue eyes?" she asked when he paused to wonder at the effect she had on him.

"Indeed, yes. Do you know much of Greek culture?" he asked, drawing her away from the reference to his mother's side.

"One island-hopping holiday with my parents when I was thirteen." She gave a gentle laugh, as if embarrassed by the idea of being a tourist.

He looked at her, imagining her as she might have been then.

"What?" she asked, in response to his scrutiny.

"I am trying to picture you as a girl of thirteen. It's very hard because you are such a woman."

Pleasured by his remark, she looked at him with a beckoning glance, every part of her oozing lush femininity. He wanted to take her into his arms, make love to her long and slow.

"Thank you," she whispered.

"Did you enjoy the islands?"

She picked up the glass of yellow-green wine and sipped it, her eyes closing appreciatively as she swallowed. She was very sensuous. "Yes, but not fully." She looked at him. "My parents always wanted to rush from one sight to another. It was all just a list of places. I like to explore, to take on an adventure if there's one to be had."

He smiled. "So I've noticed." He took a drink of his wine, nursing its sharp, zesty flavor in his mouth, enjoying the aftertaste of pine.

"Are we still talking about the Greek islands, or something else?" She looked so inviting, her eyes filled with secret messages about what they had done the night before, what they would do again, that he almost forgot he wanted to talk at all.

He leaned forward and took her hand, meshing her fingers with his. "I'm sorry. I did slip into thinking about having sex, but you have that effect on me."

She chuckled. "The experience is mutual." She mouthed a kiss at him.

Now he was getting hard.

"This retsina is very good." She took another sip, her glance heavy with allure over the rim of the glass. "Actually, speaking of sex, I had my first, well . . . sensual awakening, I suppose you'd call it," she glanced at him from under her lashes, "in Zante."

Well and truly hard as rock. "Go on . . ."

"I was alone near the harbor one evening, watching the fishing boats come in. I felt something. Her free hand reached to the back of her shoulder. "Here."

He listened intently as he imagined it.

"At first I thought it was an insect, but then some innate reaction in my body told me what it was. It was something sensual, sexual."

She was like a drug, he decided in that moment. If the building had been on fire, he couldn't have stepped away. *So much for caution.* He rode his fingers against hers, wanting it to be their bodies meshing that way.

"I turned around, and there was a boy standing behind me, a dark-eyed gypsy. He'd kissed my shoulder." Her fingers trailed across the back of her shoulder again. "I felt both fear and the thrill that comes from . . . inside." She locked her fingers with his, and they merged for a moment, totally in tune. "It affected me deeply, and I can still remember how I could barely breathe." Their fingers intertwined, their eyes speaking without words.

She laughed, breaking the moment. "That's all that happened, but it was very special, moving."

"It's the poor youth I feel sorry for." He drew her fingers to his lips to kiss them.

"I expect he's kissed a thousand shoulders by now."

"And never found one quite so perfect . . . the virginal Abigail, how blessed he was."

She looked up from her wine and caught the message he was sending her. He wanted to be inside her. *Soon.*

"I like the idea of your sexual awakening in Greece, but I'm jealous of the youth that first stirred the woman in you."

Her lips were slightly parted, her cheeks glowing. "If we were somewhere more discreet, I'd show you that you are the one awakening me now." Her pupils were dilated, her eyes darkly suggestive.

Raw lust surged up inside him. He wanted her on her back. He rested his arm along the banquette behind her shoulders and kissed her mouth, his tongue skimming her lips, tasting her. *You're supposed to be talking to her, learning about her. Focus, dammit.*

"You have the most incredible eyes," he said. "They are almost amber, like a cat's."

She gave a mock-puzzled look. "Hmm, I thought they were a dull hazel, but I'm pleased that you see them that way."

He chuckled and lifted her chin with his fingers, encouraging her to look at him again. "No, definitely amber, both rare and beautiful." He looped a trailing curl behind her ear. "What of your heritage? There has to be some Celt in there, surely?"

"The red hair gave it away, huh?"

"Kind of, but more than that."

"My dad was Scottish. He died a couple of years ago." Sadness passed over her eyes, and then she blinked it away. "My mum is English, like yours."

"Any brothers and sisters?"

"No, just me. I've always been a bit of a loner, independent, part of being an only child, I suppose. To be honest, I always felt like a bit of an outsider. Sometimes I still do." She frowned.

Was this a confession, he wondered? How much of a loner was she, and did independence mean she looked after number one? He wanted to know and yet . . . he didn't. What he really wanted to do was forget his concern about her agenda and take her to bed instead.

"I can understand that. As a young person I had a hard time trying to decide which culture I felt part of, the Greek or the English." He hadn't meant to comment, but the thought had turned into words unheeded. He topped up their glasses. "Have you always lived in London?"

She nodded. "Yes, I'm a city girl through and through." She paused. "We share the fact that we have mixed heritage."

"Yes." He smiled, acknowledging the coincidence. "And the red hair has come down your father's side?"

"The hair is a pain in the proverbial. I have to wear it really long, or else very short; otherwise it grows straight out. I hate it."

"I love your hair." He ran his hand through the trailing strands, unable to resist contact again. "Last night, I wanted to stroke it while I was fucking you."

Her lips parted, her breasts shifting inside her dress as her breathing pattern altered.

His hands itched to touch her, to mold her breasts in his hands, feel her nipples. Lick them. Words melted away from his mind. Actions took over. His mouth covered hers, his hand cupping the back of her head beneath the hair.

Her hands moved to his chest, then one dropped lower, squeezing his thigh, roving over his cock, enclosing it. "I want you, Zac," she breathed as they moved apart.

"And I want you. Shall we go?" He couldn't think of anything he'd rather do than get her home to his bed. "My place?"

She nodded, breathing a husky acknowledgment in response.

Outside, the evening was still warm, balmy, the sky darkening into a drape of dense, blue-black velvet. Zac led her to a taxi stand a few minutes' walk away, but she barely noticed the time or the distance. She was aware most of all of his presence, his arm around her shoulders and the promise of passion in his eyes.

He gave the driver an address, then turned to her, quickly leaning into her for a deep, lingering kiss. Her body trembled beneath his hands, desire an urgent need that unsettled her every fiber.

Drawing back, he stared at her, his face in shadow, his mood inscrutable.

"Is it far?"

"No. Not in this light traffic."

She chuckled, low. It was so true of London, a city that lived and breathed with the movement of people as sure as the turn of the tides. Behind him the city lights blurred into one another. A streak of orange, green, blue light, it was too bright, too peopled. She wanted more darkness, the gloom of intimacy—a private arena in which to discover him. Stroking the soft, black leather of his jeans, she felt the firm outline of his thigh beneath. She wanted to see him naked. Through his shirt, his chest was leanly muscled, strong. She breathed his scent, a musky fragrance that said, *I am passion.*

He slid his hand against the curve of her abdomen, otherwise as still as a bird of prey watching its target. The lights flickered on his face, revealing the intensity in his expression. With one arm around her back and his hand stroking her stomach, she was captured, but not unwillingly. She barely broke from the spell when they reached their destination.

His apartment was one of several in a beautiful converted mansion on the river near Kew. The opposite side of London from where she lived. When he led her inside and flicked lights on, she was startled to find his apartment decorated in rich, dense colors, starkly juxtaposed to one another, emphasizing the sparse furnishings of the place.

"It's a bit bare," he explained. "I've just started; it's an ongoing project . . . as and when I have time."

The fact that his home wasn't properly furnished yet made her smile. *So like a man.* The reception room held only two sets of bookshelves and a striking dining table and chairs. Stacks of news-papers and books teetered up against the bookshelves, which were empty. It was a true bachelor pad.

"Such lovely rooms," she murmured. Space was such a premium in London, this felt luxurious. She was surprised. She hadn't thought about what to expect, but for an arts entrepreneur it kind of fit the bill. He'd add to it as the business established itself, she supposed.

"It's a Mackintosh design, isn't it?" She nodded at the tall, thrust-ing line of the chairs, the dramatic oval of the headrests.

"Yes, Mackintosh," he replied. "Do you like it?" His voice was so deep and resonant, every word touched her inside.

"Oh yes, I love his work. The Arts and Crafts movement is fasci-nating." She felt her gaze drawn back up to him. He was still the most attractive thing in the room. Her eyes rose across his face, and each bone carved itself into her memory.

He nodded and smiled at her.

"Are you a collector?"

"No." He smiled. "But I know what I like when I see it . . . and then I do my best to have it." His eyes swept over her, confirming the inference of his words as he moved closer.

"Oh?" she responded. The tension between them hummed in her ears, speeding along her veins. She felt as if they were moving in a slow dance, inexorably closer and closer.

His fingers stroked her cheek, sliding higher and into her hair. He was brooding, passionate. "You're an objet d'art, and I intend to have you."

Her heart thudded violently. She hooked one finger over his belt. "I'm glad to hear it."

He lowered his head and brushed his mouth over hers, slowly, subtly, making her lips tremble.

She was wired. Anticipation had built beyond anything she'd experienced before; he was throwing coal on a fire already pumping out way too much heat.

"This time," he murmured, moving his mouth to her ear, "I want to savor you. I want to take my time with you, enjoy you." His lips smiled the gentle smile of a classical statue, the secret held in their line.

She had to fight for her breath. The atmosphere between them was charged. A tremor ran through her body, a tremor of expectation and arousal. The flame of desire was reflected in his eyes.

Turning her around in his arms, one arm locked across her torso, the other hand on her opposite hip, he held her tight against him, making her remember how it had been the night before, how he'd bent her over and made her watch.

She moved her hips inside his, her eyes closing as she absorbed his total contact. His grip tightened. Lowering his head, he kissed her neck, her shoulder.

"Do you own a bed?" she murmured.

He chuckled, his breath warm against her skin. "Oh, yes." He moved, freeing her and then resting his arm around her shoulders, drawing her alongside him as he led her from the room.

She had to make a concentrated effort to walk slowly. Her panties were damp between her thighs, her pulse racing, her nipples chafing against the fabric of her dress.

He led her down the hallway and through a doorway. The bedroom was lit by a tall, elegant lamp and housed a large bed with a wrought-iron headboard formed into a frenzy of Art Nouveau swirls. The surface was covered in a black velvet comforter, like a void that invited her to disappear into it. She turned to him and saw the dark energy simmering in his eyes. "It's beautiful."

He gestured at the bed, one corner of his mouth lifted. "It will be, with you on it."

And with you over me. He looked so good; she could barely wait to have him inside her. Stepping out of her shoes, she walked over to the bed, sat down, then lay back, her arms moving across the surface.

He shook his head as he looked down at her. "The bed is nothing. The real beauty is here." Leaning over her, he stirred the satin across her abdomen, lightly moving it with his fingertips, watching her face.

"It's a Roland Mouret dress," she murmured, barely able to speak as darts of sensation shot out from the material moving under his fingers.

He smiled, gazing into the black pool of satin. "Very admirable, but I suspect the beauty that I am referring to lies beneath the dress."

She sank back into the bedcovers, inviting him closer with a pleading glance. "I hope I don't disappoint."

Slowly, he began to push the material up from around her legs, exposing her body, caressing her skin with the waves of satin before caressing it with his eyes and then his hands. As his fingers passed over her, from shin to thigh to hipbone to breast, they seemed to draw the breath from her body. She swallowed, reminded herself to breathe. When the material gathered on her breasts, she slipped it over her head and then lay back again, her hands moving restlessly in the abandoned pool of black satin above her head.

Staring down at her naked body on the bed, it was as if he had touched her; the heat in his expression was extreme. "You look like a beautiful sacrifice waiting to be offered, waiting to be tasted."

Her sex clenched, over and over again. "Please don't make me wait any longer," she begged.

He bent down to lift one of her feet onto the surface of the bed, opening her legs. His hands crept along the inside of her thighs, his fingers spreading wide around her groin, sending wild flames coursing across her skin.

Glancing down, she watched his thick black hair moving as he kissed the inside of her thighs. Each kiss was like a beautiful torture, filled with divine sensation, but she craved more than that.

"Oh please, Zac," she murmured, her body shifting, her hands clutching at the bedcovers.

Chuckling, he sank his mouth onto the mound of her sex and sucked deeply at the flesh, his teeth grazing her while his tongue moved between her folds.

Arching, she let her head fall back against the pillows. When his tongue stroked over her clit, she moaned and twisted on the bed. He reached one arm up to still her, his hand between her breasts. She covered it with her own hands, squeezing her breasts around his spread fingers. His other hand shot along her thigh and down to her foot, anchoring her. As his tongue moved, her breath came quickly, rasping in time with his movements. Pleasure roared through her whole body; but still she wanted more.

Her fingers pulled at his hand, her torso moving, suggesting more to his body, suggesting more shared pleasures. He raised his head and looked at her. His eyes were black with passion, his lips dripping with her juice. She sat up and reached for the buttons on his shirt.

"No," he said, pushing her hands away. Humor lit his eyes. "You must learn to take your time, Abby." He pulled his shirt free from his leather trousers. "You're a wild creature, and I intend to tame you."

She growled, "How?"

"By fucking you very, very slowly." He dropped the shirt to the floor.

Very, very, slowly? Why did that sound like sheer torture? *Because you're so damned horny.* Just looking at his muscular shoulders, the strong column of his neck, and the bulge of his cock inside the leather made her mouth go dry. Other parts of her were oozing moisture. Her attention was drawn to a tattoo on his right arm, an image that flickered with movement as he undressed. It coiled around the line of his bicep, emphasizing the shape of the muscle.

A shadowy smile passed over his face, partly hidden in the hair that fell forward as he bent over her body. His breath moved on her like a warm sirocco sifting the sands. "I want to be sure that your body is at its peak before I have you, and I want to find out where that peak is."

She felt sure that her peak wasn't very far away at all and was desperate for him to take her to it and force her right over the top. Zac, however, had other ideas. She watched his bare chest, exquisitely masculine, as he moved. He reached for her, yanking her legs apart. Fluid seeped from her exposed pussy. Every ounce of her intimate flesh was on display.

"So delicious, so ready . . ." His finger, firm and slick with her moisture, probed inside her.

She clutched and let out a loud moan of relief when he moved it, stroking the front wall of her sex. Shock waves darted through her body. His thumb rested over the hard nub of her clitoris, and she cried out with pleasure.

He muttered something unintelligible that sounded like it might be Greek as he bent over her, his tongue lapping at her clit. He added a second finger, flexing them, moving them in small circles and then scissoring her open. Sensation traveled through her as he sucked her swollen clit, gently, a stark contrast to the hard fingers inside her.

She lost sight of the room, her body jerking spasmodically as she came, sudden and hard. In the distance she heard her own voice crying out. He pulled out. When she surfaced, she could see that he was desperately aroused, it sent an after-tremor through her sex, drenched but suddenly bereft.

"Good?" he teased.

"Not until I have you inside me."

He eyed her possessively as he kicked his boots off and climbed out of the leathers. The bulge of his erection sprang up, long and thick, its head beautifully defined and dark with blood.

She watched as he rolled a condom on and then lay over her, his cock resting against the tingling folds of her sex. His closeness overwhelmed her with a new rush of sensations. She was intoxicated by him, absorbed by his presence. She breathed deep the musk scent of his body; it swept through her like a cloud of smoke, immersing her senses in its cover. She whimpered her frustration, and a wave of sheer lust took her over. "Please, Zac, please," she pleaded.

His eyes flashed at her, his mouth in a passionate curl. He nudged her and then drove the full length of his shaft inside her, and she gave a cry of pleasure. His cock throbbed, crushed deep inside her, and she clasped at him with her inner muscles, relief sinking through her senses.

He moved, slowly at first, and then with more impact, and with the precision of a well-oiled machine, each stroke carefully measured for optimum effect. She wrapped her legs around his hips, her hand on his buttocks, where strong muscles drove him deeper into her with each flex. Each thrust was so exquisitely full and yet bordering on pain, the sensitive flesh of her overaroused sex a riot of sensation. He had driven her to distraction, and now he was moving so in tune with her body that she felt as if she was about to come again, every time the swollen head of his cock crushed against her, so very deep inside.

"You are so beautiful, and when you come you look like a goddess," he whispered. He thrust with deep, even strokes, a controlled movement that brought them mutual pleasures while holding off his final reward. She was powerless to do anything but enjoy.

When their movements became more fevered, she bucked her body up against him. He stroked her torso, and his fingers crept against the moist line beneath her breasts, his fingers tracing the lines of her body with intimate attention. She clung to him, desperate for release. She felt a sob at the back of her throat.

He slowed, and she hovered on the brink. She clawed at him, her breath sucking into her throat as the imminent release wavered to and fro. His hands roved feverishly through her hair, and then his mouth covered hers. Hidden in the shifting cave of his hair she met his kiss with bliss—and with desperation.

Her sex was drenched, and as his tongue plunged into her mouth she moved with him again, the pressure of each thrust spreading the heat of imminent climax through her body, right up to her throat, where it seemed to burn. She spoke his name to let the heat escape.

"I don't think either of us can hold back any longer," he muttered through gritted teeth, the tension in his body attesting to it; his cock was rigid, his balls high against her buttocks.

"No," she managed to reply, her head rolling on the pillows. Her legs climbed up around his hips, locking him in against her. The mutual pleasure of it shot between their locked eyes. Their bodies were harmonized; they moved in quick, even strokes, barely parting but to press home again.

He turned his face into her breasts, drawing his tongue along her skin. They were pacing, ever faster, toward crescendo. As the orgasm came close, his hand slid over her pubic bone, pressing her mons down as he moved against her. His brows were drawn together, his eyes intense, a bead of sweat sliding slowly down one side of his face. His mouth opened, each quick stride drew a harsh breath from him.

Heat welled from her womb, as if a heavy, hot liquid was held in her pelvis. A shock wave released it, and it buoyed up against the full head of his cock, where it lodged itself deep and hard inside her.

"Oh yes . . . yes," he murmured. His body arched and bowed against hers, and finally his cock moved alone, their bodies falling still in the moment of mutual climax.

Abby was floating weightless when he stroked the final ripples of pleasure through her with one trailing hand. He kissed her gently, then disengaged. She watched him walk to the bathroom. Never before had she felt so perfectly sated, so complete. She snuggled against the comforter, sighing deeply.

When he returned, he lay alongside her, tilted her head back with a finger beneath her chin, and looked into her eyes. "You wear sex so well, Abby." Curiosity spilled from beneath his hooded lids.

She couldn't speak; she didn't want to break the spell. Her hand coiled round the place where she had seen his tattoo. She looked at the image. It showed a yin-yang symbol resting in a bed of thorns. It had a tribal quality about it, but she suspected it was personal to him. The design twined his bicep to meet at the back of his arm. She stared at the image, mesmerized by it, tracing its possible meanings.

He ran his hands through her hair, spreading the long curls loose across his pillows. "It's like flames, or the many different colors of the October trees."

"It's a mess," she murmured, taking off her earrings so they didn't get trapped in the mess overnight.

"A beautiful mess." He smiled, teasing her lips with his fingers.

She closed her eyes and let the sensation lift her, the gentle brush of his fingertips against her mouth causing her nerve endings to fly away from her control. He replaced his fingers with his mouth, gently kissing her back down to him.

She stroked his forehead, pushed her fingers into his hair, and then trailed them lightly across his face. She watched as his eyes closed, his handsome face reaching forward into her touch, strands of hair following her fingers across his face.

When her hand dropped, he pulled her across his chest, locking her there with his arms. One hand rested against his chest, the other lay over the tattoo etched into his arm.

five | five

"Open wide," Suzanne instructed as she reached over to the box of chocolates she had propped up on her spare pillow and pursed her lips as she selected one. "Here you go." She rested the chocolate on his lower lip until he moved and bit into it.

Chewing slowly, Nathan looked at her mouth. It was swollen from hungry, lust-fueled kissing. Her cheeks were pink. Both suited her. She reminded him of a gangster's moll from some old black-and-white movie.

"Good?"

He nodded. "Hazelnut."

"Right." She poked about in the box and picked one out for herself.

He watched it disappear into her mouth. He'd never been big on chocolate, but he was learning to love it. So long as she was lying naked on top of him and feeding them to him, he was prepared to eat them forever. He took a deep breath, lifting her with the swell of his rib cage.

She chuckled, rising up on her arms, peeling her breasts from his chest. They were both sticky from hot sex. They'd been at it for hours. The dim light of early dawn was already showing at the one window in her tiny bed-sitting room. She didn't seem to care that it was a weeknight. She even thought she'd be able to convince him he had the stamina to do it all over. Maybe that's what the chocolates were about.

He was only just beginning to think straight again. They'd had a lot of fun. He'd lost count of the number of drinks they'd had. All his Motorhead stories had been told, many of his Iron Maiden, too. He hadn't let her buy all the drinks though, and he'd insisted on paying for the fish-and-chips supper. Arguing over it had been fun. She was a very playful, hands-on type. In fact, it took him a while to muster a comeback when she slapped his arse and told him she was calling the cards. And now she had him pinned down and at her mercy. He couldn't have been happier.

Except the reason why he was here had wriggled to the forefront of his mind for the first time in hours. *Got to get info.* "What's it like, working in that swish office block?"

"It's OK, mostly." She gave a slightly sad smile. "Not my dream, but such is life. You find yourself places in life you didn't think you would."

"I know what you mean."

She rested her chin on one hand, her elbow on his chest. Her weight was nothing to him, but her presence—now, that was a different matter altogether. He kept trying to keep his mind on what he had forgotten during the course of the evening. He was supposed to be gathering information for Zac. "What would you want to do, if you had the chance for an ideal career?"

"I don't know, something in PR maybe."

"You'd be good at that."

"Thank you. I agree. What about you? How does being a courier suit?"

"Oh, I don't mind being a gofer. The guy I work for is sound. He's more like a friend."

"What would he think if he knew you were using work time to pick up women?"

He gave a soft laugh. "He wouldn't be surprised, but I'd like to point out that you picked me up."

"So I did, and you were well worth it." She snuggled closer and bit his chin.

That sent a jagged streak of interest down to his groin. She played rough, and he loved it. His body was strung out under her, exhausted and yet wanting more. He breathed in the heady scent of sex and chocolates. His thoughts blurred. *What is it I'm here for?* Struggling, he tried to focus. "So, um, what are the finance people like to be around?"

"Stuffed shirts." She laughed. "There is one woman I get on with, Abby, the one you brought the documents for, and she's a sweetie. She talks to me and stuff, she's a good laugh."

"A rock fan?"

"Nah, not that I know of. Although I suspect she's a bit of a rebel. She's not like the others."

A rebel. Is that a bad sign? "In a good or a bad way?"

"Oh, a good way, definitely good. Like us, I mean. She's the only one who would stop and give you the time of day, to be honest."

She leaned to one side, her breasts bouncing free of his chest. Man, he wanted to suck on them. He wanted to sit her on his cock and mold those gorgeous breasts in his hands.

She ran one finger down the length of the scar on his cheek, lifting away and then touching his lips. She looked at the smaller scars crisscrossing his forehead. "Where did you get those?"

He should've expected it; she was pretty direct. He tried not to clam up. "In a street fight."

"Did you start it?"

"No."

She nodded but didn't press him.

He sensed she was relieved. "Thought you'd brought a bruiser home, did you?"

"Hey, buster, you're the one in the manacles." Gesturing up at the headboard where she had him handcuffed, her eyes twinkled.

He laughed aloud, the tension of the moment breaking. "Good point." That wasn't why she'd manacled him, though. She'd told him she liked the sexual power. He'd been surprised, yes, and it had driven him nearly insane with lust, but having her in charge about shot his head off. What a buzz. He was convinced he'd lost the power of speech when he finally got to come.

"Do the scars bother you?" He was concerned, wanting to know what she thought of him.

She shook her head, her soft curls bouncing. "I think it makes you look sexy."

"That works for me." He rolled his hips from side to side, causing her to grab him and hold on tight.

She gave her trademark naughty giggle and put her hands on his shoulders, lifting up. Moving her hips against his, she let her legs splay to either side of his body and then rode her pubic bone up and down the length of his cock.

If he wasn't getting hard before, he sure was now. "Jesus, woman."

"Seems like you might be ready to go again." She captured her bottom lip between her teeth, her eyelids lowering as she assessed the hardness of his cock.

"You better believe it." He instinctively moved his hands; the handcuffs rattled and held.

Clambering to her hands and knees, she shuffled down the bed until she could see his cock. She nodded approvingly. Grabbing a condom from the handful she had scattered over the bed at the outset of the session, she quickly unwrapped it. Looking at him, she licked her lips.

He groaned, rattling the cuffs again. His cock was throbbing, his back arching off the bed. She made an oval shape with her lips and rested the condom there, before ducking her head down to roll it on with her mouth.

Oh yes, that felt good.

She moved slowly, eking out the sensation, her head gradually lowering till she had him against her throat. He had to close his eyes and grit his teeth.

Mounting him again, she looked as if she couldn't get enough of it. A feeling of honor belted out inside him, adding fuel to his lust.

"Your pussy is the sweetest place on the planet, Suzanne." It was snug, hot, and slick from the time before.

She grinned and squeezed him tight inside her, her head rolling, her mouth opening wide and letting out a pleasured sound. He jutted his hips higher, lifting her, shoving as deep as he could within his restraints. She rode the movement, her expression challenging him, like some demoness from one of his comics—and he was ready to offer her his soul.

With agile hips she pumped up and down, her body angling back and forth as she rode him, squeezing and crushing his cock until his balls were riding high, braced for release. Sweat had gathered in the crease of his neck, between his thighs. He didn't think he could come again, but he did, with spine-wrenching finality, the ejaculation emptying his balls of what little fluid he'd managed to muster for the repeat performance.

She was moving fast, grinding onto his cock, one hand rubbing her clit. When she shuddered to finality, he wanted her in his arms.

"Undo me, please," he whispered.

This time, she did. Every other time he'd begged she'd denied the request. That had driven him wild. She rubbed his wrists and shoulders as she freed him. He barely noticed the stiffness and sat up, snatching her into his arms, keeping her on his cock as it shrank, his head going to her neck and breasts, where he kissed her reverently.

Her body was limp, soft, and warm as it lolled against him. Holding her was too good; rolling into the bed for sleep this way was the only option. He lifted her and tucked her in against him, disposing of the condom and moving her easily onto the bed beside him.

His gaze traveled round her room, taking in the stacks of CDs, action movie videos and magazines, cushions and candles, her crazy collection of teddy bears—all of which has been modified with punk gear and piercings. A massive close-up image of a shark about to bite dominated one wall. Her quirkiness was everywhere. He liked it.

His hands roamed her body, stroking all the places he'd wanted to touch when she'd been in charge.

She sighed sleepily under his touch.

"You feel so good. Can we do this again tomorrow night?"

She snuggled against him. "I can't. I promised I'd babysit for my sister, but any other night would be good." She looked up at him, locking her arms around his neck.

"Every other night?" The words were out before he'd even thought about it.

She chuckled, sounding sleepier but just as naughty as before. "I'll give it a go, as long as you can dredge up some more good gig stories for me." She winked.

Dynamite comes in small packages, he reminded himself, as she rested her head on his shoulder.

When Abby awoke into the early morning light, Zac was lying next to her, his arm loosely about her waist. He was watching her, a small frown on his forehead.

She let her eyes fill with him, while her other senses awoke slowly to his presence. Her mind confirmed what had passed before. She hummed with pleasure. "Good morning."

He smiled and moved his hand to her neck, stroking the surface gently, awakening her further with his touch. After a few moments she looked at the morning light that streamed over his shoulder from the window. It was Tuesday, and she had to be at work first thing to deal with the sale of the shares.

"Damn." She sat up and looked around for a clock. A small, elegant, silver oval on the bedside table told her it was after six. She was supposed to check for Adrianna's papers and call the broker to notify him to trade on the exchange before eight.

"What is it?" Zac pulled her back toward him. He kissed her mouth before he let her reply, and she was momentarily absorbed into his aura again.

"I have to be at work soon." She drew away reluctantly.

He looked at her while his fingers stroked from her throat down across her breasts, his touch drawing her closer to him. She breathed in determinedly and climbed from the bed. Lying on one side, the black sheet draped over his hip, he watched as she dressed.

Abby couldn't take her eyes off him as she fumbled into her dress, found her shoes. He looked like pure sex, spread on the decadent bed, tempting her to come and enjoy his body again. The dusting of black hair across his chest tapered into a line that led the eye down. She looked at the shape of his abdomen, the firm ridges of muscle that went from beneath his rib cage to disappear under the sheet. The black material hid his beautiful cock from her view, and she wanted to go over and pull the sheet off him, to take pleasure in looking at his cock, too. But she knew that if she did, she wouldn't be able to leave.

When she walked over to collect her earrings from the bedside table, Zac rolled over, put out his hand, and grabbed her wrist as she reached out.

"Will you call me later?" A sudden sense of tension emanated from him.

She looked down at his eyes, sparkling azure in the morning light. The dark line of his brows failed to shadow their brightness and their question.

"Yes," she replied, wondering why it was like this, the tension between them when arranging to meet again, as if it was a secret affair. Why didn't he ask to call on her? Did he think she had someone else, and he was a bit on the side? He still held her wrist tight in his grasp.

"I'll give you my contacts," she said, wondering if that was it. She hadn't thought. "I haven't got my card on me." He slowly pulled her down to him, to his mouth, and kissed her, one hand resting around the curve of her breast.

"But I will call," she murmured against his mouth, and he released her.

"Perhaps not soon enough to satisfy my insatiable lust for you," he whispered, his eyes growing dark.

She stood there looking at him, mesmerized. He was making it difficult for her to leave without actually doing very much at all. Her mind was unable to believe that she had to walk away from him; her body was unwilling to do so.

He smiled, kneeled up on the bed, stretched, and got up. His cock was long and hard, half-risen. Her sex clenched. Her sense of purpose floated away.

"I'll phone for a taxi," he said, breaking the hold.

She turned to watch as he walked from the room, leaving her standing by the bed. She listened to his muted voice in the next room. When he came back and stood in the doorway, she took in the look of his naked body. The way he wore it with such nonchalance was unbearably sexy.

"Two minutes," he said. He looked her up and down, his expression unfathomable.

She walked over to him. She wanted to say something, to voice the desire that held her captive. His strange thoughtfulness while he watched her made it difficult, even though she had to admit it was hellishly sexy. Enigmatic was good, but she was experiencing a yen to unravel the more mysterious aspect he had to him.

She laid her hand along his jaw, moving against the graze of stubble that met her touch and then reached up to kiss him. "Soon?" she whispered.

His expression was guarded, but he smiled in response, his eyelids lowered, his eyes on her mouth. "Soon." He grabbed a robe, pulled it on, and led her to the door. "How about dinner tonight?"

She smiled. For some reason, she'd felt as if he wasn't going to make a follow-up date, but instead leave it to her, like some kind of test. Outside, the taxi sounded its horn. "I'd love to," she said and reached up for a hurried good-bye kiss.

Just over an hour later, after changing clothes and freshening up, Abby was on the phone to their broker at the London stock exchange. The release documents were, as promised, on her desk when she got in to work. Once she'd got the ball rolling, she set the FTSE index screen to streaming and tucked into the breakfast bagel she'd ordered in. There was nothing to do now but wait to see how the stocks fared; then she could write it up and move on.

After she'd eaten, she sent Caroline an e-mail requesting her legal advice when she had a minute; then she stretched and stood up, looking out the window and down at the busy street below. When she'd first taken over the office, she hadn't liked to get too close to the window. She always felt like she might fall through it. Then time assured her of its invincibility, and now she would lean into it, imagining what it would be like to fall through the space into another world. The people swarmed on the street far below. She was high on life, her affair with Zac, her work on the Ashburn portfolio.

She looked at her watch. Just a few minutes to wait for the results. How many hours till she met Zac? What was he doing now? Where was he? She wondered. She shook the thought off; she had to survive at least another few hours before she could have him again. It was killing her.

There was a knock at the door, and before she had time to answer, Tom walked in. He was carrying two stemmed glasses and a bottle of what looked like Bucks Fizz.

Abby stared at him, bemused.

"Well, Abby, what an absolute coup on your behalf. I've been watching the FTSE, and I think we can anticipate a celebration." He walked over and put the glasses down, then perched himself on the edge of the desk while he unwrapped the foil on the bottle and glanced at the computer screen.

"Yes. The company has been in sustained growth for several months now," Abby replied as casually as possible, trying not to re-act to his unexpected appearance. The bottle was chilled; he'd been prepared for this. How did he know about her deal, and why was he so interested?

He turned the bottle, easing the cork free, glancing over her as he did so. When it popped, he poured out two glasses. He smiled and then passed her a glass, watching her as she took it.

"Thanks. This is a nice surprise. I didn't realize you did this sort of thing." As soon as she'd said it, she wished she hadn't.

"I don't." He gave a slow, suggestive smile. "Cheers." He clinked his glass against hers, winking.

He *was* harboring a personal interest. A sinking feeling hit her. She sipped the drink unwillingly.

"How did you convince Adrianna it was the time to sell?" He si-dled nearer.

She reached over and fiddled with her mouse, then changed the angle of her VDU to create a sense of distance between them. "I hap-pened to read in the gossip magazines that the company owner was going through an expensive divorce. I did a bit of scouting and found there were rumors about redundancies. The owner preferred that to selling his own stock . . . something to do with the wife benefiting if he did. I only had a couple of days to action this sale before the news made the company seem unstable for the foreseeable future."

He shook his head in disbelief. "Gossip magazines?"

She shrugged, withheld a smile that she would have given readily had she not felt so uncomfortable in his presence. "The information is out there, so I figure why not check its accuracy and use it. I didn't mention my sources to Adrianna, only the redundancy aspect, but she agreed that it would affect the share price. The divorce case goes to court today. It's a great time to sell."

"I always knew you were unconventional, but I have to admit I'm stunned."

Stunned into leaving me alone, with any luck. She took the opportunity to move, taking her seat at the desk. "I hope that the formidable Adrianna will be pleased with the result. It may help to win the contract renewal."

He nodded, eyeing her legs as she crossed them.

The phone rang, and she snatched at it, grateful for the interruption. It was the broker. She wrote down the figures he quoted next to the price paid and the growth percentage over the past month. Tom moved behind her to read her note.

"Superb," she said as she put down the phone.

"The client should be very pleased with it." His hand went possessively to her shoulder, and he reached down to give her a kiss on the cheek. "Let me take you to lunch at Fat Francos, my treat."

She tensed. No matter where she moved, he'd moved closer. And now he'd kissed her cheek under the excuse of this good news. She pulled away and stood up. "Thanks, Tom, but no. Take the others. I've got to move quickly. I have some ideas on investing the profits, and I want to act on them, pronto, to get them into the scheme of things before the contract renewal meeting."

He looked disappointed. "Shame. Another time?"

Damn. Mercifully, there was a knock at the door.

"Come in."

Caroline entered, bristling with purpose, her notebook in her hand. "Oh, sorry, am I interrupting?"

Tom gave a mock grimace, indicating that he was sorry Caroline had joined them.

Abby shook her head. "Not at all. Thanks for coming so quickly." She looked at Tom, explaining, "Caroline is going to go over a few potential properties for the Ashburn portfolio, to see if I'm missing anything."

He nodded and took his leave.

When he'd gone, Caroline looked at the glasses and the bottle with curiosity. "Oh lordy, have I forgotten your birthday?"

Abby shook her head. "I think he's trying to show faith in me, now I'm working on my own with this portfolio." She smiled, genuinely glad to have Caroline around. It was getting difficult to keep saying no there.

Caroline flipped open her notebook. "So, what can I do for you?"

Abby reached over to her top drawer and lifted out a folder. "I'd like you to look into the paperwork on these three properties, see if there are any loopholes we need to know about." She paced about, her mind alive with thoughts. "Blayne Castle, the first property on the list, that's the one I'm particularly interested in acquiring, if the client agrees to it. I think it could be restored and converted into an exclusive hotel. We will need to know if there are any potential problems with planning permission." She watched Caroline thumbing through the pages in the folder. "The auction is on Thursday, but I need to put the proposal to the client by close of business tomorrow. Could we be ready by then?"

Caroline looked up and nodded. "Sure. I've got a couple of things to tie up for Ed, but he's flying out again this evening, isn't he?"

Abby nodded. "I think so."

"I'll be finished on his bits and pieces soon. I'll be able to get onto this midafternoon, at the latest. There should be enough time."

After Caroline had gone, Abby checked the share prices. They had dropped immediately; no doubt the scent of bad news was picked up on the exchange after the Ashburn shares were pulled. *Better to be a leader than a follower, especially when the ship is going down,* she mused.

She sent the news on the share sale through to the formidable Adrianna. Once that was done, she picked up her mobile phone and sent a text message to Zac.

> Now you have my contact number. Can we make dinner at 8? I need to go home and change. Soon. Abby

It was hard to get back to work after thinking about Zac, but it was important to focus. She had to begin her property recommendation report for the next day. She also had to monitor the investments Ed had made on the account, as well as going full charge ahead with her own ideas. That way she could prove to herself that she was capable of working alone on any type of project. She was determined to succeed, and her motivation and energy levels were high; they were being fed by a powerful force, her affair with Zac. Her phone blipped.

> 8 is good. Let's meet at The Bankers Draft and go from there. Soon. Zac

Smiling, she crossed her legs high on the thigh, giving herself a quick clit squeeze. She promised herself tonight as her reward and got to work.

When she broke to pick up some lunch, she stopped by Ed's office, hoping to find him alone for a brief chat. He'd started to become a nagging voice in her conscience. They'd never been exclusive, but she felt the need to tell him she wasn't on offer anymore.

The door was open, but she found him arguing with Penny. He looked up miserably when Abby walked in.

Penny stood up. "I believe congratulations are in order," she snapped. Her voice and attitude were positively terse. Her gray eyes almost looked green.

Abby smiled. It looked as if Caroline was right about this one. They weren't bosom buddies, but she hadn't seen Penny deliver an outright flare of jealousy before.

"Thank you, Penny. It's so nice to have your support." As she walked by, Abby patted her on the shoulder condescendingly.

Penny snatched up her papers. "You obviously got charge of the easier account," she spat. She turned on her dramatic designer heels and walked swiftly out the door.

Abby looked at Ed with an inquiring expression.

He shrugged. "She's not taking things too well. All this hassle." He waved his hand over the piles of paper on the desk.

"That's what it's all about though, Ed, isn't it? Making things work to your advantage? I haven't always been so lucky with the investment advice I've given. This time I have been." *In my personal affairs, too*. She smiled to herself as she followed her own thoughts for a moment.

He didn't glance up but nodded vaguely. He looked like a forlorn puppy, and she thought twice about launching a discussion on personal matters just then.

"Anyway, I popped in to see how you are and to ask when your flight is."

"Thanks, Abby, coping." He smiled wearily. "We're on a flight this evening."

She nodded, wished him a safe journey, and headed back to her office. She was thinking about that evening, too, but with more pleasant prospects. She smoothed her skirt down over her thighs and closed her eyes, savoring the anticipation.

Zac sat in traffic, tapping his steering wheel. The multistory car park where he was headed was in sight, but the traffic was crawling. He normally traveled into work by tube, but with the immanent prospect of having to shoot out with papers for his mother to sign, he had decided to motor in for the rest of the week.

Yesterday had been a true test of logistics. He'd sent Nathan in with copies of previous documents, and he'd had to pay highly to get the release documents couriered out to his mother after hours and back to Abby's office before she returned to it the next morning. His mother had agreed to Abby's proposal readily enough. She'd even said she'd get onto George about setting Zac up as a signatory, but he'd managed to put her on hold for the time being. This was getting complicated, he realized with a wry smile.

His phone blipped, and he read the text, smiling when he saw it was from Abby. The traffic was solid, so he took the chance to reply immediately. She hadn't been far from mind anyway, and now she was back in full Technicolor detail, his mind running with plans for the evening. After she'd gone that morning, he'd sprawled on the bed for quite some time. His mind was filled with images of her, her beautiful body and the way it responded so acutely to him, her face when she was in the throes of ecstasy; he was fascinated. She was so expressive and so feminine, sometimes wanton, a delicious mixture of blatant candor and subtle feminine allure. The fact that she was a finance whiz to boot seemed somehow ironic. He couldn't help wishing now that they'd met under different circumstances.

The traffic crawled on, and he pulled into the car park and handed the valet his keys, telling him to keep the car ready. As he walked down the street toward the venue, he wondered if Nathan had found out anything useful. But would that help? He was now involved in a complicated affair with a potential Mata Hari. Was there an easy answer to how this was going to pan out?

The blinds were open in his office, and the door through to the adjacent room stood open. Nathan was in there, sitting at the computer terminal.

He looked up as Zac approached. "So this is you getting back in touch with me first thing?" He chortled, well aware of the reason why Zac had not got back to him sooner.

"All right, already." Zac put his keys on his desk. "What have you found out?" Looking over his shoulder, he saw that Nathan had the Robertson dossier propped beside the PC, open on the staff information pages. On the screen, he could see that he was looking at information about Abby's university days.

"She's a clever girl, got a first in business management. Won some sort of prize for her accountancy dissertation project."

Zac nodded. "What about now?"

"Standard stuff: she goes to the gym, she works hard. She's well-liked by the other staff in house."

"Do you think she has strong loyalties to Tom Robertson?"

"Hey, what do you think I am, psychic?" Nathan chuckled. "OK, here's the full lowdown. She's been there almost three years, she works with the team, but she does seem to be a bit of a loner—at least that's how it sounds, and I don't think she hangs out with them a great deal."

"Figures," Zac replied. Abby wasn't the typical finance expert, and far from the cliquey sort, which didn't make things any easier for him.

"I can't see any obvious signs that she's dealing with anybody else, outside of her work colleagues. There isn't time in her schedule."

Zac nodded. "Let me know if you turn up anything else."

"I was about to pick up some coffee." Nathan stood up and followed him into the main office. "You look like you could use some."

"Cheers, yes." He flicked open the diary on his desk.

Nathan nodded over at it. "We're expecting the delivery guys with the installation for the Cordover exhibition in the main gallery. It's not due before two. You've also made a note to do the press release for the exhibition today. That's about it."

Zac looked up, nodded.

"Are you still going to Paris on Thursday?"

"Yes, I've got to move on that club if I want to buy it. Why wouldn't I be?"

"Thought you might have changed your mind, what with your new playmate and all."

Zac responded with an admonishing glance.

Nathan still hovered expectantly.

"What?"

"Tell me if I'm out of line, but the way I see it is that she either knows who you are—in which case something isn't quite adding up—or she doesn't know, and if she doesn't know, she is going to find out at some point."

Zac sat down behind his desk and flipped open his laptop. "Yes, if she doesn't know, it's only a matter of time." He rested back in his chair, drumming his fingertips on the arms. "I just need to know why she's lying to me."

Nathan shrugged. "Maybe she's one of those compulsive liars. Who knows?"

"Her work seems to be the only thing she's lying about though. Everything else she tells me fits into place."

"But if you're not telling her that she's working for you," he ventured, "isn't that just as bad?"

Zac shook his head, suddenly annoyed. "I haven't told any lies."

Nathan lifted his eyebrows. "No, you just haven't told the whole truth."

Bloody hell. He had a point. "If you weren't my best buddy, I'd fire you."

Nathan gave a hearty laugh. "Sometimes we all need to hear an objective view, right?"

Zac gave him a sardonic smile. "Where's this coffee you mentioned?"

"I'm on the case." He sauntered off, grinning happily to himself.

What a fine mess, Zac realized. He felt almost despondent, nothing like the contentment he'd experienced earlier, watching her sleeping in his bed that morning.

When she had found her way to him he'd thought, *What the hell?* thinking it wouldn't affect his more respectable interests in her work, but things seemed to be changing rapidly. He was already completely fascinated with her, and he didn't relish the idea of their affair coming to an end too soon because of business complications.

By the time Nathan came back with coffee, he had decided to let things run their course, which was kind of where he had started first thing in the morning, but there was an unbidden sense of urgency running through him now. That feeling annoyed him more than a little, because he hated to be rushed.

He accepted the double espresso and glanced over his e-mail while he tipped sugar into it. "Jesus," he exclaimed, as he read the mail bearing Abby's name. It contained a short report relating the details of the share sale. "This woman's got the Midas touch, and it looks as if she traded in right on time. The share price dropped almost immediately."

Nathan popped the lid on his giant latte and grinned. "In that case, let's hope she thinks you're good in bed. You might get to keep her."

Zac threw him a warning glance. "Now you're just pushing your luck."

But Nathan continued to grin as he left the office, leaving Zac alone to consider his peculiar state of affairs.

Yet again, Nathan had a point.

six | xis

After an afternoon where he'd spent every spare moment brooding on his sorry state of affairs, Zac's mood had grown surly and disagreeable, at best. Standing in The Bankers Draft, he knocked back a vodka and tried to shake it off.

He knew why he felt this way. It was frustration at the turn of events. He was about to spend the night with the most beautiful, desirable woman he could wish to have, a woman who he was pleased to give his every moment of time and attention to, and yet he knew he wouldn't be able to speak to her the way he wanted to.

He wanted to ask how her day had gone. He wanted to celebrate her success on the stock exchange and ask her how she knew it was the right time to sell. He wanted to show her his respect for the way she worked and talk about it; he sensed there was much more to Abby, so many details to discover and appreciate. Fate had not dealt him a good hand, though, and he felt caged by their circumstances.

Perhaps that's why he had decided to take her to his father's restaurant, Glykeria, the smallest of his three London eateries. They could have gone to one of hundreds of restaurants, but no. It was almost as if he wanted his real identity to be brought out in the open by chance, but deep down he knew that might throw everyone into chaos. What would she do if the truth came out now? *Depends what her motives are.* She'd either leave in disgust because he hadn't said anything, as Nathan seemed to hint, or dump him in annoyance that her own plans hadn't worked out. Whatever those plans were. It looked like a no-win situation.

When the door to the pub swung open and Abby sashayed in, all those niggling doubts began to fall away from him. She was there, and she looked delicious, wearing some sort of filmy dress the color of the sea. It floated down into layers around her shins. The straps of her sandals crisscrossed over her elegant feet and wound themselves around her ankles. Slender threads of jewels at her throat and wrist caught the light as she walked over to him. The fabric of her dress pooled enticingly in her cleavage and shimmied over her body in all the right places when she moved. She didn't appear to be wearing a bra. Yes, his attention was all hers.

"Sorry I'm late, I had to wait an age for a taxi."

"No worries. Shall we go straight to the restaurant?"

"Mm, sounds good." She took his arm. "I've got quite an appetite."

"I like how that sounds," he commented before he kissed her, long and hard.

As they were walking, he glanced at her quizzically. She was like a drug, making him forget the doubts he had when he wasn't by her side, making him only experience the pleasure of being with Abby, like a siren of the sea calling to him, entrancing him.

She was observing him, too, as they walked, her steps perfectly in time with his. "So where are you taking me? This feels a bit like a mystery tour."

So does our relationship, he thought with a bizarre sense of irony. But she was smiling at him so happily, her eyes bright with anticipation. His more primal aspect urged him to enjoy the moment, to make it last, to be inside her again and again—for as long as their relationship could possibly last.

"I was thinking we could eat at a good Greek restaurant I know. It's not too far from here, if you'd like to give it a try?"

"Oh yes, that sounds great."

She stared up at the sign as they neared the door. "Glykeria. What does it mean?"

"Sweet. It's like something sweet."

It was how his father had felt about getting his own restaurant up and running, the way he himself felt about The Hub, now, in fact. This restaurant was the smallest of his father's chain, and the most friendly. The tables were arranged in varied group sizes between demurely placed pillars and foliage. It was his father's first venue, and Zac had fond memories of being taken there for a special treat as a child.

He didn't recognize the young waiter who came forward to seat them, but within seconds Stefano, the restaurant manager, had spotted him and was cutting a fast path through the tables to greet them.

"Zachary, you should have phoned, I would have saved our best table."

"No need, Stefano." He shook Stefano's hand warmly. "I don't want any fuss," he winked, "just a private evening and some of your good food for myself and my guest."

"I understand. Follow me. We have something discreet over here." Stefano bowed in greeting, looking at Abby with open admiration, then ushered them to a secluded table. After seating them, he supplied them with menus and left them in peace.

"Now this is perfect," Abby said, reaching across the small table to stroke his hand.

At that moment he felt he would give up everything he owned just to be with her, to have her body close to his. He felt a fierce desire for possession of her flesh and blood. "It is. I hope you will enjoy the menu. Do you know much about Greek food?"

"Only a little," she replied.

"From the island-hopping holiday?"

"Yes."

She seemed pleased that he had remembered. How could he forget that particular tale? He'd practically leapt on her as she described her growing awareness of her sensuality and what it did to her.

She glanced at the menu. "I'd like you to choose for me."

"Really?" He was amused. For the seemingly independent Abby, it struck him as unusual, but then he had so much to learn about her, didn't he?

She nodded. "I put my trust in your expertise." She said it as if she was referring to something much more intimate than a restaurant menu. "Oh, except I'd like to try the retsina again, if they have a good bottle." She winked.

Why did that small thing bring him so much pleasure?

She was smiling to herself as she listened to him speak in Greek to Stefano, giving his choices for the meal.

He turned back to her. "What are you thinking?"

"About the islands. I'd like to go back one day. My mother is there now, coincidentally."

"You said your father died, yes?"

"Yes, and since then, my mother has been going back to all the places they visited together. She's become quite the traveler in her mature years. I think perhaps she's trying to recapture the memories. It's sad. I think she senses now how much more they could have had from life if they had just tried to enjoy each moment as it happened." Her mind drifted, and he drew her back with his caress. She laughed at herself.

Her mind fascinated him. "People don't realize the important things in life until they are taken away. Is that what you think?"

She nodded. "It's not something we sit down and think about enough, yes. If we did, we'd be a whole lot better armed to prioritize life as it happened."

"What's important to you, Abby?" He couldn't resist asking, even if it was a loaded question.

She looked straight at him, and her glance teased him in a way that made his chest ache. She stroked his hand, running her fingertips over the back of his fingers, trailing her nails over his knuckles. "Outside of this, outside being here with you, now?"

His spine tensed with a sense of delicious anxiety, his body alert to her every move. "It is good, isn't it?" Even as he said the words, it felt like the understatement of the year. It was more than good. Deep down, he knew it was the best he'd ever had. He wanted her so badly. He arrested her fingers with his, locking their hands together. The way she looked at him when he did so made his loins flood. Her pupils were dark, her expression hungry.

The wine waiter arrived with their retsina. They pulled apart to allow him to pour the wine.

"But what else?" he asked, when they were alone again.

"My work, I suppose . . . being professional."

"Professional," he repeated, with a sinking feeling.

She smiled, her eyes filled with secret memory. "I had this one secondary school teacher that I really liked, and she said something that has always stuck with me. Remain professional, no matter what life throws at you, no matter what the situation is, and you will do well in life. So far I've managed to remember that, and it served me well."

Zac felt as if he'd been hit in the solar plexus. The words she spoke meant everything to her; he could see that. But because they were about her job and its place in her life, they put an instant barrier between them, a barrier he wanted to kick aside but didn't know how to overcome. They also threw a new light on his doubts about her integrity. Had he mistrusted her unjustly?

"Kind of like the old saying about keeping your head, when all around you are losing theirs," she added when he didn't respond.

He attempted to muster a response. "It sounds like a good motto to live by." He felt like he was the one losing his head right then.

Stefano arrived with the selection of starter dishes he had ordered and mercifully broke the awkward moment.

Zac distracted himself by tempting her with the offerings, telling her about their preparation, their ingredients, and their history. "A selection such as this we call *mezethakia*. It means that which opens the appetite."

"My appetite is never satisfied when you are near," she breathed in response.

He followed her remark by offering her a *dolmathes* and a smile.

She listened to him while she tasted the exquisite stuffed vegetables, the rich dense flavor of the garlic-smoked bacon, the light spinach and cheese found in the pastry-wrapped envelopes.

"Food has always been very important to Greek culture, and it's been immortalized in many great literary works," he explained. "But eating is often very informal, so that it becomes an art that pervades the everyday." His fingers lifted a tiny hollowed cherry tomato stuffed with pine nuts and cheese to her lips.

"I know which flavor of Greece I'd like to taste every day." She blew him a suggestive kiss and then sipped her wine to hide her smile.

He feasted on her image; the wine arresting each moment in a capsule of pine-needled memory. He wanted this to last and last. "Abby, I shall forget to eat at all if you continue to make such erotic comments."

Her laughter made him feel warm.

The main course arrived. Stefano himself continued to serve them, but astutely let them be private, too.

"What a feast, a real banquet," Abby said while he served the main course.

"A beggar's banquet," Stefano replied. "It is the restaurant philosophy. These are the everyday flavors of Greece." He told her how the baked red mullet was cooked, with lemon and olive dressing, and why the grilled aubergines, tiny potatoes, and shallots braised in balsamic vinegar were the right accompaniment.

Stefano liked her, Zac noticed as they chatted. It made him wonder if his parents might like her, too, but then he couldn't imagine anyone not liking Abby. His mother would take to her for sure; he had no doubt about that whatsoever. They were kindred souls.

"What are you smiling about so secretively?" she asked when Stefano had gone.

"Sorry." *I'm trying to work out what my parents would make of you.* No, he couldn't tell her that. And why was he even thinking like that? It wasn't something he usually did when he got involved with a woman. Was it the strange juncture of their lives through his mother's business, or something else? Once again he felt like rattling his cage of circumstance or throwing a spanner in the works.

She was still looking at him, waiting. "You're a very mysterious man, and that's one of the things I like about you, but my curiosity sometimes gets the better of me."

"What are you curious about?"

"Well, have you got a wife and family you haven't told me about?"

He laughed. "No. Why do you ask?"

"You seemed faraway, and yet you were smiling. I wondered if I was a bit on the side."

"Abby, you're far too all-absorbing to be a bit on the side." It hadn't even occurred to him that she might think that, but his mind had been following a completely different path, he realized, and chastised himself for being so blinkered.

"Am I your bit on the side?" he asked cautiously.

"No." She smiled.

He was relieved, yes, but it didn't make him feel much better.

Zac was pensive this evening. He might deny it, but Abby could see he was. The shadows cast by a small copper-encased lamp lit him strangely from above. Abby had to touch him to reassure herself that he was there.

When they were sitting over black coffee and a platter of rich, syrupy baklava, she noticed that his eyes seemed to hold a dark question. It was as if he was trying to decide whether to walk away from her forever or draw her into his aura never to be released. Her hand went to his when the thought occurred to her. "I feel as if you're going to walk away from me."

"Perhaps you read minds?"

She froze.

He smiled. "I have to go to Paris later in the week."

Her body clenched with a sudden feeling of loss. She sank back in her chair, unable to voice any objection but feeling deprived of him already.

He reached into his pocket and drew out some photos. "It's a club in Paris; I'm thinking of buying it." He passed her the photos. "I have this idea about a chain of Hubs, one day."

She looked at the pictures with interest, glad that he had included her. There were a couple of interior views and an exterior. Inside she saw a cavelike design of interlocked rooms, bars, and a dance floor. It was full of character, intrinsically Parisian in style. Outside, the entrance was discreet but caught the eye with its Art Nouveau ironwork. It was a fascinating little property, one that she would be pleased to look at herself on behalf of a client. She smiled when she found herself wondering whether he needed a full-time investment advisor.

"I think it would be great investment," she murmured as she looked over the images, roll-calling all the excellent features that caught her eye. "European cities are having a renaissance in the holiday market, weekend breaks and so on. Character venues will always appeal."

After a moment she glanced up, aware that he hadn't replied.

He was watching her with a curious look on his face. He was probably wondering what on earth she knew about it. She'd told him she was a receptionist, after all.

"I listen to them talking, at work. They deal with a lot of top-notch property." Why hadn't she remembered? The answer was, of course, sitting in front of her. He was such a distraction. She made a mental note to clarify what she did for a living, but she didn't want to bring it up tonight and break the current flow.

Thankfully, he spoke, covering her awkwardness. "Of course you listen. I'm glad you think it's got potential."

His eyes had that shuttered look that made her want to know what he was thinking, to know more about him, to see the real man who was so alluring beneath what he revealed to her.

He tucked the photos back into his jacket, then picked up the menu and described to her the range of liqueurs that she had to choose from before they left.

"This is sex in a glass," she commented, while sipping her Metaxa appreciatively.

"Do you think about sex all the time?" he teased, pleased that she liked the Greek brandy.

"Not quite," she replied, chuckling.

"Isn't it inconvenient, when you're working, for example?" He wasn't going to let it go.

"No. Sometimes I think my sex drive fuels everything I do."

He was laughing quietly, his hand partially covering his mouth as he looked at her. He was enjoying some secret thoughts.

"Don't laugh; you're embarrassing me. Anyway, circumstances prevail; I'm with a very sexy man." She gestured at him.

He actually looked embarrassed. So, it was possible. She congratulated herself inwardly and stored the moment away. She suspected it was a rare treat.

They stared at each other across the table, their mutual attraction making heat and energy flow between them. It charged their bodies with its suggestions, with its demands. Her lips parted, and a hungry sigh climbed out and spoke to him. His hand slipped down her bare arm and stroked it firmly.

"Witch," he murmured, his voice a low hiss.

Her hips rocked forward instinctively and pressed her sex down into the hardness of her chair. His eyes fell as he took in the movement of her body, and his hand paused on her arm. He glanced up.

"Are you always like this, Abby?" He spoke in a low whisper.

"No, it's you. I want you."

Their mutual passion was total, uninhibited. His mouth crept into a smile, and his fingers moved back to the thin strap of her dress at her shoulder. "You're making me hard."

"You're making me wet."

"Tell me about it."

She didn't reply. She was watching the candlelight flicker in his eyes as her body took in the movement of his leg against hers under the table. She slipped her foot out of her sandal and lifted it until it crept between his legs.

His eyebrows rose when she slunk down in her chair and put her bare foot over the bulge of his cock in his pants. He moved his hand under the table to close over her ankle.

His hand was warm and firm. He stroked her calf muscle, and she felt her eyes start to close as she savored it.

"Tell me more." he whispered. He leaned forward in his chair.

"Inside, I'm creaming for you, Zac."

His eyes narrowed, his passionate mouth growing taut with restraint as he listened.

"When I move . . . I'm sticky with it." She shifted in her chair. "My G-string is clinging to me."

"Open your legs." His expression left her no choice.

Her legs wavered apart, and the cool air teased her. She trembled slightly.

"Touch yourself."

Across the table, the force of his will controlled her. She snuck her hand under the white linen tablecloth and pulled up her skirts, slipping her fingers under her G-string and resting her hand over her mons.

His gaze dropped as if he could see through the table, then lifted again. "Do it, make yourself come, now. I want you to."

Curving her foot over the hard bulge of his cock, she pressed her foot over him as she squeezed herself. Dipping her fingers into the damp entrance to her sex, gathering the sticky fluid of her desire onto her fingers, she stroked them up into the tender groove of her aroused flesh. Spreading either side of her clit, she squeezed, her knuckles gently nudging free a spasm of ecstasy. A quiet whimper escaped her.

His mouth was braced in a tense smile as he watched, his expression wolflike in the extreme.

Her hips began to rock against her hand, where she rubbed slowly at first, then faster and faster, her clit buzzing with pure delirium.

The air stirred as someone walked by, but she didn't register more than that, looking only at him. His fascinated expression urged her on, until she was pressing so hard the peak was seconds away and she had to clamp her lips together to stop herself from making a noise.

"Oh, Abby, you look so beautiful, especially when you are about to come."

He can tell. It pushed her over the edge; a blaze of energy suffused her groin, followed by hot waves of relief pooling over her entire body, her fingers coated in her juices.

"Let me taste you."

His request made her groan. She felt so horny that she could climb over the table and straddle him right there and then. She pulled her hand out from under the table and laid it over his. He lifted it to his lips and licked her fingertips. Her body shuddered slightly, caught on the brink of a new wave of lust.

"That's only made me want you even more," she commented.

"That's just as well, because you're going to have to have me, and soon." He gave her a dark smile. "I want to take you down a dark alley and find the nearest wall to stand up against so I can fuck you." He gave that slow, wolf smile that she loved so much.

"Let's do it then." Was it the thought of him leaving for Paris that made her reckless, she wondered fleetingly, or something else? *Him? Just him?* But she wanted to do it as much as he did.

He threw a wad of notes down on the table, gesturing at the waiter as he did so, then stood up, abandoning the drinks.

She retied her sandal strap and followed his lead, smiling as she reached for his hand. They walked away from the table and out of the restaurant, almost racing one another into the street, moving quickly along the pavement. As the sounds and music of the restaurant faded behind them, her heart pounded; she felt dizzy with arousal, deviant, barely in check.

After a few moments he slowed and turned into a small alleyway. "Come on," he said, taking her hand.

Her pulse rate soared. It was perfect. When they reached the middle, he glanced around. They were between two tall buildings in a narrow cobbled passage that was lit at each end but dark at the center point.

Abby pulled on his hand, drawing him to a halt. "Here's good," she insisted, pointing to a narrow ledge of brick jutting from the wall, hungrily grabbing at him for a kiss, pulling him up against her as she backed toward the wall.

He ran his hand over the fabric covering her breasts, his breath coming thick and fast.

She balanced her hips on the narrow ledge and clutched at him, one leg climbing against him, inviting him in. She wanted fast, clandestine sex, and she wanted it now. "I want you really badly."

He glanced back down the alley. There was no one in sight. He lifted the skirts of her dress, shimmying them up around her thighs and hips, tearing her wet G-string down the length of her legs. Abby clutched at him, one leg climbing against him. His hand slipped into the warm, damp groove of her sex.

"I wouldn't have missed that show in there for the world."

Crazy laughter bubbled up inside her, alongside the desire that carried her. She was high on his presence, every moment sending her farther into orbit.

"I must taste you. I want to lick you clean." He kissed her hard, his tongue thrashing with hers, and then he pulled away and squatted in front of her, moving between her thighs. His mouth sank over her mons, kissing her deeply, while his hands spread her open. "Exquisite," he whispered, then ran his tongue up and down from her hole to her clit.

She trembled, her hips pressing forward to take his caresses. His stubble ground against her, electrifying her skin, while his tongue thrust inside her sex, seeking out and devouring her as he kissed and caressed her, inside and out. She whimpered when the tension began to climb back up through her pelvis, his mouth bringing her quickly back to climax again. Her hips moved instinctively, tracing the innate movements of carnal pleasure without the need for thought while he led her back to that special place again.

As if sensing the imminence of her release, he centered his mouth on her clitoris, sucking gently, teasing it to fruition, his fingers moving against the sleek walls of her inner sex. He pressed a digit against the swollen pad of flesh on the front wall of her sex, and she almost lost consciousness for a moment as the second climax took her, racking her body with dense throbs and spasms that spiraled out from his mouth.

She was still catching her breath when she heard his zipper. She'd grown accustomed to the dark; she could see him holding the thick, hard shaft of his cock in his hand while he rolled on a rubber. She reached her arms around his neck and put one leg up against his flank, inviting him in.

"I could eat you forever," he whispered against her mouth. He lifted her other leg around his hip and pushed her body up the wall, easily strong enough to hold her.

She moaned her approval, urging him on. His cock nudged inside her. He eased the head a little farther, and then lunged deep. For a moment she was still, holding her breath, completely taken with the feeling of being filled suddenly, her sex sensitized to the max by what had gone before.

Then she breathed out. He pulled back and then drove himself inside her, thoroughly. She groaned with pleasure, her head thrown back by the force. Above them clouds scudded away from the moon, flooding them in its eerie glow. Her legs locked around him, and she twined her hands around his neck and then across his back, grasping at him with feeble hands. It felt like dirty, illicit sex—and it felt so, so good.

His thrusts became deep and fast, his body driving her up against the wall. The straps of her dress slid down and he placed a fevered kiss on her breast where it jigged up. She ground her hips against his to pull him in to the hilt, her back riding up against the rough brickwork of the wall.

She gave a breathy laugh, her hips arched. Her body was burning up with the feeling of being stretched to capacity and that oh-so-delicious nudge up against her very core when he landed against it, sending a roar of heat through her groin and releasing a flurry of sensation in the pit of her stomach each and every time.

She heard a sound, and saw two figures pass the end of the alley. Their voices faded away, and they obviously hadn't seen anything, but Abby couldn't help picturing how they might look to a passerby, indulging in a furtive, surreptitious encounter up against the wall, clothes asunder, and the image only served to throw fuel on her fire.

"I'm coming."

"I know. You're on fire," he groaned. His face contorted when she came, her body clutching at his cock.

"It's you, your cock, it feels so damn good." Her voice lifted in pleasure. "I want to see. Let me see it, Zac?" she asked. "Wank for me like I did in there, please, Zac?"

"Now?"

"Yes."

He moaned quietly and thrust faster, then pulled out. "Bloody hell, woman, you know how to drive a man insane," he muttered. He reached down and locked her hand over her sex.

She could feel the reluctant control in his touch.

He ripped the condom off.

She stared at the fiercely pulsing head of his cock. It was so swollen; the sheen of it glistened in the moonlight. His fist rode it faster, his body arched before her to fulfill her request. She glanced up; he was watching her face. His eyes were like hot coals, burning with lust for her as she looked on him. His eyebrows were drawn close together, concentration holding them. Her lips parted, fingers rubbing her clit.

His mouth opened, and his hand moved faster still, then it slowed to a complete stop.

She looked down and saw the upward surge of the flesh in his hand. As it pumped and spurted, ribbons of semen flew between them. She gave a small cry at the sight of it and then Zac's hands fell against the wall as he leaned into her and clung to her, his body shuddering in release, his mouth kissing her neck hungrily.

"I want more, more than this," he whispered against her throat. "I want to fuck you all night long."

"Good," she replied. "Because I haven't done with you yet."

They kissed hungrily, shared promises captured in their embrace, staying in the dark alley for a long while, their bodies pressed close against each other. She only turned away from him when voices rose up, and a crowd of people passed the end of the alleyway.

He bent to straighten her skirts.

"What a gentleman you are."

"I do my best." He stood up.

"I thought someone might see us."

"You sound disappointed."

"It turns me on, I have to confess."

He growled, "Tell me more."

"Well, during the Shock Tart show, half of me wanted to watch; half of me wanted to be up there on the stage with them, being sexually provocative like that, in front of a crowd of onlookers."

In the moonlight, she could see his eyes gleaming with interest.

"Now, that I'd pay to see."

She gave a throaty laugh. "Oh, but I wouldn't charge *you*, Zac."

"It could always be arranged." He kissed her neck, his breath hot on her tingling skin, making her chuckle and writhe against him.

"I suppose you do run a theater, with a stage." Laughter bubbled inside her.

"Unfortunately it's fully booked this week."

"Shame," she teased.

"Another time or place." He glanced down the alley again. "Do you suppose we can make it back to my place before I have to have you again?" His eyes met hers, and she saw the twinkle of amusement in his expression. "I shall want to fuck you, properly . . . soon. I want to come inside you."

She knew what he meant. He meant really come inside her. Her sex gave a pang of longing. "I want that, too. We could try to make it," she added.

Music and traffic noise traveled through the night air, greeting them as they emerged from the alley. Zac hailed a taxi. Inside, he turned to her and lifted her chin with one finger, his expression suddenly serious. "Look, we've got tomorrow before I go away, but why don't you join me in Paris on Friday evening? We could make a weekend of it."

Her heart leapt. She could see he was being cautious, as if unsure whether she would want to go. She looked up at him; she couldn't think of anything she would like to do more. "Yes," she replied. "Oh yes please, Zac." She didn't try to hide the pleasure his invitation gave her.

He stroked her hair, then ran his fingers over her cheek, his smile showing her how glad he was. "I can sort you out a booking?"

"No, that's OK. I'll organize it."

When he kissed her, she could feel his mouth smiling against hers. She ran her hands under his jacket, drawing his hips closer to her. Paris, far away from everyone, just the two of them. Her body began to pulse with anticipation.

• • •

On the other side of the city, Nathan was at The Hub, standing by the sound-mixing board, watching a band rehearse, when he felt his phone vibrating in his hip pocket. He pulled it out and saw from the screen display that it was Suzanne.

"This is an unexpected surprise."

"I've been thinking about you," she whispered.

He could barely hear her. "That's good news, but why are we whispering?"

"The little one has just gone off to sleep."

Of course, she had said she was babysitting. "Hold on while I move somewhere quieter." He walked away from the stage into the corridor at the rear, where the sound was muted. As he did, a picture of domestic bliss featuring Suzanne at the center settled into his mind, and he smiled. Settling down wasn't something he ever thought about, but now that Suzanne had been dropped in his path, he found that he rather enjoyed the image.

"That's better."

"Can you hear me now?" she whispered.

"Oh yes."

"Is that music I hear? Are you at a gig?"

"I'm at a rehearsal. I do some sound mixing. It's a new band, and they're just trying out the stage for acoustics. They're pretty good. I thought maybe you'd like to come down and hear them play on Friday night?"

"Oh, Nathan, I'd love to." Even though she was whispering, he could hear the excitement in her voice. "I've just been thinking about how much fun we had last night."

Listening to her whisper down the line had put a big smile on his face. At the base of his spine, that intense thudding sensation had kicked in. "Me, too; in fact I don't know if I feel like waiting until Saturday for a repeat performance."

"Me neither."

Thud, thud. His cock was straining against his jeans. "What are you doing tomorrow night?"

"Seeing you." She gave a quiet, soft laugh that trickled over him in the most maddening way. "You could pick me up from work about seven?"

"Sure thing, dynamite girl. I'll be there."

seven | nɘvɘƨ

Nathan put Zac's double espresso down in front of him and peered at his face with a frown. "Blimey, who died?"

Zac responded with a wry smile. "I'm about to do something I may or may not regret for the rest of my life." The screen saver on his laptop chose that moment to spring into action, which threw him. He teased the mouse, reread the e-mail he'd typed, and hovered over the Send button.

"Is it something I should know about?"

Zac shrugged. "I'm bringing the Robertson Corporation end-of-contract meeting forward. I've requested it be next Monday rather than the following one, and I'm going to attend myself."

Nathan's eyebrows lifted. "I take it this is because of Abby?"

It may well be because I'm going insane. Life had been bizarre, to say the least, since he'd met Abigail Douglas. What had started as a situation where Abby's possible private agenda bothered him had somehow flipped over, and he now felt as if he was the one leading a double life—that he was the one with something to hide. And he didn't like that feeling one little bit. "Yes. It is about Abby. I've invited her to spend the weekend with me, but after that I want this thing resolved. No matter which way it goes."

"Are we done digging for information on her?"

"I think so."

Nathan nodded slowly, as if weighing up his response. "Do you want to keep seeing her?"

Zac didn't hesitate for a moment. "In an ideal world, yes."

"In that case, are you sure you want to do this?"

"You were the one that told me the truth would come out at some point."

Nathan pursed his lips. "True."

"I don't want to throw off her concentration while she's busy working on the portfolio. But for the sake of my sanity it has to be soon, hence the compromise."

Nathan opened his own giant latte and took a mouthful, watching with a speculative expression.

Zac hit Send. As soon as the e-mail was gone, he had the crazy urge to call her. He picked up his mobile phone as soon as Nathan left the room and turned it in his hand, thinking it over, trying to quell the impetuous need he felt to control this situation.

He wanted to see her; he wanted to spend every minute with her that he could, in case it all fell apart. Would that help though? Wouldn't it be better to keep some distance, just in case their relationship did crash and burn? Logic didn't seem to help. He had to face it. He was falling for her.

· · ·

Abby stared at the e-mail in astonishment. Adrianna wanted to bring the meeting forward by a whole week. *Damn.* In her mind, she had three weeks to prove herself. She'd hardly begun to do what she had planned for that space of time. She hadn't even secured a property deal yet. *Keep your head,* she told herself. *You've taken significant steps. That is all you can do, given the lack of time.*

She looked at the e-mail again. It had been copied to Tom, so there wasn't any point in trying to negotiate; he'd just insist they put the client's request first.

There was a knock at the door, and Caroline came into the office. She walked over and dropped a stack of papers down on Abby's desk. She frowned when she noticed Abby's expression. "What's up?"

"The Ashburn renewal meeting has been brought forward, just when I'm getting a grip on it."

"That is a shame, but you've stamped your name all over it already from what I hear." Winking, she grinned. "Everybody's been talking about it. Besides, this client is pretty much bound to renew, so you'll be fine."

Caroline had a point. "I hope so. I'm away this weekend, so I'll have to do all my prep by Friday."

"I've got something that will cheer you up."

"Is it about Blayne?" Her spirits lifted immediately.

"Yup. I've been in direct contact with a senior Dublin heritage advisor. They would be happy to support your proposals for the property."

"That's fabulous news."

"The previous owners have let the estate run down over the last twenty years, but it's not beyond repair, far from it. Apparently they've been concerned about it being bought for land use alone, for cattle. The inland part of the estate is good pasture, but the heritage in the property could be lost if that was the main focus, so your interest was good news to them."

"That's interesting." Her mind was turning over with ideas. "I must make a note to mention the land potential in my report, as an added incentive. The client could rent out part of it, immediately, to gain income while doing the restoration work."

"Sounds great, you're onto a winner."

"I'm so pleased," Abby replied. "Now all we need is Adrianna's OK, and I'm good to go on the auction."

"So, spill. Why is this account so important? Is it because you're flying solo and concerned it look good?"

"Yes, and I've set myself a challenge with this account. It was a good opportunity to test myself. I wanted to see how well I could do on my own."

Caroline nodded. "It's been good for you; we can all see that."

"The important thing is that I will be able to advise Adrianna to purchase Blayne Castle and start early planning and restoration phases with the profits from the share sale."

"Nicely done," Caroline replied.

"Yes," Abby said with a smile. "If I pull the deal off, it will be a real achievement. The portfolio manifesto was weighted toward property, but I wanted to do something unique. I'm going to send my proposals through to her this afternoon, and then get in touch with some architects. I'd better get back to the heritage people, too, and keep them on board. I'll be pushed for time on this, but I'll try to get a full outline of the proposals ready for the meeting on Monday."

"Have you met her?" Caroline asked.

"The formidable Adrianna? No, not yet."

Caroline laughed. "Good title. She is quite formidable and a little eccentric. I met her when Tom called me in to look at the special terms in the contract for her account."

"The daily reports?"

Caroline nodded. "I hope I'm like that when I'm her age. Sharp as a saber and easy on the eye."

Abby nodded. "I've been looking forward to meeting her, I have to say. Ed said that she's a very interesting person." She paused a moment, her thoughts distracted as she saw the castle being whisked away from her hands by its rightful owner. "I do hope the Ashburn account is extended so that I can monitor its progress after it has passed out of my control." *That's if I even stay here.*

"Well, you could always watch from afar," Caroline replied. "And go visit the castle when it's all done, knowing it was your idea."

"Yes, I could do that." Abby's mind was drifting to her private image of the castle, with a dark prince and a big white bed.

"Now you're talking." Caroline chuckled.

From her bag, Abby's mobile phone began to chime.

"I'll leave you to it," Caroline said, tapping the stack of papers she'd left for Abby and heading out.

"Cheers. We'll talk more later."

Abby glanced at the display on the phone. It was Zac. Her stomach gave a little flip, her emotions spinning. As she went to answer the call, she wondered how just seeing his name on her caller ID could evoke such a strong reaction from her. "Hello, Zac, there isn't a problem about tonight, is there?"

"No, I just had to speak with you, I was wondering . . . Can you meet me for a half hour, now?"

Yes, her body answered, her pulse racing. She glanced at the clock. It was midmorning. "I guess I could call you lunch," she replied with a naughty smile. "Why?"

"Why do you think?" His voice was tight with need.

He wanted her. There was a sense of desperation in his voice that freed a thrill inside her, one that plumed through her entire body.

"Tomorrow I'll be in Paris. I know we're meeting tonight, but if I can grab you for a half hour now . . . Abby, I'm desperate to put my hands on you."

"Oh, Zac," she murmured into the phone, her womanly center melting in response to his words.

"I'll get a taxi and come for you."

"Yes, I can be outside the building in say . . . twenty minutes."

By the time she put down the phone, she was as eager for the interruption as he sounded. She had to write her report for the formidable Adriana, but she had the afternoon to do that. She wanted to spend every moment she could with Zac; she felt as if time were short. It had to be his imminent departure for Paris that gave her that feeling, but she would be there with him soon enough. Maybe it was because she felt he could just as easily disappear from her life as he had entered it. She was getting all the signs that this was an affair, a fling. When she was with him, she couldn't help hoping for it to be more, but could she really take the risk with a man like Zac? A man who was as elusive as he was the embodiment of every fantasy she could possibly have. *Don't fall for him; he's not the type.*

She looked at her watch and grabbed her bag. Whatever it was she was doing with him, she sure as hell was going to enjoy every minute of it, Paris included.

In the lady's restroom, where she was touching up her lipstick, Suzanne came in and darted over, grinning.

"Hey you, how's the love life?"

"Couldn't be better."

"Excellent. I'm pleased to say mine is looking up, too."

Abby rolled her lipstick down and shoved it into her bag as she looked at Suzanne. "Yes? Tell me all."

"Well, whoever is employing the men down at that courier company has good taste, I can tell you that much." Suzanne laughed. "The next one that came in was just as sexy, and this time I snagged him." She winked.

"Ha, that is great news. You have fun. I want you to tell me all about it." She glanced at her watch. "I've got to dash now though, I've got a lunch date."

"Now let me guess. It wouldn't be with Mr. Tall, Dark, and Handsome, otherwise known as Zac, would it?"

"You're too good at this game." Abby hugged her and then set off, her spirits high.

In the foyer, she could see the busy London street thrummed with movement and noise. The sun was high in the sky, lighting up the crowded pavements between the tall buildings in the heart of The City. She took a moment to absorb the atmosphere as she walked out of the tall glass and steel revolving doors. The street was buzzing with energy, and so was she.

Zac leaned forward and gestured to the driver. "Pull over, just ahead."

The driver slowed and signaled.

Zac leaned across the backseat and opened the door for Abby. She moved, leggy, sophisticated, and beautiful, toward the car. His pleasure at seeing her immediately turned carnal. His cock had hardened as soon as he caught sight of her standing on the side of the road, and it was pounding in his pants by the time she climbed in.

She was immaculately presented for the corporate world in a

125

cream-colored fitted skirt and jacket that brought out her coloring and showed off her figure superbly. Beneath the jacket she wore a camisole that gaped endearingly as she climbed in, letting his gaze rest lovingly on her bare cleavage for a moment. High heels and the short skirt showed off her long, elegant legs to perfection, and Zac simply stared, not trusting himself to say anything about her appearance.

She was smiling, her cat's eyes twinkling with pleasure. He reached over to kiss her long and hard on the mouth.

"Where to?" The driver had a smirk on his face as he observed the two of them clinched together in the backseat. Miles away, Zac had forgotten they were on one of the busiest streets in the city, and on a double yellow line at that.

"Just drive," Zac ordered.

The driver shrugged and set off. "Your call," he replied, glancing happily at his meter.

She leaned into him, and he captured her in his arms, her breasts crushing against him as he held her. *All woman.* "All mine." The words escaped him as he kissed her neck.

"Yes," she breathed, her fingers moving through his hair.

He kissed her mouth, his tongue tasting her. He couldn't get enough.

"Abby, I need to be inside you."

"You want me now?" she asked, amazed.

His mouth twitched on one side. He nodded.

"Here?"

He gave her another nod.

"Right here," he said quietly, and his hand moved up and down against his pants, rubbing the bulk of his cock.

"But . . . how?"

His eyes narrowed, and he slid his body forward on the seat, jutting his hips out toward her. Glancing at the back of the driver's head, he unzipped his pants and closed one hand around the stem of his erection that pushed eagerly from his shorts. He held it in a light grip, moving in slow, even strokes.

She watched the movement; she shifted on the seat. She glanced up.

Zac tried to control his breathing. The cab was pulled up at a traffic light; people were walking across the road in front of them. Alarm bells were starting to sound in his head, but the thrill of the moment held him. He fixed her eye with his, staring blatantly at her.

She nodded, her lips softly parted; it was all the encouragement he needed.

"Driver." He leaned forward as the cab pulled away from the lights, glancing around to try to figure out where they were, hiding his eager cock from view. "Pull into that alleyway," he instructed.

The driver grumbled but quickly hauled the vehicle into a narrow alley between two tall buildings, barely much bigger than the cab itself. He braked sharply just before making contact with the Dumpsters housed there, pulled on the brake, and turned round. "A little more notice would be helpful." He stared at the fistful of money Zac was holding out to him.

"Get out of the cab and wait at the end of the street." It was an order.

"Hey, I'm not about to leave you with my cab, oh no, I'm not falling for that one."

"Take the keys then." It was uttered through gritted teeth. "Lock us in if you like; just get the hell out for a few minutes."

The driver looked again at the sizable amount of cash being offered.

Zac spied a packet of cigarettes on the dash. "A week's wages in return for taking a cigarette break?" he pointed out, harsh need biting into his blood.

The driver snatched the cash from his hand, grabbed his cigs and the car keys, tipped a salute to the pair of them, and promptly left.

Zac glanced after him, watched him take up a sentrylike pose behind the car and light a cigarette, then slumped back in the seat, turning his attention to Abby once again.

She was sitting on the edge of the seat, looking dazed. Strands of her hair had fallen free from where it was clipped back high on her head. She was eyeing his cock as if about to devour him.

His cock twitched eagerly.

Her eyes rose to his. "Now?" She whispered.

He nodded, a dark thrill running through his veins. She looked so gorgeous, her arousal blatant in her expression, her lips parted, her pupils dilated. She reached to kiss him, her lips soft and lush, tender beneath his. Her scent intoxicated him; he wanted to hold onto her forever.

Her fingers moved across his thigh to his cock, where it reared up from his shorts. Another wave of lust pooled in his groin as her head dropped toward his lap, her lips parting.

Zac mouthed a string of silent curses at the ceiling of the cab as her lovely mouth closed over the engorged head of his cock. Her lips molded over its swollen tip, slowly sinking onto it, and then her tongue swept over the surface while her fingers reached for his balls.

His hands fisted against the seat when she took it deep into her mouth, riding it in and out, her moves threatening to make him come far too quickly.

"I have to be inside you . . . Abby." He was desperate for her, angling his hips on the seat. "Give it to me; I want to feel you here, now." He pulled a condom from his pocket, his hands near useless as he tore it open. He managed to roll it on, one hand closing tight around his shaft, the other reaching for her.

She hauled her skirt up around her hips and wiggled out of her thong, her shoes dropping to the floor of the cab. She straddled him, her legs folding against the seat, her thighs enclosing his hips.

When she rose up in front of him, he pushed her chemise up and sucked heavily on her breasts. His hands rested at her waist as he moved over her nipples with his mouth.

She was wet, like honey, and his cock slid up against her clitoris, the full head of it rolling against the swollen nub. She opened her mouth wide and rubbed herself against the hard surface of his cock, catching the sensitive skin on the underside.

He breathed out loudly; each sensation was inexorably torturous and pleasurable. She led the head of his cock along the hot folds of skin that lined her sweet entrance and let it press home there, the flush of arousal heightening across her face and neck. Her perfume, heavy with musk and honeysuckle, was tempered with smell of her sex, as intoxicating as nectar to him.

An almost unbearable demand throbbed inside him, and he drew her close, his hands around her waist.

She sank down onto him in one gliding movement and settled herself on his hips.

The pull of her body sucking in his cock was exquisite. He groaned, his head going back against the seat of the cab. He closed his eyes, savoring the pleasure of his cock thrusting up inside her tight sheath, and he moved his hands from her waist over her breasts and up into her hair as it fell against him.

"Abby," he breathed. "Oh, Abby." His voice was heavy. She lifted her hips, riding up with a flex of her knees on the seat on either side of him. He groaned, and she began to ride his shaft in regular movements; she gripped the back of the seat and freed her movements, taking his hardness into her with determination each time and then grinding down with utter determination and a cry of pleasure.

Their need was entirely in tune, and she laughed and looked down at him, her face radiating the rapture she felt.

"Oh yes," he said and gave a low laugh. The desperation had gone; this release was what he wanted. Longing had been replaced by outright pleasure. He sprawled on the seat, his hands resting on the bunched fabric of her skirt around her hips as she moved over him with abandon, looking down at him with the laughter still on her face.

She reached forward and stroked his hair free with her fingers. Her mouth was opening as she rocked slightly and massaged the head of his cock deep inside her.

His hands held her buttocks, and he leaned his face into her chest, every moment sending him closer to the edge. He felt fierce; he wanted to lock her body to his. He bit his lip; he was going to come, and he wanted to wait for her. He felt her begin to quiver and reach. He moved his head back to look at her again, and his hands tightened on her waist.

"You fill me so well," she whispered, leaning over his face and breathing the words to him as her body sapped the strength from her voice.

He swelled further inside her at her words, his cock rigid, his balls in an iron grip. He was sweating from the intensity of the thumping orgasm building there.

She tilted her hips higher, clutching at him with her strong inner muscles.

"Oh sweet Abby, I am going to come."

She flexed her back and worked her hips smoothly and rhythmically on him. He felt her sex quivering; she was close, too.

When his cock began to reach, he crushed his face into her breasts, and her arms enclosed his head there. He held her tightly, and they did not separate, coming violently at the very same moment.

Abby tottered back to her office and sat staring out at the skyline, trying to gather her faculties. It was fortunate she had done so much that morning. Zac's impromptu get-together had thrown her completely. In fact, she felt as if she'd been hauled onto the side of a fast-moving train the week before and hadn't been able to put her feet down on the ground since.

He certainly wasn't predictable, and that thrilled her, but she knew there was more to it than that. She couldn't stop thinking about him. The sex was something else; she wanted to be locked up with him for a long time.

He fascinated her. His self-control seemed to be something that he could wear at will and was equally happy to fling aside. Their whirlwind affiar didn't make any sense, although she didn't want to analyze their relationship too deeply, just enjoy it while it lasted.

She glanced at the time display on her monitor. Only a few hours to go, and she'd be with him again. *And you've got an important report and release documents to prepare.*

Later that afternoon, Zac stood up from his desk, pacing as he waited for the documents Abby had e-mailed to print out. She had to have a signature by early morning to bid for her recommended property in the auction. He glanced at his watch, calculating how much time he had. He had to get the papers out to his mother's house for her to sign, drop them at the couriers' and get back to his apartment before Abby arrived at nine. Luckily he'd asked her to come over later, anticipating something like this, and it was just about doable.

He lifted the first sheets of paper, scanning the details of the property she had selected for purchase. He couldn't withhold a smile. She certainly didn't play safe, but as she'd said in her proposal, it wasn't often an opportunity like this came onto the market. With only ten days for the account to run to renewal and even less until the meeting, he'd have assumed she'd be looking at something safer, something that would have been easier to assess what the long-term investment potential might be. She'd put together a superb proposal, though, including the heritage response on planning, suggested architects, costing, the whole shebang.

Why? He went over the deal again and again but couldn't fault it other than that the castle was a bit of a way-out project. It was an interesting choice, for sure, but not entirely practical in view of the short-term portfolio management. Mind you, she would be hoping for contract renewal on behalf of her company. Besides which, he couldn't point the finger. He'd taken on exactly the same sort of risks when he'd bought a run-down cinema, boarded up and rotting into decay, to convert into his dream venue, The Hub.

They had similar tastes in property, he mused.

He flicked on through the pages. She'd suggested two architects, and both of their résumés were attached. Impressive stuff. She'd even included a quick reckoning of how long it would take to recoup the cost of conversion. After her exceptional trading on the stock exchange, which had saved them huge potential losses, it would be hard to find fault with her work.

Neither he nor Nathan had turned up anything other than positive information, and Nathan's feedback from the receptionist merely painted a picture of the woman he knew, a genuine live wire with talent and character, not someone with a hidden agenda.

She'd lied though. Why? It kept niggling away at the back of his mind, screwing him up good and proper.

Right now there didn't seem to be a reason why he shouldn't agree to go for the castle, unless he was blinded to it by his intense need for her. He frowned at the scanned photo of the castle, then at the clock. The minutes were ticking by.

"OK, lady," he murmured, "I'll get you your signature." Snatching up the rest of the papers, he grabbed his car keys and headed for the door.

eight

eight

Once he was sure that Abby had reached the end of the street, Nathan approached the door to the building and made his way swiftly toward the elevators. It was getting late, and the place was all but deserted.

Suzanne grinned when she saw him. "Just the man I wanted to see."

Nathan darted a look down the corridor, which was in semi-gloom. "On your own?" He wandered over to the desk, where she was sorting stuff in her backpack. Her computer screen was still on.

"Yes, everyone's gone home, so I've just got to switch off here and activate the alarms, and we can get on our way."

He watched as she tidied her desk and switched the VDU off. She was wearing a pair of white hipsters and a pink top with a wavy hem that lifted every time she bent or moved, revealing her bare midriff. She made his mouth water.

Distracting himself, he did a survey of the reception area, his attention quickly snagged by a set of framed photographs on the wall.

Suzanne sidled alongside him. "I'll give you a run-through of who's who, if you're curious."

Nestling her in front of him, he stroked her arms from her shoulders to her wrists. He bent to kiss the top of her head. He didn't tune in to what she was saying as she pointed along the photographs, naming names. He didn't care anymore. He was here for her.

Her body against his felt warm and alive. It had his cock up and ready for action inside a heartbeat. He pressed against her back, letting her know. He bent his head. "I want to fuck you," he whispered against her ear.

"I thought you wanted to look at photos." She glanced back over her shoulder, her eyes twinkling.

"Soon as I touched you, I was distracted."

She turned in his arms and ran her hands over his chest, squeezing his pecs as if measuring him. "We could do it here . . . now, before we go. A quickie?"

He flexed his muscles beneath her hands. "Sounds good to me."

"It would be very naughty of me, doing the wild thing right here on the premises." She bit her lip, her eyes filled with mischief. She moved her hands to embrace his cock through his jeans.

The hot spot at the base of his spine was thudding. His balls were solid. The notion of doing the wild thing on the premises had been intercepted by all his radars. Curving his hands around her breasts, he rested his thumbs against her nipples where they were sticking through the fabric of her top. "How about I put you over the reception counter and do you from behind? That way you can keep an eye on the door."

Laughing aloud, she eased away. "You'll have to catch me first." With that she darted off down the corridor.

Chuckling softly, he shook his head. He headed after her, pacing at first and then moving into a slow jog.

She was fast on her feet. She'd disappeared around a bend and was at the end of a corridor, where large double doors stood open. Following her through them and inside the room, he was confronted with a huge oval table.

"Blimey. It's a boardroom."

She laughed and darted to the opposite side of the table. She put her hands flat on the table, challenging him to follow her.

"We could do it right here, on the table," he suggested.

She shook her head, laughing.

"Why not?"

"Because I wouldn't be able to keep a straight face when I'm called in to minute meetings."

He could just picture it. "Fair enough." He laughed, moving again.

As soon as he made it halfway around to her, she was off again, lengthening the distance between them. When she reached the double doors, she stopped. She ran her hand down her zipper, wrapping it over her pussy, rubbing hard, staring at him and smiling her naughty smile.

When he caught up to her, he reached for her, putting his hand over hers in her groin, squeezing it tight.

"I want your cock there."

"So do I, like now. How about right here on the floor?"

He could see her thoughts were racing, deviant little ideas turning over in her mind. *What a minx.*

Her eyes lit. "I know just the spot to do it." Drawing away, she walked out through the doors, beckoning him to follow. About ten feet back along the corridor, she stopped and flung open a door. "In here, quickly. It's Robertson's office, the head honcho."

The chase had got his blood pumping fast. He didn't care where she wanted to do it, as long as they did it soon. He stepped inside. She'd thrown herself on a large leather sofa along one wall. He dropped down beside her.

Her mouth was eager, her kiss inviting him deeper. Nathan couldn't respond quickly enough. His hands found their way around her waist. Her body molded up against his. He drew back and plucked at her hipsters. She growled in her throat, a sound that made his blood rush faster.

She rose to her knees in front of him and shimmied her top off in one quick movement; her hips swayed, her breasts bouncing free of the constraint.

He was riveted by the sight.

Wriggling out of her hipsters, she eased back down onto the sofa, straightening her legs out, stretching them suggestively. "Touch me."

He ran his hand down the inside of one thigh, then back up the line of the other. Her pelvis flexed up. Her eyes were filled with naughty humor, and it was so very inviting. How could he resist? He reached between her thighs, his hand nestling in to cover the white cotton panties stretched over her pussy. He wanted it bare.

She moved her hips again, nudging up against him. He felt her heat, the fabric scuffing gently against the palm of his hand. He was hard as steel. He looped one finger over the line of her cotton panties and pulled them off. His gaze swept over her.

"Dynamite," he whispered.

She whimpered, her face flushing.

He smiled. "You're pure dynamite, Suz," he repeated.

She blew him a kiss, giggling with pleasure. He had to love that. She was a total firecracker, and yet she seemed so natural.

He looked down at her pussy, his eyes following the line of her body where it curved between her thighs.

She wriggled back on the sofa, whimpering, when he brushed his fingers over her abdomen and down into her cleft, delving lower, feeling the soft, damp flesh of her pussy give way.

She swore aloud. Her face was flushed, her hair tousled and hanging over her face. "Get your cock out."

The quiet instruction lit his desire further. *Now*, his body demanded. His cock thudded insistently. No turning back. He took a deep breath.

She growled when his erection sprang out from his jeans when he unzipped. He pulled it free, fisting the rigid shaft in front of her.

"Oh yes, I want it," she whispered, glancing from his erection to his face and back. Her hand stroked over its length. "Fuck me with your glorious cock, Nathan, right here."

Her words pumped through him, making him fiercely proud. His cock twitched in response to her eyes on it.

She moved, her body opening toward him.

"Turn around," he whispered.

The smile she gave him at that moment was blatantly naughty. "What?"

"You heard. Turn over and give me a look at that beautiful arse of yours, quickly."

He could see she loved the idea, but she moved slowly, turning to kneel, looking back over her shoulder at him, her lips slightly parted in anticipation. She was teasing him to the max, aware of his urgent state.

His gaze passed down from her face and the tumble of curls that framed it, down the niche of her waist, to her heart-shaped bottom. Her knees were pushed into the leather, her thighs angled for balance. Her hips swayed.

Nathan swallowed. "Lean over the back of the sofa," he whispered, his hand sliding on his cock. She leaned over the back of the sofa, and he had donned a condom and knelt down behind her, between her open legs. He lifted her body around the waist to haul her hips back against him. His hands moved along the inside of her thighs, the shaft of his erection hard between her open thighs.

It was her turn to be teased. He nudged the swollen head of his cock back and forth between the soft, damp folds of her pussy and clit, lifting her body to access her.

She squirmed and gasped, her arms out against the back of the sofa. He increased the pressure and speed, one hand on her hip to steady himself.

"Oh God, Nathan, I'm going to come." She began to shudder.

He continued the assault, stemming his own interest with a thumb and forefinger locked at the base of his cock, watching as her body wriggled and lurched. Her body arched, and she moaned when she came; pushing back as her hips bucked up.

He pinned her body down with his hands on her shoulders.

He was so close to losing it. He eased inside her, his blood pounding. Her hips were angled to take him in, her flesh melting onto his cock.

"Your pussy is hot as hell," he uttered and eased deeper.

Suzanne cried out, her head falling back. He leaned over her back, his arms around her waist, holding her locked into place. He moved his face into the curve of her neck, his mouth sinking against her skin; she felt so good, she smelled so good. He drew back and then reached further inside, each thrust making him crave more.

"Oh, this is so wrong," she said, driving back onto him, "doing it in the boss's office—I'm so bad."

"You surely are." He squeezed her buttocks in his hand; giving her an occasional slap as she met his movements, matched each rhythm.

"That's good," she whispered, struggling for breath.

He molded her flesh in his hands and then spanked her again. "Naughty girl, doing dirty things in the boss's expensive chairs."

Oh yes, she liked that a lot. He could see her hands tightening on the leather upholstery, her knuckles turning white; then her sex contracted and began to spasm. She had him so very deep. He felt the heat of her climax sucking at him. He tightened his hands on her hips, holding her. "Don't move," he begged. "I'm going to ride you hard while you come. Can you take it?"

She moaned, her body shuddering on the brink. "Hurry," she cried, her voice low and forced.

He put his hands on her hips and began to slam home. She cried out in ecstasy. And again. He was there. He thrust home. Her head rolled back, her body clutching at him, over and over.

His body jerked, and he came in a sudden, dazzling rush, his essence churning into hers, and for a few moments, he lost contact with everything except the clutch of her body on his.

"That felt so wrong, but so right," she said, smiling, when she broke free, her body wavering.

He lifted her back, drawing her in against him, kissing the top of her head. She was the craziest woman he'd ever had the pleasure to be around. Somewhere far, far away he heard a voice telling him it was too good, that it couldn't last, but Nathan ignored it.

• • •

The gym was mercifully cool, Abby noticed. They had their air-conditioning on full blast, and there weren't many people around. The day had turned steamy, humid. There was a storm brewing. She hadn't wanted to go back to her apartment before seeing Zac, so she'd pulled on a tank top and army trousers and shoved a change of clothes into her bag, together with her gym gear. She could go straight on to Zac's from there.

Tom had given them all membership at the nearest gym as a Christmas bonus the year before. Mostly she went with Caroline, early mornings or lunchtimes. She'd never been there at night before. Obviously, its position in the city catered mainly for the day-time surge. It was usually full of business types and was strangely different at night. Abby was able to wander around the equipment without interruption.

As her body worked with the rhythmic movements of muscle against machine, she breathed in a regular pattern, visualizing her muscles flexing. Her eyes closed. She was more alive than she'd ever felt, her body fired by a regiment of hormones that readied themselves for release, for battle.

She felt the lycra stretch over her rib cage as she flexed. She imagined it was leather; she could almost hear the creak. She was thinking about his legs. She was thinking about his skin. She wanted to feel it against her own. She opened her eyes, and the white wall in front of her reminded her of his shirt, that first day in the elevator. She laughed at herself and gave up on the machine.

She took a quick shower and then a quirk made her decide not to wear the dress she had brought with her but instead climb back into the vest and army trousers. Her blood coursed ever quicker in her veins when her taxi pulled alongside his Mercedes. He was there. Her heart beat triumphantly.

When he opened the door, he stood smiling silently, a towel over his shoulder. He was wearing loose-fitting black trousers; his torso was naked. He must have just stepped out of the shower. Wet hair hung over his shoulders. A trickle of water ran over the skin of his chest, slowing as it met the dark shape of his nipple. "What a pity I didn't arrive a bit earlier," she said as she walked in.

He shut the door behind her and rubbed the towel against his head as he looked down at her combat gear. She watched the line of his triceps as he reached up to bend his arm back. He flung the towel over a chair and put his hand on her bare arm. His skin was still cool from the shower; hers was burning hot.

"I'm glad you're here," he said and reached down to touch her mouth lightly with his.

She wanted to respond fiercely, to climb all over him, but he brushed gently on her lips and then released her arm with a gentle stroke. "You smell good, like the sea," he said, breathing against her skin. It made her feel weak.

"Would you like a drink?" he asked, and his eyes roved over her body before they returned for the answer.

Her hand went to his wet hair, and as she touched it a few drops of water ran down her arm. The erotic charge of it hung heavy between them, like the humid air of the night. Eventually, she nodded.

He picked up a shirt that looked as if he had dropped it as he went to answer the door and stopped to put it on.

"No," she said, following him, her hand reaching for the bare skin of his chest. "Don't cover up." She drew the material slowly back down his arms, her hands taking the opportunity to touch his shoulders as they passed. She seemed to move in slow motion, brushing the material where her hands wanted to go on his arms.

He took the shirt from her and tossed it aside.

She stroked her hand across his shoulders and down to trace the line of his lean torso. Then it wandered up to circle his arm around the tattoo.

He captured her wrist with his hand and her gaze with his eyes. "Abby . . . your drink awaits." He strode off, and she followed a few paces behind. She found herself in a small kitchen with a tall, thin, glass door that opened onto a tiny balcony. It had a Mediterranean feel about it. She walked over to the open door and gazed out at the river.

He moved behind her, and she felt the cold slide of glass on her bare arm as he joined her with two glasses of champagne. She gasped and then laughed. She was thinking of the day before. How much better it would have been if it had been Zac with champagne, instead of Tom with Bucks Fizz.

They stood in the doorway. They drank from their glasses and from each other's eyes.

"It's an excellent view of the river," she said, not looking at it but at him. He nodded. The air was so charged she almost felt rays of light crashing from her body to break up the humid air around them.

"Come inside. I want to see what you look like sitting in one of my Mackintosh chairs." He slipped his arm around her waist and led her back. His hand lay on her hip. It felt right, it felt good, and it belonged.

"Your throne . . . Witch Queen." He drew the chair out for her.

She sat down on the beautiful piece of furniture. She leaned back against the dramatic headrest, the lines of the upward struts cool against her back.

Zac stood and looked at her. "Very suitable," he said with a dark smile.

She could see the desire in his eyes. Could he see it in hers? She suspected it was even more obvious than his. She crossed her legs, and his eyes followed the movement. He glanced up. "The bottle," he said and wandered off to the kitchen again.

She looked around the room. He'd put some of the books onto the shelves, and that made her smile. She stood up and wandered over, drawn to the library full of keys to his mind, to his soul. Her fingers ran over the spines of the books, almost as though she could take all their knowledge from them with her touch. She saw titles she recognized, books that stood as well-read and creased on her own shelves. Others were unknown to her. She fingered them curiously. Would she have the chance to know this man better, to recognize his literary tastes?

She heard him come in behind her, then the sound of the bottle being put down. He closed on her, and she felt the touch of his bare chest against the back of her shoulders. She leaned against him, her eyes closing.

His hands slipped around her hipbones, the thrusting line of his body pressed against her back. "You don't want to read now, do you?" His mouth was close to her ear.

She smiled and moved her hand forward to the shelf. "Well . . ." She felt his mouth on her bare shoulder. She slipped a book out, and he leaned forward to take it from her. She glanced down at the cover; it was an Eastern love text.

She looked at him. "I thought I might learn some of your secrets," she said suggestively.

He smiled and put the book down; his hands sliding back to her hips. "I don't want you to learn all my secrets too quickly." He turned her away from the shelves. "Your champagne will be getting warm." Then he walked over to sit in the chair she had abandoned; it was a subtle invitation to follow.

She felt as if they were two jungle creatures stalking each other in the moonlit heat of the tropics. She stood for a moment and then followed his path, pausing only when her legs touched against his knees. He handed her the glass she had abandoned and then pulled her gently onto his lap.

Her free hand went to his shoulder, steadying herself, and then it slipped down to his tattoo. She followed the pattern with her fingers.

"What does it mean . . . to you?" Her eyes were still on it.

He laughed quietly, his head dropping back, his hands drawing her closer up on his hips as he leaned back.

"I had it done when I was a troubled teenager," he replied. "It expressed the way I felt at the time. Part Greek, part English, my mixed blood made me unsettled."

She let her gaze wander over the bones of his face while he spoke.

"I felt like I didn't fit in anywhere, that both races were somehow familiar yet foreign to me." He was watching her reaction as he spoke.

She traced the line of the yin-yang symbol and its bed of thorns with one curious finger. "But you seem so comfortable with yourself now." She tried to imagine him as a troubled youth. The idea made her wet. She crossed one leg over the other, her knee drawing up to be met by his hand as it moved over the surface of her trousers.

"I came to realize that there is no norm; most people feel that they don't fit in at one time or another."

He could have been talking about her feelings toward the people she worked with; it was so strange.

He broke into a smile then. "I grew out of it, I guess, and adopted all aspects available to me."

"The multifaceted human character?" she said, reminding him of their first conversation.

He nodded and stared into her eyes, as if he could climb into her thoughts.

She sipped her champagne, and her breast brushed against him as she leaned back to swallow the liquid. His fingers rose to her throat and touched it as she swallowed.

"Everyone has a secret side, Abby, only in some people it is more developed than others." His mouth curled. "You have a dark side, do you not?"

She looked at his teasing smile. His lips were so perfectly carved. She wanted to drink her champagne from his mouth while he kissed her.

His eyes were glowing; he seemed to be reading her thoughts as they flickered suggestions.

"You know me so well," she murmured. Her wrist slid between the chair and the back of his bare shoulder, the glass disappearing into his hair.

His hand climbed up her leg to her waist, then reached up to cup her breast from beneath. "Fate decided that we should meet."

She leaned toward him; his words and actions infused her with the need for more of him. "Do you think we were lovers in another life?" she whispered, her sex creaming as the thought teased her.

"Probably," he said, and she seemed to see the confirmation in his eyes. His hand closed on her breast, and he moved against the surface of her vest slowly.

Her womb tightened in response to his touch, and she felt her breasts straining against his spread palm. She focused on his lips but moved hers past his face and sipped her drink. Then she crawled her lips back over his cheek and kissed his mouth, letting the liquid spill slowly into his opening mouth. She moved her hand from his arm to his neck, to feel him swallow, and then she chased the liquid with her tongue. Their kiss endured until his body jerked.

She dropped back and realized that she had spilled her drink across his shoulder. It was running over his chest toward his waist. The sparkling patterns of liquid invited her to follow them. She looked at him hungrily, climbed off his lap, and pushed open his thighs to kneel between them.

He sat back and watched her, his eyes narrow, his mouth tense with contained passion.

She chased the clinging bubbles of champagne back up from his waist to his nipple and sucked, teasing it with her tongue as it hardened. She looked at the pleasure showing in his face, and then she lifted her glass and ran the remaining liquid over his chest, a little at a time, her mouth catching it, spreading it over him and drinking in the taste of his body with it.

He swore quietly, his body moving at each splash on his skin, each suck of her mouth.

She felt his hand in her hair, heard him putting his own glass to the floor so he could touch her while she moved on him. His skin tasted so good she drew it into her mouth, sucked, kissed it across his chest. She took a subtle bite where she could feel the bone at the base of his rib cage, and then her mouth moved down to his navel, her tongue sinking into the hollow to draw out the pool of champagne that lay there. As her tongue stirred, a well of desire whirled inside her body, sweeping her into its charge.

The glass dropped from her hand, and she heard it roll on the carpet. She reached for his belt, the button, and the zipper. She felt his fingers tighten in her hair as she pulled him free, his cock reaching, like the root of a tree moving through the earth to find its sustenance.

She moved her face into the heat of his loins, taking in the dense, rich scent, nestling against the fur of him, her fingers sliding up the silken surface of his erect shaft. He was so swollen, so hard with energy and passion, that it took her breath away. Her sex throbbed; the primal force contained in him was being mirrored in her own body, like a magnet seeking its equal force.

Her lips caressed the surface of his cock, feeling the hot skin, the smooth, ridged flesh. Her sex was pounding, and she plunged her mouth over his shaft, taking it deep, filling her mouth with him, tasting him and pleasuring him. She caressed each slight ridge, her fingers gently moving against his shaft.

She heard him give the muted sounds of deep pleasure and breathe out her name. Her arms pressed against his hips as he leaned back against the chair, his hands still twining in her hair. Her fingers moved into his trousers, sliding around the weight and tautness of his balls. She heard his breath coming quicker, felt the movement of his balls riding up. The energy was fantastic; she felt it surging up in her mouth. She wanted to feel the release, taste the essence of him on her tongue and in her throat.

She lifted her mouth from him, licking him upwards as she did, her fingers still moving on the base of his shaft.

His fingers hung in her tangled hair like creatures captured in a net.

She looked at the throbbing tip of his penis, the slit that gleamed a pearl-like dew with the promise of more to come. She felt his finger touch her lips. As she looked up, their eyes met.

"You are so very delicious, Zac." Her voice was husky.

He stared at her with the pain of absolute pleasure. He pulled at her hair with his fingers, his mouth moving silently.

She smiled and then took his penis into her mouth again and slid quickly down to its stem, nudging him along the roof of her mouth to her throat. He gave a mighty moan, and his thick, hot juices pumped into her mouth, swirled into her throat, and she swallowed him, each drop like nectar to her.

When she kissed the last drop from him and looked up, he was still braced against the chair, his eyes closed. He looked like a dark overlord conquered by pleasure. She leaned against him, her arms resting on his chest, her face close against the moist surface of his abdomen. His sated penis glued itself close to her cleavage. Her breasts ached, and her whole pelvis pounded with hot, animal instincts.

He stroked his hands over her shoulders and across her back, lifted the material of her tank top and slid his warm hands underneath. He moved one hand to her chin and caressed it, sweeping her hair back where it clung to her face.

"It's so hot," she whispered.

He nodded; the heat was all around them. He fastened his pants and drew her up, lifted her in his arms and carried her to the bedroom. She rolled against his body as he carried her and linked her arms around his neck. She felt so heavy with heat and lust she wondered how he could lift her.

He laid her down on the bed. "Let me get you something refreshing."

She lay back on the bed, watching him walk away, sinking into the cool, black sheets. Soon they would be heated through from her body. It had to be the hottest night of the year. There was a storm coming, she could hear it, sense its approach.

When he returned he was carrying a platter of fruit. He sat down on the edge of the bed and proceeded to cut it with a small paring knife.

She lay back and watched him. His face was cast in shadow, and it heightened the dark sexual look of him. She heard a crack, and he reached toward her mouth with a small, dark, passion fruit broken in his hand. The juice and seeds were spilling through his fingers. She sucked them from his skin slowly, the taste of the cool fruit only just managing to distract her from the feeling of his fingers in her mouth.

He was smiling, and she continued to suck at him long after the juice had gone, holding his gaze with hers. He pushed her gently back onto the bed and reached for another passion fruit.

She opened her mouth, but he shook his head. "This one's for me." He cracked it over her chest, and she gasped as the cool juice slid down her skin and into the material of her top. He leaned over her and licked the juice from her, his tongue chasing it in quick swirling movements that spread flames under her skin.

This wasn't cooling her down at all, quite the reverse. He reached for another fruit and dribbled it slowly onto her breasts, the material soaking with juice, revealing the erect tissue of her nipples. He followed the juice with his mouth, communicating his desire through her body via the electric current at her nipple.

"Zac," she whispered. Her sex was slick for him. But he continued his attentions at her breasts, moving from one to the other until she trembled with desire. When he sat up, she looked down at her vest. It was saturated with juice.

"Oh, dear. What will I wear to get home?"

He smiled. "You can always borrow something of mine . . . Do you have to go at all though?"

She frowned, her eyes closing. She had to be up early to get to work, check for Adrianna's papers and prepare for the auction. "Yes. I have something important to do at work, first thing. I have to go later . . . because it's too difficult to leave you in the morning." She looked at him; she feared he wouldn't understand that she really wanted to stay.

"I'd like to keep you here all night, in my bed." His fingers squeezed her nipples slowly as he spoke.

Her heart raced at the thought of it. She groaned and leaned back against the pillows.

He slid a cold piece of mango against her throat and then leaned over to eat it from her skin. The sensation of his grabbing mouth against her throat sent a wild thread of electricity across her chest.

"We'll be together at the weekend," she murmured.

"I can hardly wait." He looked at her again.

She nodded, her breasts rising and falling with desire.

He sank down to kiss her cleavage, pushing the material of her top down with his chin. His lips were like steel branding her with his mark. She wanted him to brand her everywhere. He lifted his head and began to rip the vest with his hands, tearing the material slowly, revealing her naked skin inch by inch.

The sound seemed to twitch inside her sex; it begged to be opened up to him, too. Her body curved up to him on the bed as he took her naked nipples into his mouth in turn. As he sucked, arousal tugged deep inside her, and she whispered her need close to his ear.

He leaned back and began to undo the buttons of her trousers. She hummed her approval and wriggled free of the material. He touched her mound, as if testing the fruit for ripeness, then reached to the platter and brought a slice of guava to her mouth. She bit into it. Its spongy flesh was ice-cold, and she tore it gently from his fingers. She took the next piece of fruit from his hand and offered it to his mouth.

"We could be on a tropical island now . . . the heat, the flavors, the storm that's coming."

He knew which storm she meant, but he shook his head. "No. We are only borrowing the flavors; the real heat is our own." His voice led a tremor through her body. She was unable to reply. "Anyway, if it were a tropical island I would have to protect your beautiful white skin from the wicked sun." His hands spread a sticky path across her body, her skin sticking eagerly to his fingers. "I would rather take you to a beach in winter. A snow-filled beach . . . where it would be so very cold you would need me to keep you warm."

Her eyes closed as his fingers trailed their sticky prints along the insides of her thighs. As her lids lowered she saw Blayne Castle imprinted there. It stood near a windswept cove. In her mind's eye she could see the snow falling.

"I think I know the place," she murmured, as his juicy fingers met the juice that came from within her.

"Will you show it to me?" he asked, his fingers pausing their movement.

"Maybe." She smiled at him.

He stared at her, his eyes flashing with passion, with warmth and humor; then he reached for another slice of mango and touched it along her pussy lips.

It was cool torture to her, and she moaned quietly against the back of her hand. He slid the fruit gently inside her. It was beautifully cold and firm against her hot skin. She stirred her hips. She wanted to plunge down onto his hand, but she also wanted to climb away for something else. Her whole body throbbed with dense waves of heat that emanated from a heavy spot within her womb.

"It wouldn't be too cold for you?" He was smiling wickedly at her as he moved the mango inside her.

The cool, fleshy fruit and the tease of his fingers brought about a desperation, an agony of need. She breathed out. The air crackled with the imminent storm. A thunderbolt rumbled in, signaling its approach.

"No, not with you there to warm me."

He dropped down to eat the mango from her, the heat of his lips and tongue taking the coolness away and replacing it with a heat and energy equal to her own.

He drew her first climax from her with his mouth, teasing the anxious surface of her sex folds with his tongue and inviting them to enjoy his caresses. He sucked gently at her, taking her juice from her inner sex and offering it to her ripe clitoris with his cupped lips.

She was buoyed up, weightless—strung out by the dynamism and intensity of his touch on her sex. There seemed to be a direct link between him and the thunderous skies over their heads, through the medium of her body. As she lifted and came, Abby heard the sound of her own voice echoing through the room, like a rain bird in flight above them.

They lay still together for a moment until a flash of lightning began a new moment, a new movement. They shed their remaining clothes and met one another as the flashes of electric light captured them in the flow of the elements—the elements outside and those within. They were driven, fueled by the energy of nature. They climbed over one another, searched deep, pressed high, reached farther. As the skies began to open and the heavily scented rain flew out to them, she rode him, and their naked bodies slid together in frantic movements, sweat-drenched movements. They sought the prize. They offered it to one another.

He rose up, and she locked her legs around his hips when she saw the look of intense fever in his face. He sat up into her embrace and reached for her breasts, sliding his hands over their hot, damp surface, reaching for her throat.

She looked down at him and peeled his damp hair from his face, her hips rocking back and forth. His eyes communed with hers, and his hands twined around her neck as she moved against the full shaft of him inside her. The climax was coming close. A trickle of sweat gleamed on the bone of his temple, and she reached down to take it with her tongue, arching her body over him. He sank his head into her neck, his arms enclosing her, locking them together. The sounds in his throat were pleasured, pained.

She felt her womb begin to contract, and her arms fled over his back as her flesh tightened around his penis.

"Zac," she whispered, "come to me now!" Her nails flew across the skin of his back, and he came at the very moment she wanted him to.

They stood by the window, looking out at the wet ground. The air smelled fresh, damp.

"Shall I order you a taxi?" Zac asked, stroking her arm gently.

"Yes, thanks." She turned away from him to get dressed before she changed her mind about going home.

He walked to the wardrobe, but Abby went to the chair, where she had spied his abandoned clothes earlier, and picked up the shirt he had worn that day. It was white with a tiny black line coiled in barely visible patterns on its surface. She held it up and breathed his scent on it. She turned to him.

"Can I have this one?"

He nodded, came over, and slipped it around her, buttoning it gently. It was cool and crisp against her skin.

She smoothed it over her breasts. "Now I have you with me whenever I want, even though you will be in Paris."

He opened his mouth to reply but thought better of it and kissed her instead, before reaching for the phone. After he'd booked a taxi, he folded a piece of paper into her hand. "This is where I'll be staying in Paris. I'll tell them to expect you at the reception desk." He looked very serious. "I want you to come, but I will understand if you can't." The words seemed to be drawn unwillingly from him.

"I will be there." Her bruised lips reached for him again, pressing their wearied kisses to his. To be without was the only real pain.

He traced the outline of her body slowly with his hands, memorizing its shape. "I'll be looking forward to your arrival."

She reached to stroke his face. "Me, too."

He dressed and walked her to the taxi. When she got in she wound down the window and he leaned on the doorframe.

"Paris?"

She nodded, and then reached forward to touch his lips. "I'll get away as soon as I can . . . I think I can last until then."

"If you can't, let me know, and I'll fly back."

She laughed and blew him a kiss as the car pulled away.

As the taxi drove into the night, she looked at the time. It was one o'clock. In eight and a half hours she would be bidding for her chosen property in the auction. Zac had deepened her desire to win Blayne Castle. Now she wondered if they would ever be there together in the future.

nine|nine

Fitzsimmons of Twickenham, one of London's finest property auctioneers, was housed in a fine neoclassical building with double doors that sprang twenty feet high, flanked by twin Corinthian columns.

Zac stood outside, eyeing the building, doubting his own sanity. He knew he shouldn't be there; he just couldn't resist coming along to see if Abby managed to secure the castle. After their encounter last night, he wanted to see the dream realized, to be there with her.

Pushing his shades higher on his nose, he glanced up and down the street in case she was about to pass by. He was pretty sure she'd already be inside to get a good seat for the bidding. It was a one-room auction house with a clear exit; the place had been a chapel at one time. She'd be focused on the bidding; she wouldn't even see him if he stayed at the back of the crowd. He could just observe and leave as soon as he knew.

It was a crazy thing to do; if she spotted him she'd likely find out about the link between them, and he wasn't quite ready for that yet, but he couldn't resist. Besides, he wanted to see her again. He shook his head. It was only thirty-six hours until he had her to himself in Paris, if everything went according to plan.

A few stragglers went inside. He glanced through the doorway and noticed they had to stand at the back. Full house. That was good. He knew the layout, and he'd have cover. Ironically, it was the same auction house where he'd bought the venue he converted into The Hub. He glanced his watch. The auction would have begun.

Without allowing himself to analyze his actions further, he darted up the steps, picked up a catalogue at the reception desk, and found a place at the back of the crowd.

The auction was well under way and, aside from a quiet murmur here and there, the auctioneer had the crowd's full attention. Anticipation filled the air. Zac craned his neck, looking for Abby. After a moment, he caught sight of her in the front row on the right-hand side, so he dipped left and skirted the edge of the standing attendees until he had a good view of her.

Fitzsimmons senior was taking the auction. Zac lowered his head. Fitzsimmons and Zac's mother went back years. Many of her adventures in property had been started here. Flicking open the catalogue, he saw they were only one property away from Blayne Castle.

He wondered how Abby would play it. She looked immaculate, cool and sophisticated in a fitted jade-colored dress, her hair hanging over her shoulder in a ropelike plait. She held a clipboard folder in her hand, the catalogue on it. Why did he feel so much pride as he watched? He wondered.

When Fitzsimmons opened the bidding for Blayne, she chose her moment well, waiting for the competition to make themselves known before showing her interest. There were two other interested parties. The first was an agent who relayed everything via his mobile phone to his clients, the second a father and son team who looked like they might be building contractors. The two parties took each other up in small increments.

Abby sat wordlessly, waiting, until the head of the building contractors shook his head and dropped out. The agent looked smug as he reported the news back to his client.

Abby lifted her numbered identification card and made a bid. She'd taken it up in a double step, causing a murmur to run round the hall, but Zac knew from the proposal that she was still within the agreed limit. She was signaling her intent to win. Her glance dipped from Fitzsimmons to her bidding opposition, her demeanor not giving anything away. She was good at this. He couldn't help smiling. He wanted her to get it so badly.

Realizing he'd moved out from the crowd to observe, he shifted position. As he did so, he saw a familiar face standing a few feet away in the crowd. The man was smartly dressed, probably in his fifties, and he was watching Abby closely. Zac tried to place him.

At the front of the hall, Fitzsimmons began to push the agent for another bid. Zac glanced back; the agent looked annoyed as he spoke into his mobile phone. He nodded, gave another bid. Fitzsimmons pointed his hammer at Abby for her reaction. The crowd was riveted, their heads moving as if they were at Wimbledon, the bidding being the ball knocked back and forth between Abby and the agent.

Zac turned back to the older man who looked so familiar. He was staring at Abby, a smug, possessive smile on his face. That's when Zac remembered; he recalled him from the dossier photographs. This was Tom Robertson, Abby's boss. And something about the way he was watching Abby grated on Zac's nerves. He must have accompanied her. But why wasn't he sitting with her?

He heard Fitzsimmons prompting the bid, glanced back. Abby moved, taking the bidding up to the limit that they had agreed upon. This was it. If the agent put in another bid, she'd lose the property. Fitzsimmons looked back at the agent, who held up his hands and shook his head. *She'd won.*

Zac gave himself one more second to absorb the pleasure he saw on her face before he turned away to make a hasty exit. As he did, he discovered that Tom Robertson was just ahead of him, making his own quick departure.

Zac's emotional response to the other man was primal and edged with territorial anger. He wanted to stop the guy, ask him what he was up to, and warn him off, and yet he knew it was he himself who was acting dodgy as hell here. He was shocked at his own raw, possessive reaction.

I'm in love with her, that's why. The truth hit him hard and fast. There was no denying it. The question was: What did he do now?

When Fitzsimmons slammed down the hammer and pointed at her, Abby was delighted. She had won the castle for her client. She smiled to herself, thrilled to bits.

The guy who had been bidding against her glared across at her. She tucked her identification card under the clip on her clipboard to distract herself from his expression. Despite her pleasure at winning, something was niggling at her. She felt uneasy. It must be the hostility she felt from the other bidder. He was sending daggers; that's what it was. She glanced in his direction again and saw him storming off, his mobile phone slammed shut in his hand. Her clipboard fell off her lap, and she had to bend to retrieve it. The person seated behind her rescued it and passed it through the chairs.

Turning to say thank you, she caught sight of her opponent moving fast through the crowd at the back of the hall—and there, too, she thought she saw a glimpse of another much more familiar face. *Zac?*

She froze, blinked, and looked again. The flash of black hair disappeared into the crowd. What was he doing here? He was supposed to be in Paris. Her blood ran cold. Was he following her? She turned back into her seat, clutching her clipboard to her chest, her heart running an erratic race. *It can't have been him. I'm mistaken. It was someone else.*

It looked like him though. It didn't make any sense. He said he'd be in Paris today. He hadn't said what time, but what would he be doing here? How would he know? *Unless . . . unless he's following me.*

Her hands were shaking by the time she gathered herself enough to leave her seat and approach the auctioneer's assistant at the side of the hall, to go through the payment details for the property. She could barely think straight. Zac was a mystery man, yes, but she'd never felt as if there was a reason to be afraid of him until now.

When she left the building her mind was filled with questions. She recalled that feeling of being watched before, a sense of awareness that someone was taking an interest in what she was doing. She darted to the edge of the pavement and hailed a taxi.

By the time she got back into the office, she'd got herself well and truly spooked. *Stay calm.* She was adding things up wrong, had to be. She'd know if there was something dodgy about Zac, surely? She'd felt so close to him. She would know. It was just someone who looked like him. Yes, she'd felt odd recently, like she was being watched, but there had to be an explanation.

In reception, Suzanne was talking to two clients seated in the waiting area. She nodded discreetly when she saw Abby waiting for her at the desk, winding up her chat.

"What can I do for you?"

"This is going to sound odd, but did that guy you're seeing mention the name of the courier company they work for?"

"Not that I remember, why?"

"Neither did Zac. I just . . ." She looked at Suzanne's face, her happy expression. She couldn't bring herself to cast a shadow on her happiness. That would just be cruel. She didn't even know for sure it had been Zac. She shook herself. "Oh, I just wondered."

Suzanne gave her a concerned look. "Are you OK?"

"Well, kind of." She really needed a friend, but maybe Suzanne wasn't the right person, not if she was getting involved with this courier guy. She'd give Marcy a call.

"Excuse me, Abigail?"

Hearing her name, Abby turned to see Tom's PA sauntering toward her.

"Tom wants you to drop by his office as soon as possible."

Abby nodded. "Will do."

"Ew, that doesn't sound good," Suz commented when the PA had gone.

Abby shrugged. "No." Usually he visited the staff on their own territory, unless it was something very important or confidential. This was the last thing she needed right now. "He's been a bit . . . protective, since I've taken over Ed's work," she explained, with a decidedly charitable view of Tom's interest in her. "I suppose I better get it over with."

Suzanne gave a concerned frown and squeezed her arm affectionately. "Good luck."

Dropping her paperwork on her desk as she passed by her office, she went straight on to his door.

"Abigail, thank you for stopping by so promptly." Tom stood up from behind his desk and gestured at the low easy chairs that were set to one side of the large room, around a coffee table.

She glanced at the view as she took her place. Tom's office occupied the cornerstone of the floor, a suitable spot for their leader. With floor-to-ceiling glass and dual aspect, the view extended over the city to the left and to the right-hand side toward the river and beyond. On a clear day, you could see practically all of London, right out along the Thames.

She sank into the soft Italian leather of the easy chair, smoothing her fitted dress over her thighs as she did so. She was aware of his eyes on her as she took her place. She hoped he wasn't going to try to get cozy on her again. Adopting what she considered a tidy pose—knees together, ankles crossed just above the straps on her elegant sandals—she rested her hands loosely over the arms of the chair.

"I thought we should have a chat about your work." He walked over to the drinks cabinet. "Would you like a drink?"

"No, thank you, Tom," she replied.

He poured himself out a large measure of whiskey and strolled over to sit next to her.

It struck her as odd that he was drinking spirits at this time of day, but part of her thought she could probably do with a swig herself to steady her nerves.

His immaculate shirt and tie gleamed in the bright sunshine that edged into the office. He was so well-groomed that he looked rather artificial.

"I've been watching you closely over the past few days." He

wasn't actually looking at her as he spoke; his eyes were focused on the heavy crystal tumbler that he turned in small circles, making invisible patterns on the marble-topped coffee table in front of him.

Watching me? She felt a chill come over her, above and beyond that of the air-conditioning. The hairs on the back of her neck stood up. "What do you mean?" She tried to keep any defensiveness out of her voice, but in her current state of mind it was difficult.

"I'm taking a special interest in you. You must know that by now." He polished his comment with a smile. "I saw that you were attending the auction house when I was checking your targets on the network. I had to come down, just to see how you did."

A mixture of anger and sheer relief hit her. It wasn't Zac she had to be worried about; it was her bloody boss! She stared at Tom, weighing him up. *Keep calm.* She prided herself on remaining professional, no matter what the circumstances. "You were there?" *How dare he?*

Tom nodded and gave a quiet chuckle, still avoiding eye contact. "It was a great performance." He shifted in his seat.

Her fingers tightened over the arms of the chair. He'd been watching her. He'd been the one making her feel uneasy. Not Zac. Her heart beat out a triumphant tattoo.

"Why didn't you tell me you were going to be there?"

"No need."

In that case, why are you telling me now, you creep?

"The important thing is that I am around and available for you. You've had a lot of extra responsibility, and I wouldn't dream of letting you cope alone." He glanced at her, clearly trying to gauge her reaction. "Last week, I told you I was there for you, but so far you haven't called on me." The last comment had a chastising tone to it.

"Things have been proceeding well."

He ignored that. "You do know I care about you, Abby, don't you?"

She fought against gritted teeth to speak. "I'm sure you care about all your staff," she responded coolly, her skin crawling. She tapped her fingers on the chair arm. The leather, mercifully silent, did not betray her annoyance. Her mind raced with the dismal immediate options that faced her. She could hardly confront him and tell him his so-called care and interest was akin to being stalked, but at the same time, she wanted him to stop making veiled passes at her. He was clearly abusing his authority.

He looked at her over the edge of his glass as he took another swig.

She waited to see what he would say next.

He took a deep breath and smiled at her. It held an unwelcome fondness. "I think we both know how well you've been doing, but I felt we needed to discuss it in more casual circumstances." His pause was deliberate. "I was disappointed you didn't take me up on my lunch invitation after your good work on the stock exchange."

She felt herself flushing with annoyance and bit the inside of her lip in an effort to keep calm. She gave what she hoped was a cool nod in acknowledgment of his remark.

"In fact, I have been wondering if you wouldn't have been a better choice for the Pascal account. I feel quite sure you would have had it well in hand by now." He cradled his drink.

She gripped the arms of the chair. How the hell was she going to deal with the situation? It was difficult; the options were few and the pitfalls many.

"But then you would have been in Geneva for much the time . . . and I wouldn't have wanted that."

His intimate look sickened her. Even though she had never given him any encouragement or shown any signs of interest in a relationship with him, he had made certain assumptions about her.

She decided that evasive tactics were the best strategy. "There's always a certain element of chance, of luck, involved in these matters. I was very lucky to have been assigned the Ashburn portfolio. However, if you think I could contribute to the Pascal account, I would be willing to join the team out there for the benefit of the company." She had no intention of going anywhere farther than Paris in the near future. She was calling his bluff with one of her own.

"Quite so." His expression was tight. Obviously he wasn't pleased with her response.

Taking up the initiative, she attempted to redirect the conversation. "Incidentally, I've received a request for the end-of-contract meeting to be brought forward a week. I was surprised by that . . . I was somewhat concerned about my property investment, but seeing as you were there and let me go ahead with it . . . Have you any comment?"

Shaking his head, he looked down at his glass. He spoke slowly as if he was thinking of something else, perhaps planning his next maneuver.

"No. Most clients tend to make a noise when they are displeased, and Adrianna's been very quiet since you've been in charge." He gave her a quick smile.

"Good," she said.

"I'm aware of the revised date." He glanced up at her. "They want all the relevant staff to be present, myself included." He dismissed the subject with a gesture of his hand. "Nothing for you to worry your head about." His tone, no doubt meant to be friendly, was unbearably patronizing.

She nodded, curtly. *Now what?*

He put his glass on the table. "I notice you haven't made any flying visits to Geneva, to be with Ed." His voice was low, intimate.

Aside from annoyance at his assumption about her and Ed, he was again treading a dangerous path into personal territory. And yet she didn't want to deny there was anything going on between her and Ed, in case he took that as some sort of green light. Dear God, how could he put a member of his staff in such a position?

"Is there any particular reason for that, Abby?" It was a completely inappropriate question, and yet Abby felt compelled to answer. It struck her how distorted the whole scene was. His behavior verged on sexual harassment.

She kept her look cool, distant. She needed to get out of the situation without hurting his ego, without damaging their professional relationship. But most importantly, without giving him any indication of interest. "The account I'm working on at the moment has to be my priority within the Robertson group. Personal matters—of any sort—should not intrude on the work one does."

He stared at her and then nodded lightly, his expression frozen, revealing nothing. He acted as though their conversation was nothing more than a business negotiation.

"I'm glad you feel that loyalty to your work," he replied and sat back in his chair. "Perhaps when the Ashburn portfolio has passed the trial period and we have persuaded them to renew the contract, we can all take a breather and relax a bit more?" He gave her a questioning look, a slight hint of annoyance in his expression.

She adopted what she hoped was an efficient smile and took the chance to stand up and take her leave.

"Abby."

She turned back.

He eyed her up and down, pointed a finger at her, and winked over it, as if lining her up in his sights. "Keep up the good work, kiddo, you've got style, and I admire that. Remember . . . I'm watching you."

Patronizing and blatant; it was all Abby could manage to muster a false smile and walk out of the office without further communication.

When she got back to her own office she thought about what he'd said. What a farce, what a horrible, tawdry setup. She balked at what had gone on. He'd been the one giving her the creeps. It hadn't been Zac at all. As far as she was concerned, today had dotted the i's and crossed the t's on her resignation. She stood at the window, looking out at the view. Yes, it was time to move on. Too much in her life had changed. She was ready.

Sitting down at her desk, she picked up the phone. After that ghastly business with Tom, she needed a hug. Zac was out of town. Suzanne was too close to this. Her mother was cruising the Med. She needed to talk to someone though, and soon.

She tapped Marcy's number in to the phone.

"Hi, Marcy. It's Abby."

"Hey, sweetie, how you doing?"

"Oh good, fine." She laughed, feeling suddenly exhausted. "Actually it's been a bit crazy at my end. I wondered if you wanted to do the girl thing tonight. I could bring some wine over."

"Sounds good to me."

"Thanks, Marcy, I appreciate it. I'll come over around eight."

Zac pulled into his parents' driveway, pausing a moment before he switched the engine off. He was in a very different mood than he had been the last time he'd visited the week before. He stared at the dash. He was happier than he'd ever been, but at the same time verging on miserable. His life felt like a complete mess. He had to get order back so that things could move forward. Since Abby, he'd lost it. Completely. Not in a bad way, of course, but it was time to sort his head out, make some concrete decisions and take action on them.

He wanted her badly. Seeing her boss ogling her was the last straw. He wanted Abby for real, whatever that meant. A full-on relationship, he guessed. When he saw her win the bidding, he wanted them to be sharing their workdays, their ups and downs, every moment. No subterfuge, no secret affair.

It was all he could manage not to pick up the phone and call her again. But he knew he needed the time away. He needed the space to think straight—he'd got himself into a fine mess, and he had to figure out the best way to resolve it without making her think he was a demented stalker who had deliberately misled her.

He'd been knocking a plan about. It was tentative and riddled with possible complications, but his instinct was driving him. At least he hoped it was instinct—and not insanity.

He had a lot to do before he flew out that evening. Top of the agenda was convincing his mother he would deal with Monday's contract meeting at Robertson's. When he'd brought the property purchase documents over for her to sign the day before, she'd been pleased with his level of involvement. She was also eager for the time to pass until the trial period came to an end. He gave a wry smile. No doubt because she couldn't wait to whisk the portfolio back into her own jurisdiction.

His gut feeling was that he had to be the one to deal with the contract meeting. How the hell he was going to handle it was yet to be decided. Abby's work on the portfolio had been outstanding; he didn't want to jeopardize that by throwing her a curve ball. He wanted to figure out the best approach for Abby. Telling her before-hand could result in chaos for everybody concerned. She had every right to walk out on both him and her boss. Not telling her at all went against his conscience. He wanted to do the right thing regarding Abby, but timing was crucial.

He'd suggested Paris on the spur of the moment, but even now he felt it was the right thing to do. He wanted to be somewhere with her that was away from their real lives and all their intricate complications. He wanted time with Abby, the woman. Not Abigail Douglas the investment manager who in just a few days' time would find out exactly how entwined their lives were. He had to know how she really felt before that moment, and whether she wanted more from their relationship as much as he did. If she did and his instincts had been well-founded, he'd find a way to make it happen. He flipped off his shades and climbed out of the car.

As he approached the terrace he caught the sound of music spilling out of the house. Dimitri, his father, was sitting on the loungers, his thick, silvering hair falling forward as he brooded over a newspaper. When he caught sight of his son, his face lit. He dropped the paper and stood, his arms outstretched in greeting.

"What a surprise."

"It is. And it's good to find you at home. The restaurants are coping without you?" Zac quizzed as he embraced his father.

"Apparently so." His father shrugged it off, laughing. He was so much more amenable than his mother about passing the baton.

In the background the music changed to what sounded like tinkling waterfalls. Zac nodded toward the house. "What's that I hear?"

"Your mother." He rolled his eyes, chuckling. "Come and look; I guarantee you won't believe your eyes."

He was right. There on the hidden, private lawn at the side of the house his mother stood, wearing what looked like a karate suit, with her arms outstretched as if bathing in the music that came from the speaker at the window.

"What the hell is she doing?"

"Tai chi."

Sure enough, she changed position.

"We'd better not disturb her. Come, we'll wait on the patio."

"I was talking to Joseph Sullivan the other night," Zac said as they walked. "He mentioned that you were looking at a new bistro."

His dad glanced over his shoulder as if he expected his wife to appear by his side at the very mention of business. "It was tempting, but I want to stick to my side of the bargain. No more expansion."

Zac smiled. His father had tried everything with Adrianna. Agreeing to limit his own work was just one method.

"Were you at one of the restaurants?"

"I was, but I bumped into Joseph at a pub in the city; he was doing an extra shift there."

Dimitri shook his head as he sat down. "So I hear. I'm worried about him."

"Why not give him the extra shifts he wants?"

"I think he should be with his wife at this time. He doesn't have to worry about money, I told him so, but it seems to be part of his makeup."

"He's only going to do the hours elsewhere, somewhere he won't get overtime rates, and he'd rather be working an extra shift in his own job. Why not ask him for a bit of extra work to prep the cellar supplies for the time he'll be away on paternal leave?"

"Not a bad idea, and I suppose you're right." His father looked at him with a curious glance. "You're good with people, Zac. I try too hard to make them what I want them to be."

"You can't force other people to live by your ideals. You can offer them options, but there has to be some level of compromise."

"Yes, but we all try. It's part of being older and thinking you're wiser; at least that's my excuse." He gave a wry smile. "You seem to have hit the nail on the head though. I'm proud of you, son."

"I know that, and I'm glad."

"I understand you're also overseeing the investment management for your mother?"

In more ways than one, Zac thought to himself, frowning. "She told you?" He was surprised.

His father nodded.

"That's what I came to discuss today."

"Not trouble, I hope?"

"No, well, I hope not." He'd come here with a deal, one that might or might not be negotiable.

"Your mother is finally starting to let go of it and relax."

"So I saw."

"Incredible, huh?" He beamed.

"It is, yes." *Does that bode well?*

Later, when she joined them, he noticed that she looked better than she had in a long while. Could a week really make that much difference in a person's life, changing their attitude, changing what was important to them?

Even as the question ran through his mind, he realized it could, because it had happened to him—and the realization hit him like an unexpected left hook. He'd not only fallen for Abby, but she had changed his life, his priorities and goals. Most of all his desires—her; he wanted to keep her as part of his life.

"You look startled, Zachary," she said as she joined them.

He shrugged. "Yes, I'm surprised to see you like this, so chilled, but then I suppose it might be possible, even with your errant son in charge of your valued investments," he teased.

"Having someone I know and love watching over the business end of things did make it easier, I confess." Her eyes glistened with emotion, even though she was smiling.

The tenderness he saw in her expression made his gut churn. What would she think if she knew how unprofessional he'd been, that he'd been having an affair with their agent, that he'd been involved in some sort of masquerade?

A masquerade, yes, and for what?

It all came crashing in on him. He'd been kidding himself that it was because he mistrusted Abby's motives. At first, maybe, but he'd quickly seen how honest, loyal, and hardworking she was. No, his real reason for the masquerade was selfish. He was falling in love with her, and he couldn't step away, no matter how unprofessional it was. No matter how duplicitous it was not to have told her who he was, that he was the one replying to her daily reports.

His father was stroking his mother's hand, smiling happily. Zac hadn't seen them this way since he was a child, when they'd been happy and carefree. He wanted them to stay like this, to have that closeness again. Lord knows they'd earned it. And he couldn't help hankering after a taste of it for himself, too.

He sat forward in his chair. "Mother, I will find a way for this to work. I'll take full responsibility for your company from this moment on. You'll have to put your trust in me though. I want that to be total, and I want it right away. If you do, I promise I won't let you down." He hoped to God that he wasn't promising her something he wouldn't be able to deliver.

Curiosity lit her wise eyes. She looked at him for further explanation.

"I want to represent you at the board meeting. I've gotten involved with the management now, and I want to be the one to deal with Robertson on my own terms. I've notified them that we want the meeting brought forward; I'm ready to give them notice."

His father darted a glance at her with uncertainty, his brow furrowed.

It was what she had wanted, but at the same time it was a big step, handing over her whole life's work. A company she'd built from one property deal she'd made as a young woman who'd inherited two hundred pounds from a distant great-uncle and found a way to make it work for her. Was she ready to pass it all over on the turn of one promise? No matter how much she had wanted him to get involved, it was as her agent, her representative. What he was asking for was very different.

She looked thoughtful but calm.

His father lifted her hand and raised it to his lips.

She smiled at him fondly. "I suspect you two have been plotting this together."

His father shook his head. "Zac is taking a big step, but this is a decision only he could make for himself." He glanced back at his son. "But I admire him for doing so, and I'm grateful for what he offers us, if you will accept it on his terms."

She gave a deep sigh. "Yes, Zac, and I suppose you're right. If you take over, you don't want your old mother meddling in things."

He shook his head. "That's not why—"

She put up her hand to stop him. "It's all or nothing. Always has been."

"Do you trust me to deal with it?"

She nodded. "I trust you to deal with it." There was a moment's silence, wherein the three of them took in the significance of what had been said. "Now, I think this calls for a celebration," she added, "Do we have champagne?"

His father stood, darting off with a decidedly cheerful look on his face.

When he'd gone, she leaned over to Zac. "I knew that once you got involved, you wouldn't be able to resist," she whispered to him proudly.

The sense of happy resolve in her expression was too good; he didn't want to shatter it or any of her illusions. It wasn't quite as simple as that, but there was a way to make it just as agreeable.

There was no turning back now. If he wanted to keep the company on an even keel and win Abby, he had to see his plan through.

ten | nǝʇ

"So let me get this straight." Marcy knelt up and grabbed the bottle, topping up their wineglasses. "You've met this hunk—and he sounds pretty damn sexy, I agree—but then you thought he was following you, but it turned out to be your boss?" She put the bottle down and pulled her khaki tank top and shorts straight as she resumed her cross-legged pose.

Abby frowned. "Well, yes, that doesn't sound quite right, but basically that's it."

"I want to hear more about the hunk in a minute, but Abby— your boss?" Her eyes rounded. "I mean . . . you poor love. You're going to need the name of a solicitor, aren't you?" She was deadly serious.

"No, don't worry. I'm not going to let it go that far. At the moment he hasn't really stepped out of line. He's hinting like crazy, and he's been taking an interest in what I'm doing above and beyond what would be considered normal, but it wouldn't stand up at an employment tribunal. I'm not going to let it go any farther though. I'm out of there."

"No, don't let the bastard push you out of your job." Marcy was starting to look irate.

Abby shook her head and reached out for Marcy's hand, squeezing it. "He isn't. I've had itchy feet for a while. This has just given me that extra push. I've always had this dream about having my own company. I think I'm ready."

Marcy's expression softened, and she squeezed Abby's hand back. "Well, that's good news. But if he does anything before you move on, just walk out that door. Promise me."

"I promise."

"Good." She picked up her wine and took a long slurp. "Now, back to the hunk." She smiled. "I think you'd better start at the beginning. And don't skimp on the details."

"He walked into my life one day, and it hasn't been the same since."

Marcy waved her hand. "Describe him, I need an image to work with."

Abby chuckled. "Tall, dark, and handsome, cheekbones to die for, long black hair, blue eyes, very unusual. He's part Greek."

Marcy lolled back against her cushions, then rolled toward the portable fan that she had stood next to them, flicking the speed up a notch.

Abby shuffled. Her dress was riding up on her thigh. She wasn't dressed right for sprawling on the floor, but she didn't care; the wine saw to that. She felt as if they were sitting in a harem. Marcy had a big Persian rug in the middle of her sitting room floor with massive scatter cushions for seating. The heat and the fan gave it that exotic edge—women talking together in the harem, talking about sex and desire.

"There was an instant connection, it wasn't just an attraction, and it was like we connected on some other plane."

"Oh dear, Abby's in love."

It was so odd hearing it said aloud. "Do you think so?" She knew the answer, but she needed to hear the verification again.

Marcy raised an eyebrow. "Tell me more about the connection. How did you meet?"

"We first saw each other in an elevator, of all places. I wanted him instantly. He sent my hormones into overdrive. I never wanted a man that bad. There was this other couple in there, fooling around." She smiled as she remembered. "Zac and I looked at each other, at them, and back. There was an instantaneous sexy dialogue going on between us, only we weren't actually speaking." She moved, stretching her legs, squeezing her thighs together. Just thinking about being in the elevator with him was turning her on.

"I thought he was a courier; he was delivering papers. When he walked into our offices, I told him I was the receptionist."

Marcy frowned. "You lied?"

She nodded.

"That is *so* not like you. Why on earth did you lie?"

"I know, and I really wish I hadn't." She shook her head, remembering that her mother had drummed into her to always be honest. She'd told her that a liar needed a good memory to keep up the facade, and that lies built the foundation for other lies. It wasn't as bad as that, but she'd found that backtracking wasn't easy, once you'd done it. "I'll sort it out, but I was so fed up of men being intimidated by my job. I mean . . . I wouldn't have cared if he was a courier, but I didn't want to take the risk that my job would be a turnoff to him."

"He's *not* a courier?" Marcy looked thoroughly confused.

Abby laughed. "He was delivering the papers as a favor, and I really don't think he will be intimidated by what I do. I'll tell him as soon as we get together."

"So what does he do?"

"He's in arts management. He runs The Hub."

"Aha, now it all falls into place." Marcy smiled.

"Yes, I owe you for getting those tickets. I saw him that night, and he invited me to come back again. When I did, we couldn't keep our hands off each other."

"Go on," Marcy whispered, fascinated.

Abby sipped her wine. "I still feel as if he's a bit of a mystery to me, that I hardly know him. I mean, I like that about him, but it's also beginning to bug me." She laughed at herself.

"You're too keen; just let it all develop in its own time."

Abby nodded. "He's worth it, I know that. I've been trying to work out what it is about him though."

"You mean apart from the fact that he's gorgeous and sexy and you've fallen in love with him?" Marcy laughed.

"Yes, apart from that." It *was* funny. "I mean . . . it's not as if I haven't had plenty of hot sex before, but this is different. We are a good match in bed, but we don't just connect physically. There's an emotional, mental stimulation, like there's a flow of energy there, too. Sexually, he unleashes me, lets me run wild. He brings out the woman in me—the real woman, the lusty, honest woman. He notices that, he seems to adore it. I can let go, truly be me." Saying it aloud was making her craving grow.

Marcy watched as she ran her fingers along the base her throat. "This guy really affects you." She rolled onto her belly and reached out one hand to rest on Abby's thigh. "I can feel the heat coming off you." Her eyes were filled with mischief and interest. She pushed her fingers a little higher, until they disappeared underneath the hem of Abby's fitted dress.

"Yes." She swallowed. She was aroused, undeniably horny because she was able to talk freely about Zac, and Marcy's hand had anchored the sense of crazed longing, her fingers like a magnet drawing her nerve endings into focus. "Marcy . . ."

"Don't worry," she said reassuringly. "I'm just enjoying what this guy does to you. I love watching other people get off. Can I persuade you to share it with me, just a little?" Her hand was completely under the fabric now, her expression wayward, her fingers moving between Abby's thighs, gently easing them apart.

A tremor ran beneath her skin. "But I . . . you're my friend, Marcy."

"I'll still respect you in the morning."

Abby gave a crazy laugh, dizzy with wine and desire. "That's not what I meant. I don't want it to come between us."

"What, my hand?" Marcy grinned. She stretched her middle finger out and touched the surface of Abby's panties, her nail scratching infuriatingly at the cloth, sending Abby's clit wild.

"Oh . . ." Abby could barely reply. "You know what I mean."

"It doesn't have to come between us; just keep telling me about him and enjoy it. We'll always be friends; this doesn't mean I want to get engaged or anything." She winked.

Abby laughed. It wasn't as if she'd never touched anther woman. There'd been a girl at the university. After a party, they had ended up petting and wanked each other off. And that nail plucking at her panties was teasing her into a frenzy. Her clit was throbbing with the need to be touched.

"Tell me more about Zac."

She sighed. She was aching for him, aching to be in his arms again. "This might sound crazy, but I believe that I started truly living when I met him." She closed her arms over her chest, locking the memory of his touch against her body.

"Touch your breasts. I can see you're dying to."

That fingertip on the surface of her underwear was driving her mad. She moaned, rolling her head against the cushion, her eyes closing. She squeezed her breasts through her dress and bra, hard, answering the demands of flesh that ached for contact.

Marcy climbed across the cushions, her eyes shining, her lips parted in a suggestive smile. "I can't resist." She kissed Abby on the mouth.

She was so soft, her lips damp, gentle but sure, her breasts squishing against Abby's own.

"You're so naughty, your underwear is soaked through," she said accusingly, as she pulled back, with laughter in her eyes. She put her hand fully over Abby's mons, cupping it, pushing the heel of her hand against her aching hole. Abby's clit was crushed in the embrace, gloriously crushed and pounding. Her legs fell apart. Marcy's fingers massaged the plump flesh of her mons. She watched, lips parted and eyes riveted, glued to Abby's reactions.

Being watched so closely and handled so cleverly, Abby couldn't hold back. The orgasm was so close, and Marcy was doing all the right things. She writhed back on the cushions, her hips riding against the willing hand.

Marcy ducked down between her thighs to suck her pussy through her panties. Her tongue pushed the fabric into her hot niche, and then rode against the bump of her clit.

"Oh, oh!" Abby jerked, her whole body tuned to that spot, her actions automatic. She half sat, crying out, when Marcy lifted the damp fabric to one side and sucked her clit, kicking her over the edge hard and fast. Pleasure rolled through her, her body shuddering from release.

By the time she'd grounded, Marcy was sipping wine, lazing on her side. "Mm. Yes. He's good for you, I can tell. I like him already."

Abby gave a weak laugh. "You needed physical proof?"

"No, but it was fun seeing you get all worked up over him, then letting rip."

All worked up over him? Well, yes. She couldn't deny it. Zac could get her stirred up when he was hundreds of miles away. Besides, Marcy was right. He was good for her in lots of ways. It was less than two weeks since she'd met him, yet her whole being was focused on him and the connection between them. It was feeding her with vitality.

"And you said he's away at the moment?"

"Yes, unfortunately . . . it's killing me." She laughed, embarrassed at her confession.

Marcy didn't bat an eyelid. "I know that feeling. You're living in love's shadow."

Abby gave a deep sigh. "That's one way of putting it."

"Poor Abby, you have got it bad. So when will he be back?"

"Oh, I'm meeting him in Paris tomorrow, for the weekend."

Marcy looked surprised. "Only twenty-four hours to go? I don't know what all the fuss is about."

She gave a raucous laugh, and Abby couldn't help joining her. *Yes.* Her body gave a throb of anticipation. Only twenty-four hours to go. *Bliss.*

Abby climbed and climbed, but her breath was trapped and she finally gave in and slowed her pace on the cross-trainer. She glanced down at the mileage. It wasn't quite far enough to get her to Paris; she would just have to wait and catch the flight instead.

The early morning trip to the gym was meant to burn off some of her excess excitement, but it didn't seem to be helping. She'd barely slept; she was restless as a cat in heat. She smiled and turned to Caroline, who wrestled halfheartedly with a rowing machine next to her.

"You seem to be thriving since you took control of the Ashburn account," Caroline said. There was a note of admiration in her voice.

"Thanks for saying so." She took her pacing right down to a dawdle, thinking about the sense of achievement she'd been getting from the work she'd been doing. She had thrown herself into it totally with an energy that came from her private life, and she had thrived.

Was it really time to go it alone? She gave a mental shrug; she was almost ready to dare herself to do it, wasn't that a good enough reason? Of course it was.

"Ed and Penny aren't doing so well," Caroline continued. She pulled wearily on the mock oars and then uttered a few words before reaching again. "They seem to get deeper and deeper into the mess. I'm glad I'm not out there with them; it must be hell." She shook her head and paused a moment.

Abby thought briefly of Ed and the Ashburn account and then put both from her mind. "Come on, I'll buy you something decadent for breakfast; let's indulge ourselves." Abby said, and stepped off her cross-trainer.

"Good idea." Caroline smiled, obviously pleased to be able to abandon the rowing machine.

They went to a café that seemed to be placed strategically next to the gym, to tempt people from their path with the pastries in the window.

"I'll have to get to the office soon," Abby said, glancing at her watch. "I'm expecting the architect to phone. He's visiting the site early this morning and said he'd call me right away."

Caroline looked startled. "Good grief, I didn't think you would be able to get somebody to go out there this quickly."

Abby grinned. "I think it was a tempting project for him, and I didn't want to waste a minute on this one." Her mind drifted, and then she added, "If something's worth doing, then do it and enjoy. That's my motto."

Caroline sat back in her chair and studied Abby for a long moment. "What is it about you? You've been different recently."

Abby scooped up the last of her Danish pastry. "I'm enjoying life, that's all," she replied. It was the simple truth.

Zac stood by the window in his hotel room, sipping his breakfast coffee in the morning sunshine. It was going to be another hot day. He had a lot to do, but all he could think about was Abby's arrival. It was as if she had planted a deep sense of yearning inside him, one that he couldn't shake. *You're well and truly hooked; face it.*

He picked up his phone, looked again at the text message she'd sent him the night before, smiling.

Soon. I want you so much. Let it be soon. Abby.

He set the phone down and looked around the room, hoping that she would like the suite. He wanted them to share a weekend that she would always remember, no matter what happened on Monday. He strolled toward the dressing table and glanced down at the box he had placed there. He had procured her two gifts. A small token of

his feelings for her, and something that he hoped would fulfill her secret fantasies of being watched. He'd got so turned on when she'd
confessed about her desire to be watched, just thinking about it now
made him hard.

He shook his head, smiling wryly. "Abigail Douglas, you're a
downright liability."

The architect phoned shortly after Abby got to her office. He
was a keen, energetic sort. She'd read about his work for other restoration projects throughout Ireland and thought he sounded a likely
candidate. His reactions on visiting the site reassured her that he was
the man for the job. He was as fired up by the proposals as she was.
She asked him to describe the place to her. His lilting Irish accent
and heavily descriptive words about the castle floated her across the
sea to the romantic haven.

"Tell me, do they get much snow there in the winter?" she asked,
trying to keep her voice as professional as possible.

"Snow?" He sounded unsure of what to reply, as if he was afraid
that it would count against the project if he said the wrong thing.

"I'm sorry. Castle in the snow. It's just an image I have. It's personal, not really important."

The architect sounded relieved. "Yes, there's usually a few smat-
terings of snow in the early part of the year, through to the spring."

Abby took a moment to enjoy the thought of it before she picked
up the list of questions she wanted to run through with him and
transformed herself into a more businesslike character.

After the call, she found herself trying to remember what her life
had been like just a couple of weeks before. She'd become more adventurous at work and in her private life. The sensual aspect of her

nature had only been partially formed two weeks back. It had been fully realized through her union with Zac. He had somehow freed her and enabled her to explore that side of herself. She smiled out at the London skyline.

"The cat who has got the cream," she whispered to herself.

She spent the early afternoon updating the accounts and completed her summary report on the investment portfolio, one eye on the clock. She was striving to complete her duties and reach her goals, but she knew deep inside that the desire for completion was an extension of the desire for fulfillment in her private life. She wanted the sense of physical realization that pervaded her other life; she wanted the clarity she felt when she was with Zac, the heightened awareness of every living, breathing moment that he brought to her with his presence.

By midafternoon she had got the documentation finished. The Ashburn meeting was scheduled for first thing on Monday, and she'd laid the ground for the presentation that she was going to give on their work with the account. She was pleased with it, despite the truncated time she'd had on the project; she had more than proved her value. She picked up her weekend bag and got ready to leave the office for the airport. Now for her personal reward: Paris and Zac.

As she passed down the corridor she heard a sound from Ed's office and paused outside the door. He must have made it back for the weekend. She tapped lightly, opened the door, and walked in. As she did, her footsteps ground to a halt. Ed was there, and so was Penny. She was sitting on the desk, her skirt around her waist, her thighs spread. Ed was sitting in front of her looking at her crotch with wide eyes, his fingers probing, like a schoolboy carrying out an experiment over a Bunsen burner.

saskia **walker**

Abby bit back the rising laughter. The litmus paper must have been turning blue, by the look on his face. Penny looked completely ridiculous. Her jacket had fallen backwards, and the sharply angled shoulder pads stood out on her back like twin humps. It was a travesty, seeing a sexual act performed with such a lack of grace.

They both turned at the sound of the intrusion, and Ed's mouth fell open.

Abby turned on her heel immediately and walked out, shutting the door quietly behind her. She darted past the reception—luckily for her empty, because she was beginning to chuckle aloud—and headed for the elevator. When she was safely inside it and the doors shut, she dropped her bag and gripped her stomach, leaning back against the wall, thankfully alone. Even as she walked from the building she had to keep her hand over her mouth to quell the laughter that still surged up inside her.

She hailed a taxi, and as she climbed in, she realized that she probably would have noticed something between them earlier on if she hadn't been so distracted by her own private life. Ed had been different, he hadn't been pursuing her as usual, but she hadn't taken it into her consciousness fully.

"Heathrow Airport," she said to the driver and settled back into the seat just as her phone bleeped.

It was Ed.

"What is it, Ed? I'm just on my way out of town."

"I'm sorry, Abby."

"No, I'm sorry I interrupted. I didn't know."

He mumbled into the receiver, his tone shameful. *Poor Ed.*

She pressed her lips together and then let out what she hoped sounded like a sympathetic-sounding sigh. She didn't want to hurt him by being too glad, even though he'd clearly moved on. She adopted a restrained tone. "Listen, Ed, it doesn't matter, really, we were never really an item."

"But I . . ."

But what? "I can't talk right now, let's just let it go."

"Monday, can we talk on Monday?" He was still pushing, for some reason.

Monday? She'd shelved Monday for the time being. All she could think about now was the weekend. Nothing seemed to exist past that point on the horizon.

She agreed for the sake of peace, hung up, and dropped her phone in her bag. As she did, she noticed the black calling card for The Hub that Zac had given her, lying there in the bottom of her bag. She lifted it and moved it in her hand, watching as the eye winked at her and lured her in. It zapped her with its electric stare each time she turned it.

She remembered their first encounter in the elevator, the electric connection between them, intimate, intensely sexual. Then at The Hub. His arms around her had arrested her life forever. She'd been released into a new realm of experiences through the union of their bodies. Things would never be the same. Working with the Robertson group was over, too; she had come to a new departure, no matter what.

She felt like she could fly to Paris on her own wings. Would Zac be part of her future? She hoped so. It might have felt like a secret affair at first, but it wasn't really. It was a turning point.

eleven | nɘvɘlɘ

Abby strode out of the Charles de Gaulle Airport terminal building and waved for a taxi. She gave the driver the address and then rested back into the seat as the car covered the ground between the airport and the center of Paris.

Anticipation pumped through her veins. Her nerve endings were reaching out for Zac. They didn't need to be awoken. They were already awake, expectant. Since she'd met him she'd become consciously aware of every inch of her body—when she walked, when her clothes brushed her skin. Each sensation was a magic reminder of their joining. She crossed her legs and shifted the fabric of her skirt across her thighs with a secret smile.

The taxi pulled up in an elegant boulevard not far from the Tuileries. The hotel was stylish, fronted by massive wrought-iron-enclosed glass doors that were flanked by pillars. Matching tall, wrought-iron-framed windows echoed the doors on the refined facade. A liveried doorman clicked his heels and bowed when Abby walked up the steps.

The ornate reception area was filled with opulent velvet sofas and potted palms. When she gave her name, the receptionist presented her with a key and an envelope that bore her name.

"Monsieur Bordino will return shortly. The room is on the second floor. If there's anything you need, please let me know or call room service."

"Thank you," she murmured and glanced inside the envelope. It contained a slip of paper. She walked to the elevator. When the doors closed, she slid the paper out.

Soon.

The one word was written in large, slanted letters across the page, underscored with a determined line, and signed with his name. She smiled and curled the piece of paper in her hand.

The brass key fob bore the room number, and when she unlocked it, she paused as the door swung open. She wanted him to be there, but he wasn't. Walking through the door, she dropped her bag as it shut behind her.

The room had a courtly appearance. Rich furnishings and heavy, flowing drapes gave the place a regal air. It truly was a Parisian salon. She glanced at the bed; it was huge, covered in a thick damask quilt that invited the body to sink into it. The headboard reached upwards in a network of gilt spires toward the heavy velvet wall hanging behind it.

A movement caught her eye. The glass doorway to the balcony was open, and a long, white lace curtain billowed into the room. It was as if he had stepped out there for a moment, and she followed the movement.

Lifting the curtain aside, she stepped out and found herself on a balcony enclosed by more wrought iron. It overlooked a small court-yard, where a cherub trickled water from an urn into the circular pool that surrounded him. The building closed the courtyard in on all four sides, and she glanced at the other windows, wondering how many pairs of lovers the shutters masked from each other. Two pigeons fluffed themselves up on a ledge nearby and looked at her as if she were intruding on their private lovemaking. She smiled and walked back into the room.

The heat of the day was waning, but it was still hot. She slipped her jacket off and moved her camisole over her breasts as she walked back across the room, cooling her skin. She spied Zac's leather jacket hanging over a chair and ran her fingertips over its shoulders. Then she bent down to breathe the smell of it, seeking his scent hidden in its folds. His presence was near. She stood up and walked into the bathroom.

It was a marble cavern with a huge tub in the center of the space. Ornate brass taps and a mirror that sprang the length and height of one wall gave the place an air of grandeur. As she came back into the bedroom, a small box on the dressing table caught her eye, and she wandered over to it. It was dark charcoal kid leather, mottled like parchment and tied with black string. She didn't touch it but wondered what was inside. Just then, an unseen finger touched her, and she held her breath.

The phone rang. She stared at it. What if it was another woman phoning for him? What if she found out something, now, something that she really didn't want to know? It didn't stop ringing. She moved toward the sound reluctantly but found her hand drawing the receiver to her ear. She listened but did not speak.

"Abby?" It was his voice, its deep, intimate timbre making her spine tingle; adrenaline rushed through her body.

"Yes," she murmured. "I was worried. I thought I might intercept a call for you, from another woman."

He gave a soft laugh. "No, I told you, you're the only woman."

She lay down on the bed and nursed the receiver against her face. "Good."

"Abby, nobody knows we're here. I wanted this weekend to be about us, totally." He sounded suddenly serious.

She listened to the background noises of the place he was in, jealous of its claim on him. "This weekend is about us, and I'm here, on your bed," she whispered.

"I can just picture you," he said quietly. "I'm really glad you came. I'm finished here, so I'll be back soon."

She had an image of him striding toward her as she lay on the bed, and gave a purr of approval. "How soon? I'm ready for you now."

She heard him move against the receiver, felt him turn away from the place around him.

Her body pressed harder into the bed. "I want you, Zac." She heard his breath close to the phone.

"How ready?" he whispered.

She smiled to herself; his voice betrayed his need for her. She pressed her head back against the pillows and breathed in deeply.

"I'm getting wetter as we speak . . . I've been longing for your cock inside me." As she spoke she quivered inside, as if in confirmation of her own words. Her need was so powerful that her eyes prickled with tears. Her breath caught. She realized that the phone at the other end conveyed only the background sounds. "Are you still there?" she asked.

"Yes," came his reply. His voice was husky, constricted. "How wet? Touch yourself with your fingers and tell me just how wet you are."

Abby groaned and writhed on the bed, her sandals falling to the floor with a soft thud. Her free hand moved automatically to answer his request, her body throbbing out a joyful response. Her fingers pulled at her skirt, her thighs opening as the skirt rode up.

Her hand stroked over the hot, moist surface of her silk panties. The sensation was sheer torment. "My panties are soaked."

"Put your fingers inside."

She slid a finger down one side of the silk and beneath the material. She felt her moist sex quiver at her own touch and groaned.

"Abby?" he whispered in response.

"Zac . . . please," she murmured, as her fingers thrust inside and rubbed against the smooth, wet walls of her anxious sex. "Oh I'm so wet, the sound of your voice . . . knowing you are near . . . I have wanted you so badly." Her fingers moved, but her flesh was throbbing with longing for him. She could hear his breath against the mouthpiece; she almost felt its heat on her sex, stirring her up even more. She wanted him there.

"I can't . . . it's torture." She pulled her knees up and drew her hand away. She gripped the phone and closed her eyes tightly. "It's you I want. I must have your body against me now," she breathed into the phone, and her lips were very close to its surface. She listened to his quiet, dense breathing. "I think I'm addicted to you," she whispered.

"Good," he replied, and the line went dead.

She held the receiver to her ear and listened to the hollow echo of her own breathing. Her heart was beating wildly into the void he'd left. She lay back for a moment, then dropped the receiver and coiled across the bed, pressing herself against it as her body moved over the wide surface, absorbing the physical contact. After a few moments she rolled off the bed and paced the room.

How far away was he? How long would it be until he got to her? She ran a hand across the back of her neck and lifted her hair. She was hot and restless and wandered toward the bathroom, peeling her clothes off as she went.

Turning on the ornate brass taps, she listened to the sound of the water plunging in on itself and looked at her naked reflection in the huge mirror. Her skin was luminous in the dark marble cavern. Her hair looked like fire creeping through autumn leaves. The colors were echoed in the lick of dark flames in her groin, where the curve of her body disappeared in on itself. Her eyes were bright; she could see the heat of her own desire clearly. Her lips were full and dark with readiness for passion, readiness for Zac. Her hands caressed the outline of her breasts; they were aching. Her whole body ached for him. She turned away and slipped into the bath.

The tub was so deep that the water covered her breasts. Her toes didn't reach the end of the bath, and she stretched out, spreading herself in the water. Resting her head back, she looked at the patterned marble of the ceiling. She could see a vague reflection of herself, a white blur that rippled on the dark marble. Holding her breath, she slid down into the water until it covered her face, her hair floating up around her. She listened to her heart pounding in her ears. It was as eager to be with Zac as the rest of her body, and it struck her then that love, like blood, coursed through her heart.

When she slid up again and breathed in the warm air of the room, her wet hair clung to her cheeks and neck. It crept close across her shoulders and into points over her breasts, its touch on her skin like that of a lover.

Her skin prickled with awareness. Opening her eyes, she saw Zac standing in the doorway, leaning up against the frame, watching her. He held her skirt and lace camisole in one hand and the other slowly unbuttoned his own shirt. He ran the leather across his bare chest.

"Still warm," he murmured.

She could see from the expression in his eyes that he was just as filled with desire as she was.

He dropped the skirt, lifted the lace camisole to his face, and breathed deeply against it, his eyes closing at the touch of the lace on his face, his loose hair sliding around the material.

She couldn't move or speak, transfixed as she was by his actions.

He moved against the lace, then looked at her again and laid the camisole over the door handle.

The tap dripped. She blinked.

He walked toward her and took off his shirt. She watched the flex of his chest as he dropped it to the floor. He sat on the edge of the bath and trailed his fingers up her leg from knee to hip, over her belly and down the other leg, rippling through the water, leaving patterns of movement and sensation above and beneath her skin as he passed.

"Zac, you're here." She leaned forward, and he kissed her, long and luxuriously. His face felt warm and supple against her cool wetness.

He moved his fingers to the mound of her sex and lightly kneaded the fullness with the pads of his fingers, sending tremors through her entire groin. Her tongue touched against his, and her hands climbed to his arms. He drew back, and his eyes flashed, a dark smile on his face. He pulled a condom out of his pocket, tearing it open.

She rested her hands on the bath edge, preparing to climb out.

"No," he commanded. "Stay."

He stripped his clothes off, and she looked at his erect cock as he rolled the rubber on. It was charged, pleasure-seeking, and potent.

"I want you," she whispered.

"You're going to get me." He pushed her legs apart in the water and inserted his knee between hers and filled the space with his body. Water crashed around them, spilling over the edge of the bath.

"Zac," she breathed, laughing, as the water flowed up over her shoulders.

He followed its path. His hips moved to meet hers, his chest forcing another wave of water over her shoulders to spill to the floor.

She lifted her legs up to the edge of the bath, to lie along the sides. He squeezed her pussy, and a surge of water pushed in front of him. Her head fell back against the bath when his mouth sought her damp breasts as they pushed out of the water, her body arched up for his touch. His lips closed on her nipple, and his fingers slid inside her.

The water flowed around them, nebulous, broken only by the firm hunt of his fingers against her flesh. His teeth pulled gently at her nipple, and she moaned.

He led a line of kisses to her throat. His cock nudged against her. The water flowed around them again as he moved inside her, and she felt him wedge against her, then plunge inside, water trapped between them, inside and out.

He kissed her mouth, and their bodies moved together in the water, anchored by her legs on the side of the bath. His lips were wet, his tongue warm and firm in her mouth, skimming her mouth, tasting her. He licked her cheek, chasing a drop of water that dripped from her hair, and her eyes closed. She was entranced by the muted feeling of his body riding against hers through the veil of water. His tongue climbed to her temple, and he sucked her wet hair between his lips, his chest rising against her as he reached farther inside her.

She felt the trail of his wet hair against her face and reached forward, her eyes opening to meet his as her fingers tangled in his hair. The only sound was the splashing of water that reflected their movements. Each splash touched her mind a split second after he thrust against her, deep inside, an echo of perfection and harmony. As the touches grew faster and harder, so the noise of the spilling water became louder, quicker.

He moved his hands along the edge of the bath, lifting up as his strides became ever more urgent. He looked like Poseidon rising out of the waves, his wet hair splattered across his neck and shoulders, his muscles flexing.

Water spilled over the edge of the bath. Her body arched up, her hips bucking against his as if to free the demon that coiled inside. It was rising like the water around her shoulders, rising up to flood free. She reached forward and pressed her hand along the line of his throat as she climbed to her peak.

Zac's lips parted as he watched her climax, then she lost sight, her eyelids falling with the tide of unrestrained power flowing through her body.

He murmured her name, drawing her back to him, and as she looked into his eyes she saw how her climax had fired him.

She put her hands on his arms, holding him as he reached for his prize. The power began to fade from his eyes, and he uttered a deep, strange sound, like a captured animal. As he gave the final lunge, the water crashed again and spilled over her breasts as he came, creating a surge of movement within and without.

"Abby," he whispered.

He lay over her and kissed her again as his cock slid from her into the embrace of the water.

She glanced down. "The water wants to take you from me."

He laughed quietly and reached around to pull the plug out. As the water swirled away from them, he kissed her face, drying her skin with his mouth, moving over every bit of her. She murmured as his lips passed over her, the water sinking around her hips, trailing sensation away. Her fingers climbed into his hair, and drops of water slid down her wrist as she moved her fingers across its surface.

When the water was gone, she looked into his eyes. "I really am addicted to you, Zac, and you are feeding my addiction."

He kissed her gently, smiling. "Good; I want to feed your addiction."

When they climbed from the bath, he wrapped her in a towel and moved his hands over it, following the lines of her body through the deep fabric. He showed such acute attention to her body that she felt cosseted, cherished. She watched the movements of his body in the mirror as he attended her.

The muscles on his back flexed, gloriously strong. The damp hair on his legs drew her gaze to the taut line of his thighs and buttocks as he crouched down to dry her legs with the towel.

When he stood up again, she opened the towel and took him into it, warming his body with hers. They stood silently for a few minutes, wrapped together in the marble room.

"It's so good to be together again," she whispered, smiling up at him.

"Yes. I thought you might not be able to come. I'm so glad you're here." He kissed her forehead.

"Oh, I would have got here, come hell or high water."

He led her to the bed and laid her down, kissing her gently. They lay quietly together for a while, enjoying the reunion of their bodies.

"One night apart, and I missed you so much," she said eventually.

He nodded; there was a deep contentment in his eyes; as if he was finally happy to have her hidden away with him.

"It's a beautiful room," she said. She wanted to hear his voice again.

"Yes," he replied, stroking her cheek with the back of his hand. "Not as beautiful as you, though."

She laughed. She felt strangely buoyant, as if the water still lifted and held her body.

"I always stay here when I'm in Paris. There's a good seafood restaurant nearby. I'm going to take you there tonight, but I'll get them to send up some wine to have now, if you like?"

She nodded, watching as he moved to the phone.

He spoke in French. She didn't know he could speak French. Her heart yearned for that knowledge, for the full measure of him and the sense of completeness she instinctively knew it would bring her. She wanted to know everything about Zachary Bordino.

Zac collected the matching robes that hung in the bathroom, and when the wine was delivered, he carried it to the bedside, where they curled into a yin and yang on the bed, happily watching each other.

He teased his fingers inside the edge of her robe, brushing the skin on her thigh with the lightest breath of a touch. Her body responded, writhing with pleasure. He loved that—adored that he could affect her so easily.

"Oh, I meant to ask, did you get the club?"

"Yes. Mercifully, the paperwork was all done before you arrived."

"Will you take me to see it?"

He looked at her, unable to hide the pleasure that her request had brought. "Of course, if you'd like to, we can go there later this evening."

"Is it far?"

He began to laugh.

"What?" She tugged at the belt of his robe.

"Too far." He was still smiling. He was thinking of his rush to get to her.

She looked at him with mock innocence. "Oh?"

"I made the mistake of telling the taxi driver to put his foot down. They're all mad drivers in Paris anyway. I didn't know what I was in for."

She leaned forward to kiss him, hiding her laughter against his mouth. "Well, we'll get the metro. As long as we're together we can take things a bit slower." Her eyes reflected her amusement. She sighed. "I thought I'd never get through yesterday without you," she whispered, eyeing his body where it was exposed at the neck of his robe.

"I felt the same." He watched her with a half smile, waiting to see what she did next.

"While I remember, there's something I need to tell you," she said.

"Yes?"

"I'm not really a receptionist."

Why did he feel so strange, hearing her say those words aloud? They seemed to fly out of nowhere. He felt almost bereft. He stared at her, waiting for some big confession—guilt maybe—but he saw only honesty and a hint of embarrassment.

"Why did you lie?" he managed to ask, trying to keep his voice level.

"Because most men do a runner when they find out what I do for a living." Her eyes flashed, pure seduction reeling him in. "And I didn't want to scare you off."

That simple, huh? He could kick himself. But why did he feel such a sense of loss? *Because you haven't got an excuse to mistrust her anymore, you jackass.* Yes, he had been using it as a crutch. And now it was gone he had to stagger forward into the relationship without support. If this all fell apart, he wouldn't have his sense of mistrust to wallow in, just loss. Only loss. He didn't want to feel that, but it was edging up his back like fear.

"I'm an investment manager." She paused, waiting for his reaction. "So if you ever need any advice on what to do with your surplus cash . . ." She reached over and stroked his chest. "I'm your girl."

You certainly are.

He hadn't wanted their real lives to intrude on this weekend, but the discussion had led them there. With an effort, he smiled. He had to get her off that topic though, lest he feel tempted to confess his hidden role in her life, and have her storm out on him as a result. This was their time; he didn't want to ruin it now, not this soon. "Is there anything else about you that I should know?"

She frowned thoughtfully. "No."

He felt relief.

"Oh, no wait, there is something."

His chest tightened.

She grinned. "I dare myself to do things." Her eyes twinkled.

"What do you mean?"

"Well, when I can't decide whether to go for something, or I need to pull together more confidence, I dare myself. Like when you gave me the card to The Hub, I really wanted to go, but I wasn't sure. I wanted to see you again, so I dared myself to go."

"I see. Maybe I should try it myself sometime."

"What? Daring me to do something? Or daring yourself?" She chuckled.

He was going to have to dare himself to walk into Robertson's on Monday. "Maybe both."

She lolled back on the bed, resting on one elbow, nursing her wineglass, her hair spilling onto the quilt like molten lava.

He reached over to stroke it. "Do you always go through with it, when you dare yourself to do something?"

She nodded. "I like to respond to a challenge." She touched his face, smiling. "Deep down I wonder what the ultimate dare would be, one that I really would have a hard time deciding over."

"What, like a double dare?" He flickered his eyebrows at her.

"Why does that sound like you're thinking devious thoughts?"

"Now that I know your trick, I'm wondering how far I can push my luck."

She laughed. "Oh, I imagine I'd do just about anything you dared me to, even if it was a double dare."

He shook his head. "You do trust too readily."

"I told you, I like a challenge." Amusement twinkled in her eyes.

So she thought of him as a challenge. She certainly was, for him. "Apparently I do, too."

"In that case I dare you to tell me something about yourself that I don't already know—maybe something you've never told anyone."

"Hmm. Something I haven't told anyone." Strangely enough, his mind didn't automatically leap back to the big secret between them. It went to something else first. A matter of the heart that he thought he'd left behind long ago. As he turned it over in his mind, she prodded him in the chest with one finger.

"You're such a mystery man."

"I am?"

"Yes, but that's why I was so attracted to you in the first place."

Oh, the irony. "In that case maybe I should stay a mystery. Maybe you won't want me anymore if you know everything about me." *Never a truer word spoken than in jest.*

"I think it's too late for that," she said, quite seriously. "Remember, it's some sort of an addiction now."

He reached for her, cupping her cheek with his hand. She rested her hand over his, searching for some deep truth in his eyes.

"I think you're going to learn quite a lot about me very soon, Abby. But the thing that sprang to mind when you dared me was about another woman."

"Another woman?" Her expression changed, grew pensive. "There's another woman?" She looked as if someone had just told her the world was about to end.

He reached over to kiss her. "Hush," he whispered, "you're the *only* woman. This was a long time ago."

She flung herself back on the bed, laughing with relief. "And there was me thinking I was the shady secret in our affair."

No, that's me, my love. "You're far from that, Abby."

When she rolled back, she propped herself up on her elbow

again. "So there was another woman. What is it about her that is something you've never told anyone before now?" She narrowed her eyes and peered at him analytically, as if she could read it on his face. Humor wasn't far from her expression.

"I think she made it hard for me to trust people." Delivering that small statement somehow felt as if a gaping wound had been re-opened. "I was a lot younger, and I wasn't taking any responsibility in life; I was just out for a good time. The odd thing was, it didn't oc-cur to me that I wasn't the only one. Nathan and I hitched up with these two women, traveling through Europe on the trail of summer rock festivals. The four of us were together for about two weeks. Then she disappeared—together with my credit cards and my wal-let." It wasn't quite as straightforward as that. She'd found out he had money, and she'd ripped him off good and proper.

Abby watched him, her intelligent eyes so gently inquiring, now that she realized he was serious. "And did she take your heart, too?"

It had felt that way. He stroked her hand, smiled, and shook his head. "It might have felt like it at the time, but I didn't know what love was, back then."

She stared at him as his words sank in. Eventually, she nodded. "Friends are always telling me I trust too readily, that I don't have the thick hide I need to survive in the world I live in."

"The underlying tenderness is what makes Abigail Douglas spe-cial, but I think you probably do trust too easily. I mean . . . I could have been anybody, but you trusted me." It was as if a cruel, tor-menting demon had taken up residence in his mind, and his every thought was laden with self-ridicule. He'd have to shake it off, or he'd ruin the evening.

"Yes, but that's what I wanted. I liked the idea of a sexy mystery man for a lover." She winked at him.

He rested his fingers in her hair, teasing it out like strands of copper thread. "I think you are helping me to trust again." He meant the words. It had been hard, but he would trust Abigail Douglas with his life.

Would she ever trust him again though, when she found out who he really was?

twelve | ɘʌlɘwt

Nathan stood outside Camden Town tube station, scanning the crowds of people spilling out from the escalators. The evening party people were out in force. He spotted Suzanne's blonde hair just as her arm raised through the crowd to wave at him. His instant reaction on seeing her was satisfaction, like he was whole again. He felt like a teenager, a bit lovesick. He wanted to shout out to everyone around them, "Hey, look, everyone, this is my woman, she's with me."

She ran toward him, looking sexier than ever in hipster jeans and a black leather vest with a gauzy black mesh T-shirt underneath. A peep of black bra beneath it made him want to strip her to find out if she was wearing matching undies.

She jumped onto him, locking her arms around his neck and her legs around his thighs, like a happy koala clinging to its tree trunk. The greeting had grown familiar now, third time around. He held her bottom in his hands, squeezing her tight against him as he kissed her.

"Hey, big man."

"Hey, little lady."

She gave a throaty laugh as she ruffled his spiky hair. Her eyes were lined with kohl, her curls secured in a cute topknot.

"Ready for the gig?" He lowered her to the ground.

"Absolutely." She tucked in beneath his arm, and they walked toward the venue. Her expression gradually turned serious as they wended their way through the crowded pavements. "Listen, there's something I wanted to ask you about," she said tentatively.

He had a sinking feeling. Was she going to call it off?

"I've got a sort of a family event coming up soon, and I was kind of wondering if you'd like to come along with me?"

Relief hit him. Not only that but the sense of satisfaction was back. She wanted her family to meet him, but she'd been worried to ask. She had no idea how pleased he was. He pulled a mock frown. "You have a 'sort of' family event, that you were 'kind of' wondering if I'd like to go to with you?"

She punched him in the ribs. "Don't you make fun of me."

"I'd love to go with you."

"You don't want to know what it is first?"

"No. If you want me to go with you, I'm there already."

She wrapped her arms around him, pushing her face into his T-shirt as she gave him a hug. "It's my brother's twenty first."

"You were worried that I wouldn't want to go?"

"Well, he's not a rock fan; the music will be dire." She shook her head disapprovingly. Her expression was so serious he couldn't help but laugh aloud.

"We could convert him yet."

She smiled. "My family will want to know all about you. It might be a bit like the Spanish Inquisition."

He shrugged. "Now you sound like you're trying to put me off."

"No," she declared. "I'm really pleased that you want to come."

"Good. It's a done deal."

They'd reached the venue. She glanced at the queue and then at the sign over the doorway. "The Hub?" She frowned. "Why does that sound familiar to me?"

"The venue's had a lot of press recently; it's only been open a couple of months."

She was staring up at him, a furrow between her eyebrows. "No, it's something else." Her expression changed, her eyes lighting up. "That's it, the other courier, he gave us cards, me and Abby." She looked up at the sign again. "For this place."

Shit. It wouldn't ever have occurred to him. He struggled to find a response. *What would Zac say, if it was him standing here?* He'd find some clever way to shrug it off, but Nathan didn't feel very clever, especially not right then. He felt awkward as hell and decidedly shifty. That bothered him.

"We don't need to queue." He took her by the hand, bypassing the crowd and giving Steve, the doorman, the nod as he led her inside.

"Wow, this place is great. What is it, an old cinema?" She craned her neck, looking at the decorative coving on the ceiling of the entrance vestibule.

He nodded, relieved that her thoughts had moved on. If only he could forget it. It wasn't going to be that easy. He'd just been thrown from feeling mighty proud that she wanted him to meet her family, to feeling ashamed about the reason why he had befriended her in the first place. Instinctively his annoyance became focused on Zac, who was who knew where, having a bloody good time, no doubt.

Nathan had had enough of this. He'd got some serious thinking to do. He headed for the bar, ordering them a couple of beers.

"What's up?" She peered at him when he handed her a drink.

He smiled. She was genuinely concerned for him. He'd never had that luxury before. What had he done to deserve this woman? Her caring streak spoiled him in ways he hadn't been spoiled before. "I'm OK. I've got to watch the support people, make sure they're doing their jobs. The band has had some interest from major labels, and there will be scouts in the crowd."

"OK, I understand." She squeezed his hand, snuggling against his arm. "It's fun to be here when they are on the verge of making it."

He finished his beer and nodded at the growing crowd on the floor. "Let's get closer." The place was filling quickly, the crowd growing dense.

She followed his lead, and they moved into the pack of people, closing on the stage, just as the lights lowered and the band came out. He nestled her in front of him so she was safe from the mosh pit and stroked her shoulders.

The music blasted out, angst-ridden, energy-fueled stuff, the singer a long-haired, scrawny man with green eyes. He paced the stage and growled out to the audience, his eyes looking directly at them with a challenging stare.

People were moving in unison almost immediately, a good sign. Suzanne spooned in against Nathan's hips as she rocked to the sounds. He glanced down whenever the lights passed over her face. She was following the singer's dramatic path back and forth across the stage. He was pacing like a caged animal. Nathan couldn't help identifying with him and gave a wry smile. At the back of his mind, he vowed to make this odd situation right. He wanted to be with Suzanne, like this, but without the burden of guilt that was currently weighing heavy on him.

A whip of guitar sound licked out and locked them into the

rhythm. They moved with it, her hips riding from side to side against his. It felt hot. It felt right, too. The music crashed and ground around them, the guitarists arched over in sheer concentration as they spun out the dramatic pace of the tracks. The crowd was rapt with the experience, a mass, at one with the sounds. There was a feeling of climactic release, of escape, in the building of the current song. The singer came to the front of the stage, and his voice became solemn and low. As he let the final chords of the song free from his throat, he scoured the audience with his eyes, as if he could read their very souls.

As the next number began to take form, Nathan glanced over at the mixing board, and noticed that the soundman looked stressed. He hadn't noticed too many glitches—nothing out of the ordinary— but he'd promised he'd watch over it. Zac had wanted to do the best they could for the band.

Leaning down, he spoke against her ear. "I've got to go check on the sound. Do you want to stay here?"

She nodded up at him, pulling him down for sudden kiss as she did so.

He made his way to the sound station, glancing over the shoulder of the man at the controls. The guy gave a thumbs-up, but Nathan watched him through another track to be sure.

When he was satisfied, he straightened up and looked out at the audience, following the path of the moving spotlight that passed over them. His gaze found Suzanne immediately, and she looked at him across the heaving crowd. She smiled in recognition, some message that didn't need to be voiced passing between them.

They were becoming a couple, he realized in that moment.

He stepped toward the stage and into the corridor that ran behind it, flipped open his mobile phone, and scrolled to Zac's number.

The voice at the other end told him the phone was switched off. He tried not to get irritated; he was already annoyed with himself because he'd lost his sense of humor about this. He knew Zac was busy in Paris; he just had to make a gesture toward sorting this, or he'd go mad.

"Zac, it's Nathan. I need to talk to you. I need some advice. I know you're not going to be back in London until late on Sunday, but can we speak Monday, if not before? Cheers."

He folded the phone shut and moved back to the edge of the stage. Craning his neck, he tried to catch sight of Suzanne. He couldn't see her. Uncertainty gripped him, then discomfort. What if she'd gone?

He felt a tug on his T-shirt.

Turning around, he found her standing behind him, and his sense of humor was back, and he was laughing at himself this time.

"Hey, big guy. I missed you." She smiled up at him. "Am I allowed up here?"

"Yes, of course." He gathered her against him and found them a place to watch from the side of the stage.

"This feels like they're right in our home playing for us," she shouted over her shoulder, laughing.

The floor was vibrating beneath their feet. He snuck his hands down to rest beneath her breasts, enjoying the sexy feeling of her movement in his arms.

After a few minutes she turned around in his arms, pressed against him, looking up at him with mischief, she gestured him down so she could speak in his ear. "It's good here, I can feel the music pounding right through me."

"*Right* through you?"

She nodded, slow, her lips slightly parted, heat visible in her cheeks. "My pussy is on fire."

He wanted to feel that, too. He led her from view, taking her to the dividing wall behind the spot were the band were playing, where the wall itself thudded with the sound. He backed her against it.

"Oh yeah." Her head rolled, and her eyes were almost closed, narrowed into slits.

He put his mouth over hers, wanting to eat her up. She gurgled with pleasure, kissing him hungrily, her body rubbing up and down against his.

His cock was rock hard.

She panted; she was crazy for it. "Oh Nathan, I think I'm going to come, right here."

"Must bring you to gigs more often," he said, chuckling softly.

He groped inside her hipsters, desperate for the feeling of her moist hot spot. She was so soft and damp inside her panties, all peach flesh and cream. He wanted to eat her. He pulled his hand out, licking her silky fluid from his fingers, enjoying the rich scent and taste of woman. He grinned at her when she groaned at his actions and shoved his hand in for more, fingers inside her folds, applying pressure to her hot little clit, pushing her on.

"The guitar," she whispered, hands flat against the wall, shaking her head, denying it.

She was going to come.

He reached his hand down—forcing her zipper all the way—and thrust his finger into the mouth of her delicious cunt, just as it tightened and spilled.

• • •

Abby walked over to the dressing table and sat down. She could see Zac's reflection in the mirror. He seemed to like her forest-green velvet dress. She'd brought it because she could scrunch it into a ball, and it rolled over her body like a stocking, from bust to thigh, small shoulder straps covered in tight velvet buds the only decoration. She began to fix her hair, and after a moment he got up and walked over to her.

Leaning over, he took the brush from her hand and began to comb out her hair. He performed the task expertly, lifting the curls from underneath and drawing them up with the brush, his fingers tracing the texture of the strands as they fell back down around her shoulders.

She moved her head to follow the path he chose through the tresses, arching her neck.

"You look so good," he said quietly. She glanced up, and their eyes met in the mirror.

She took the brush from him, put it down, leaning back against him. He ran his hands down her throat and over her shoulders. She reached up against him.

He leaned over to kiss her mouth from above, and his hands curved over her velvet-covered breasts. "You should wear velvet more often," he whispered.

She felt the slide of his hair on her neck as she arched back to meet him. She covered his hands with her own, and they kissed lightly. Then he moved back to kiss her forehead, her eyelids. His touch was so light, so gentle, yet so arresting. His mouth was the only thing stopping her from floating away.

He leaned over to the dressing table and picked up the mottled box she had noticed when she arrived. Opening it, he offered it to her. "It's for you."

She took the box, and as she looked into it, he knelt down beside her to watch her face. The box held a heavy silver filigree chain that traced itself in delicate sweeps and patterns into a thicker setting at the front. It seemed to represent the irregular patterns of nature's growth. But on closer examination she saw that there were two serpents entwined at the center. Resting between their coiled bodies was a piece of amber, as if they were protecting it with their bodies or fighting over it. It was strange and beautiful, and it rendered her speechless.

"It's Lalique," he said and lifted it from the box. "I saw it, and it made me think of you. I thought you might like it." He unlatched the chain in readiness to put it on her.

"I do," she whispered. "But why?"

He smiled. "A beautiful thing deserves to be surrounded by more beauty." He stroked her face.

"I am surrounded by beauty." She looked into his eyes, feasting on him. She moved to kiss him and, as she did, his fingers slipped the pendant around her neck.

He turned her back to the mirror to examine the result. Abby let her fingers touch the necklace lightly. It was an exquisite piece and seemed to be the perfect partner for her dress.

"You have such good taste," she murmured as she looked at the chain in the mirror.

"I know." He stared at her meaningfully, and then chuckled low. "Come on. Let's go eat." He pulled her up from her seat, redirecting the mood of the moment.

Abby laughed as she fell into his arms.

He kissed her. "We'd better go now," he whispered darkly as he drew back from her mouth. "Or we might never get out of here." His tone was so suggestive, her body trembled with resurgent arousal.

The restaurant he took her to was small, no more than a dozen
tiny wooden tables squeezed into a space not much bigger than her
office. Ancient candelabras hung precariously out from the walls.
The light they gave off was increased by their reflection in the gilt-
framed mirrors. A diminutive waiter ushered them in, waving his
arm in front of himself, as if clearing a grand passage through the
tiny place for them.

As they walked behind him, Abby spied the noisy antics of the
kitchen through a curtained entrance at the back. When they were
seated, the waiter carried over a blackboard that was easily the same
height as himself, propped it on a chair in front of them, and left
them to study the enticing meals that were listed there.

Abby chuckled quietly when he left. "It's like a time warp," she
said.

Zac leaned forward conspiratorially. "Yes . . . I thought you
would enjoy it. What year do you think we are in?" He had a mock
seriousness about him that reduced her to laughter.

"Eighteen ninety-six?" she offered.

He nodded. "And you are Sarah Bernhardt, sitting there adorned
by your Lalique jewels and your velvet dress."

Abby threw her head back and laughed; she felt gloriously happy.
"And you? Who are you?" She leaned over as if to examine him
closely. "You must be a Greek prince who has come to entice me
away from my true path."

He looked suddenly serious, picked up her hand, and kissed it
gently. He lowered his eyes and then he spoke quietly in Greek. She
wanted to know what he had said but didn't want to ask. She felt as if
they were circling each other again, as if he were holding something
back. It made her want to pour herself out, beg him to use her.

He looked up from her hand but did not let it go. "What shall we eat?" he said and gestured to the blackboard, but he was still looking at her.

Eventually she turned and looked at the board. She chose lobster, and he ordered a platter of gifts from the sea. The waiter brought a small carafe of wine that was constantly replenished. Abby felt mellow, content. It was as if the candlelight warmed through her body.

The lobster was delicious and was served with honey-dipped prawns and a crazy salad that leapt from the plate in a tangle of colors. Zac constantly tempted her with offerings from his own plate. She watched him eat. His mouth was so strong, so firm and decisive. When his teeth reached for a plump mussel, she focused on them to the exclusion of all else around her. He grinned when he caught her watching and leaned forward to offer her an oyster. She shook her head but stared down at the thing as he squeezed lemon juice over it.

"This one reminds me of you," he whispered and took it to his mouth. His tongue came out and teased it from its resting place before devouring it.

"How am I ever to finish my food?" she asked. "Do you want me to starve?"

He shook his head and gave her an innocent look.

"Well, please stop it." He shrugged and returned to his plate. "There is a legend that says a young Athenian boy discovered that oysters were good to eat," he said. He did not look at her as he spoke but concentrated on his food.

Abby listened and ate. Her succulent lobster was so perfectly accompanied by his voice, she felt herself happily pulled into his story.

"As he walked on the beach one morning, he spied an oyster yawning and leaned over to touch it, to investigate." He was plucking a morsel from its shell as he spoke, and she saw him standing on the beach in the early morning sun, his naked body dappled with pools of light. "The thing snapped shut at the intrusion and bit his finger." He reached for his wineglass. "As he sucked the pain away, he discovered the flavor of the oyster and broke the thing open, to swallow the unfortunate creature." He glanced at her. "So the story goes."

Abby picked up one of her honey-dipped prawns with her fingers and took it to his mouth. His lips accepted her offering, and then he teased her fingers with his teeth, and she smiled. She felt the slide of his leg under the table. It moved along the velvet of her dress, and her own leg moved in response, caressing his in return. She sat back, stretched her leg against his, and sipped her wine.

For dessert they selected a delicate-looking tart with thinly sliced apples arranged in neat lines over its surface. Zac insisted she accompany it with brandy. She turned the glass in her hand and let her eyes slide from the movement of the rich, dark liquid to the rich, inviting look in his eyes.

"I've never met anyone like you before," he said.

It was intimate. She was moved to respond intimately. "I've never met anyone like you, either." She felt as if their spirits rose up to meet one another. The moment was intense. The clink of the coffee cups arriving on the table drew them away from each other.

Zac watched her as they drank the coffee. "When do you have to leave?" he asked, and she looked up, startled at his question.

"My flight's late on Sunday morning. I have to be ready for work on Monday morning."

He nodded and looked down at his coffee cup, avoiding her eyes. She hadn't wanted to break the spell by thinking beyond this moment, but he seemed to want to know how long they had.

"And you, are you going back to London soon?" Her voice was tentative. She was wondering when she would see him again.

"Yes, Sunday, but later in the day. There are a few things I want to finalize before I leave." He smiled. "Are you ready to see the club, Pharamonds?"

"Yes, I'd love to."

He straightened in his seat, eyes twinkling. "In the course of my research I had to look at other venues in the area, see who we could work with, who might be the competition."

She nodded, eager to hear all about it.

"I found an interesting venue that holds exclusive party events, and I procured us an invitation from the owner." He watched her as he spoke. "For tomorrow night."

Her curiosity stirred, his eyes held so much mystery.

"Exclusive party events?"

"Fetish events, anything-goes type events."

She couldn't withhold a delighted laugh. "How marvelous."

He gave a pleasured smile. "Good, but there's a strict dress code, so we'll go shopping tomorrow."

"You've really thought it all through."

"Oh yes, I thought it would give us both a chance to explore your secret desires a little bit more."

Her heart was beating fast, anticipation and the prospect of adventure and discovery tempering its pacing. "As long as I'm with you, I'm all for it."

"I'll be right there; you can bet on it."

"I can hardly wait."

He pushed his coffee cup to one side. "Come, let's go to Pharamonds; I'm eager to see what you think of it."

The entrance to the club was marked by its dramatic Art Nouveau arched doorway nestled between shop fronts and cafés. A shaft of light from a lantern revealed the stone steps that led down into the place. Abby was eager to take it all in.

It was smaller than The Hub, more intimate. The main space had a bar with a small stage and a tiny dance floor. The walls were rough-hewn stones that jutted out and seemed to guard the place like an ancient regiment. The bar was long and simple, the wooden tables dotted with candles oozing down old wine bottles. Piped jazz music fed the place with a relaxed atmosphere. It was almost full, but there were a couple of tables still free. Zac led her to one of them.

"It used to be a very popular venue, but the present owner couldn't be bothered with the music side of it, let it slide. It's really only been used as a bar for the past few years, but there's a lot of talent looking for somewhere to try out the scene. I did some investigation. There's a feeling of heritage about the place for the locale. They want Pharamonds to be a live venue again."

"Yes, I can see that the atmosphere is here. You can almost feel Piaf in the walls." She put her hand against the cool stone.

He nodded, then caught the waiter's eye and ordered their drinks.

"There are two unused rooms," he continued. "I think I could have them knocked into one, to function as a gallery. I would like to exhibit more art in my venues, to make the live music and art work together to create a dynamic atmosphere, to showcase one another."

"How did you get into this business, refurbishing venues?"

"Oh, I don't know, interest in music, teenage yen to be a musician, next best thing." He leaned forward, moving the candle that stood between them to one side. "Do you like the place?"

"Yes. It's a good sister club to The Hub. An older but more petite and mysterious sister."

"It's funny you think of it as female. So do I," he said thoughtfully.

218

"That's because it makes you want to come inside," she answered provocatively.

He laughed, flashing his teeth at her in genuine amusement. She felt a warm glow of pleasure because she had made him laugh.

"Do you think it needs many changes?"

She looked around the place again. "I see it bathed in blue light; it would compliment the rough stone walls."

He nodded and encouraged her to go on.

"Whenever I think of Paris, it is suffused with blue light, every scene. It's partly because that's the way it's most often depicted . . . ads and everything. It's always blue light, it's almost a tradition. *L'heure bleu*."

"And?" he said, astutely sensing there was more.

"Well it's about twilight. It whispers of the long pleasures of the night to come. It has an intimacy."

"You are a very visual person, Abby."

She nodded; he was right. "I see everything in images, I think. I remember everything as a series of stills." Some of them were projecting in her mind as she looked at the light casting shadows down one side of his face. She was seeing him that first time in his apartment. Remembering how he had looked as he brought her again and again to climax. "The images come back to haunt me . . ."

Her fingers were against the strap of velvet on her shoulder. As they fiddled there, the material lifted, and she felt the velvet tug against her nipples. They were painfully hard. She reached for her glass with both hands and looked down at the table. "But the atmosphere . . . it would be good to retain that?" she added, distracting herself.

"We could do that," he replied.

She noticed the "we" and looked at him. They stared at one an-other silently for a moment.

"I suppose you'll have to be here a lot?"

"At first, yes."

"Can I get a job behind the bar? I'm thinking of a career change." She was only half joking.

He shook his head. "I'd become an alcoholic."

They were still feeling each other out, and she wanted to know where she stood with him but didn't feel able to ask outright. It was as if he was holding something back. Something crucial. Would it al-ways be like this, would she never really know this enigmatic man who had her so fully entranced?

He seemed to sense her unsettled feelings. He caught her hand and pulled on it teasingly. "We haven't seen much of Paris," he said.

"You don't have to though, there's just something about being here."

He nodded in agreement. "Next time?" he said quietly, looking at her.

"I make no promises." She paused and saw the concern on his face. "I may not emerge from the bedroom for long next time ei-ther."

He reached over and laced his fingers into the straps of her dress. "You are such a tease," he whispered.

"I'm not teasing," she replied, and her hand climbed to his upper arm and circled it, closing on his body. She was desperate to get closer, to give and take. "Zac, I want you."

Urgency raced between them. They headed for the Metro sta-tion, where the rush of warm air down the tunnel made her feel dizzy with desire; she looked at him and laughed softly as her body wa-vered in its wake.

Zac watched her with hungry, possessive eyes, his mouth braced in a tense smile.

They stood in the train, and a skinny black youth got on with a guitar, farther down the carriage. He began to sing a Bob Marley song, and Abby listened as he sang in a beautiful voice but with missing and distorted words. He had obviously memorized it but didn't speak English. She smiled up at Zac and leaned into him, putting her back against his chest. He bent down to kiss her ear.

His cock was hard against her; she pressed close to it. She moved against him to the slow rhythm of the mutant Marley song, and he growled in her ear. The barely restrained thrust of his body against hers led a tremor from her thighs to her throat. Her shoulders dropped back as her buttocks rose up inside his hips. She became suffused with a craving for his thrusts, everywhere, and turned to look at him, to show him her desire.

"I want you to fuck me hard, Zac. I want you to use me, bite me. I want you to come all over me, mark me with your touch." Her fingers rose to his mouth.

Her statement hung in the air between them. Then he closed his hands over her arms and pulled her back against him. The singer moved down the train, collecting euros from the occupants. When he got close, Zac folded two notes into his hand. He grinned at the pair of them and gave them a little swaggering bow as he moved away.

When they got off the train, Zac took her hand, and she had to speed to keep up with him. His mouth was lined in a contained smile; his eyes were dark with passion. He grabbed the keys at reception and headed for the elevator. As it glided up, they stared silently at one another across the space. There was a fierceness in his gaze as it passed over her. It made her feel weak. It was that simmering passion that she always saw in him, but it was hot and hard and close to the surface, ready to blow. He wanted to possess her; his eyes were dark with passion and promise.

His fingers closed over her wrist. Her sex clenched. She reached for his mouth, and they shared a kiss that evolved from intimacy to passion. When they broke the kiss, the elevator had stopped, and the doors were open.

Inside the room, he stood in the darkness, and the light from the corridor was swept away from her body as he shut the door behind them. The only illumination stayed in a small corridor of light from the window, which fell over the bed; they were hidden in the darkness She stood close to him and listened to the sound of her own breathing. She felt the air clinging to her lungs.

He moved toward her, and she felt his hands slide around her neck and up the back of her head. His tongue teased her lips open and pushed in to line her mouth with its probing touch. He kept her head still with his hands while he tasted her deep, and she melted at the exploration. She felt trapped, caught like a wisp that had been floating in his aura. Now he was drawing her in. Her body began to tremble.

His hands went down her neck and over her back before dividing, one to follow the line of her spine, the other to move round and explore her body from throat down to her thighs in wide sweeping movements. Her skin was a whirlpool of sensation beneath his hands, his fingers the dragnet that would capture the sensations and draw them back to his focus. She felt his skin beneath her fingers as they slid down the line of his throat and inside his shirt. Her body felt the kiss of shifting material as he dragged the close-fitting velvet up over her body, to lift it over her head. The dress dropped to the floor near her feet.

He traced patterns of movement over her naked back, and she felt a fever of longing dart out from his fingertips along her spine. He stroked her nipples, tweaked them both.

Needles of harsh stimulation raced through her.

"How hard do you want it?"

"Hard, Zac, hard. Use me."

His mouth descended to her throat. She felt the pluck as her skin was drawn into his mouth. He crept between her breasts, and her hands held his head as he sucked deeply in her cleavage, his teeth grazing her. He turned his head and passed beneath her left breast, and she felt the bite of his teeth on the skin that covered her caged heart. She responded with a sweet cry of supplication and stroked his head.

He moved her to the bed, pushing her down onto it. He ducked down between her legs, and she felt his mouth press deep into the inside of her thigh and brand her heavily where her thigh curved into her groin. She moaned and gave herself up to him. She felt his belt slide over her skin as he undid his jeans, and she began to lift her legs around his denimed hips.

She heard the rip of the condom, saw him moving, her eyes growing accustomed the gloom. He climbed over her, his erection rigid against her sensitive pussy. It was so hard and hot that her body snaked with carnal lust for it. She contracted inside. "Take me, take me," she whispered. She wanted to be consumed by the brooding force that surrounded her. She wanted to offer herself as a sacrifice on the altar of sexuality.

He thrust into her, moving her across the surface of the bed with the power of his lunge.

She climbed her legs around him, moving his erection deeper inside her between each of his thrusts, until her legs hung over his shoulders, and he seemed to thrust right through her whole body each time. His hands seemed to be all over her, claiming her.

Each thrust she rode with ecstasy, awaiting the next to lift her with its power. He'd pushed her into the patch of light on the bed, and she saw flashes of him moving in and out of it as he fucked her. He bent over her, and she folded beneath him as she felt his breath come closer, louder. His hips began to move slow and deep. She felt the swell of his cock throb against the neck of her womb, then the touch of his hand between her buttocks, circling her anus.

"Ready for more?"

"Everything," she gasped, "Use me, Zac, I'm yours."

He pulled out, stroking her juices down and into the pucker of her anus. One finger eased inside her, readying her.

Her anus twitched, opened, then clenched on the digit. It felt so large. How would she manage his massive cock there?

He circled his finger, sending wild skittering sensation through her innards. Her clit was jerking, her sex clenching itself, her body turned on to dangerous levels.

"I want every ounce of you, Abby."

She knew he was asking permission but could barely respond because her entire lower body was shuddering with sensation, and words wouldn't form. Her hands clutched at the sheets of the bed. "Please," she whispered.

She felt his cock beneath her buttocks as he lifted her with his free hand. Slowly removing his finger, he eased his cock inside her, probing into her anus, his hands firm and strong on her buttocks, lifting her entire lower body from the bed to access her back passage, pulling her buttocks apart to relax and enter her. Blistering sensation roared through her pelvis and spine as he pushed his cock deeper, inch by glorious inch, hard and determined.

She was full to capacity, strung out, her spine beading with sweat, an animal speared and made boneless for his pleasure. He ground into her, slow and deep, his teeth gritted, close to spilling. In the dim light she could see the muscles in his neck standing out, his eyes barely open as he watched her. She growled and urged him on, wanting it all, her arms flung back over her head, her hair tangled across the bed. She felt dirty and depraved, yet so true and honest—giving it all, taking it all, and loving every moment.

His cock went rigid; he shouted her name. He jerked as he came, sending tremors up her spine. Gasping, he eased her down the bed, one hand moving to her clit, stroking her quickly to a rapid orgasm.

Her whole body was suffused with heat and sparkling fireworks that flew from her pelvis. Each time she felt it would drift and ease, she was dragged in its wake to the next plateau in a blissful cycle of tiny dynamite explosions. As she drifted down and her breath moved again toward a regular pattern, she felt Zac move lightly against her clitoris with his fingers, drawing a further echo of glory from her body. She began to tremble in the aftermath.

He moved, went to the bathroom. She reached up for him when he returned, and as she did, a sob left her body without her being aware that it was coming. She felt him kiss her face, moving over its surface with his warm, firm lips.

"Hush," he murmured, and she crawled against him. She could just see the outline of his face in the darkness, the flash of reflected light on his eyes when he moved. He switched on a small light by the bedside, and she squinted, as she grew accustomed to its brightness.

"You're so beautiful, every bit of you," he whispered.

"So are you." She untied his hair, her fingers wrapped in the strong strands.

"You do know that I'm falling in love with you, don't you, Abby?"

She stared at him, her heart racing with sheer joy. *He loved her, too.* "What did you say?"

He moved to her ear and breathed it ever so quietly there. "I love you, Abigail Douglas."

She smiled. "I still can't hear you."

He gave an exasperated sigh and moved to look at her face. He looked pained, desperate. "I love you, Abby." He looked at her smile and gave a quiet laugh, his expression relaxing. "You did hear me."

She nodded and reached for him. She pulled his head close and whispered his words to him, and then added many of her own, telling him—finally telling him, how much he'd come to mean to her.

They drifted toward sleep while still kissing one another gently, a new sense of awareness between them. "I don't want to be parted from you, Zac," she said as sleep took her, but she didn't hear a reply.

thirteen

Stepping out of the shower, Abby grabbed one of the big fluffy towels from the rail and wrapped herself in it. She wiped the steam that had gathered on the mirror and combed her fingers through her hair. From the bedroom she could hear the sound of Zac's voice. The door was slightly ajar, and she smiled. He was on the phone.

She walked over to the chair near the door, where she had left her wash bag, and unzipped it. Rooting around inside for her moisturizer, she paused when part of his conversation reached her.

"I understand your position; really I do. That's why I got back to you as soon as I could." He sounded concerned. "On Monday this situation will be resolved, either way. I'm sorry, but I really need you to keep quiet about what's going on here until then."

Abby straightened up, clutching the moisturizer in her hand. Discomfort nettled its way up her spine. *Keep quiet about what's going on here?* Why did that make her feel so uncomfortable? The idea of keeping anything quiet, she supposed. There was a lot about Zac she didn't know. *I've fallen in love with a virtual stranger.* She took another step closer to the door, craning her neck to hear.

His voice had dropped, but he was talking faster.

"Don't you think I know that? It's a bloody mess. I'm sorry that I got you involved, really I am." There was a pause. She sensed that he'd stood up. "No, calm down. Okay, so you went in there for dubious reasons, but you haven't done anything that dodgy, and certainly not illegal. You're letting your feelings get the better of you. Just take it easy, and we'll talk about it on Monday." Again there was silence.

Abby clutched at her towel where it was folded over across her chest, and swallowed.

"Yes, you have to do what you think is best for you, I respect that, but if it's at all possible for you to leave it until then, I'd appreciate that."

She heard the sound of him moving, putting the phone down. Gathering herself, she darted back toward the mirror. She could see the startled expression on her own face. Her heart was racing; instinct making her wary. There was a knock at the bathroom door.

"Come in."

He walked in and stood behind her.

She busied herself applying moisturizer, her mind turning over rapidly. *Keep quiet until Monday?*

He looked as if he had the weight of the world on his shoulders. There were clearly things about him that she was unaware of, potentially unpleasant things. Could she face that? Could she face finding out that there was something about him she maybe didn't want to know, but should?

"Were you on the phone?" She tried to ask as nonchalantly as possible.

"Yes, it was a work problem, something that wouldn't wait."

She nodded. What could she say? She'd overheard his conversation and noticed it sounded suspicious?

He ran his hands into her hair, lifting it and kissing the back of her neck.

An eerie combination of arousal and discomfort ran through her. "Anything I could help you with?"

"Abby," he breathed her name and turned her toward him, his hands on her shoulders. "You help me just by being with me."

"I love you, Zac. Don't you think you should share your concerns with me?"

He gave a sad smile. "I will. Trust me. I don't want business to spoil our weekend, that's all."

She tried to shelve her doubts, but as she dressed, the questions raged on. He did seem to have a lot of money for an up-and-coming entrepreneur. He could be a Columbian drug baron for all she knew. She shook her head, chastising herself for letting her worries run her imagination ragged. She was deeply in love with him. Last night she couldn't have been happier, and yet she was so easily creeped out. It had been a hell of a week, crazy. Tom Robertson and his dodgy interest in her had made her overly suspicious. But she didn't know Zac from Adam, she had to admit that. She looked at him as he poured out coffee and drank it, his body taut and infinitely masculine as he moved.

Who are you? A desperation to know had taken root in her. Could she do as Marcy had suggested, and let it unfold in due course? *Yes, I can keep my head. That's what I'm good at.*

Her instincts told her that he had a dangerous, wild card side to him—and that was undeniably what had attracted her—but she also felt that he wasn't fundamentally bad. However, she felt a level of guardedness drawing into place. She had lost her heart, but she hadn't lost all her faculties. Then he stepped toward her, so handsome and desirable, smiling at her, reaching out for her, and suddenly she wasn't so sure.

Three sculpted marble female torsos stood in the window of the shop, exceedingly beautiful and each wearing a corset. One was a traditional Victorian garment, the second a velvet and lace affair, the third a shiny synthetic fabric, almost futuristic in design. It was like looking at a history of corsetry, and Abby was fascinated.

"Looks interesting?" Zac squeezed her against him.

She nodded.

He opened the door and ushered her inside.

Abby felt as if she'd been swept into a decadent boudoir, a place that suggested fantasies could be made real. Elegant Baroque furnishings broke up the rails of sumptuous fabrics hanging around the walls. The space might just as well have been a gallery as a shop.

A woman was working on an inner display. She set down the fabric in her hand when she heard the door chime, turning to greet them. She was slim and elegant, wearing a fitted jacket and skirt that was reminiscent of the 1940s. Cinched in at the waist, it was inset with panels that were laced and corseted into the very outline of her body. The dove-gray fabric was soft, the laces around her midriff a contrast in the finest leather cord. Her narrow heels were at least four inches high.

"Hello," Zac said when she smiled their way. *"Bonjour."*

"Bonjour. English, yes?"

Zac nodded.

The woman put out her hand. "I am Gabrielle, the proprietor. Welcome." She shook both their hands in turn, her demeanor pleasant and friendly. "Is there something in particular you are looking for, or would you like to browse?"

Zac answered her. "We're looking for a special outfit for Abby, something eye-catching."

Gabrielle smiled, her gaze quickly scanning Abby as if she was measuring her up for an outfit already. "You have the look of a fiery mistress."

"How astute," Zac commented.

Abby flashed him a warning glance but couldn't help smiling.

Gabrielle gestured with a finely manicured hand. "If I might make some suggestions?"

Abby nodded. "Yes, thank you."

Gabrielle directed Zac to a velvet-covered chair nearby and then drew Abby to the rails of clothing. It was as if they had been taken into the woman's domain, a citadel of sexually charged sophistication. She selected an outfit and hung it from a bar suspended by chains in the center of the room. It looked like something an acrobat would use in circus but suited the purpose perfectly. Abby was tickled.

The item she had selected was a black velvet dress, corseted and edged with red lace, hinting at the bordello look.

"I never wear red," Abby murmured, her hand automatically going to her hair.

"Ah, but you should, you are strong enough to match up to your hair." Gabrielle spoke with surety.

"She's right," Zac commented. "I'd love to see you in red."

His smile was so intimate, and he looked so gorgeous, draped as he was in the chair. Abby nodded. "Maybe."

"I think this might be the one," Gabrielle said as she moved down the rail. Pulling out a second garment, she hung it up alongside the first. It was a corset in black, with red flames leaping up from the bustline.

"Oh, wow." Abby was completely transfixed.

"It's made of the softest leather, so will fit like a glove." Gabrielle ran her hand down one side of the corset, then outlined the detailing with one finger. "The flames are hand dyed in the process of building the garment, and reinforced so that they rise up, just above the bustline."

There was a little bit of red where the flames leapt out of the black body, and it magnetized her gaze. "It's gorgeous."

Gabrielle smiled and turned the garment on the rail, showing the length of lacing on the back. "Would you like to try it on? A fishtail skirt in a more malleable fabric would go well and allow you a certain amount of . . . accessibility." She reached for another hanger, bringing a long, supple skirt out to hang alongside the flamed corset. "I think it would be a good outfit for you."

Abby glanced at Zac.

"I'd love to see you wearing that."

It was dramatic, so sexy. And the confirmation she saw in his eyes made her squirm with longing. "In that case, I'll try it on."

Gabrielle collected the two garments and led Abby past the rails of clothes. Pulling back a heavy curtain made of midnight velvet, she ushered Abby inside the fitting room.

Abby went to take the outfit from her.

"*Non*, please. Allow me. I'm here to dress you."

"Right, of course." Abby laughed. Gabrielle was so gentle in her guiding, she felt at ease despite the newness of the situation.

The fitting room was spacious, and all three walls were decked with mirrors straight from the Baroque age, gilt framed and massive. A tall wooden figurine with outstretched arms provided the place for Gabrielle to put the clothing.

The curtain was slightly open, and she could still see Zac. He was glancing around the place, and then his gaze retuned to her. When their eyes met, her heart leapt. *I can't help myself. I love him.*

Gabrielle assisted her in undressing, glancing in the mirror as she undid buttons. "Your lover, he likes to watch, yes?"

"Apparently so, yes." *Did she know that about him?*

"And you liked to be watched."

She said it in such a sophisticated, matter-of-fact way that Abby was inspired to do likewise. "It arouses me, yes. I cannot deny it."

"Ah, you are the perfect match for each other."

Abby smiled. She hadn't thought about it that way, but it was true. Zac caught her glance and smiled back. Her heart melted.

Gabrielle bent down to move Abby's shoes and as she did she did, she caught the curtain, pulling it open so that Zac had more of a view. "We will let him see," she said as she straightened up. "But he will think that I don't know." She stepped in front of Abby, who was now naked but for her lace panties, her eyes filled with mischief.

Abby looked again and saw a brooding prince in the chair, the man who called to her essential womanhood. He looked at her with possessive eyes. "I want you," he mouthed.

"I want you, too," she mouthed back. It was so true. She couldn't deny it, or him. Despite her doubts, he hadn't done anything to harm her; he had brought her only good things and happiness. Now they were here, and this weekend was about them. Her heart was full of him, and her sex ached to be so, too.

Lifting a large powder puff from a nearby shelf, Gabrielle dipped it into a shell-like box and proceeded to dust Abby's breasts, waist, and hips with a fine coating of talc. "You must do this, before you dress in this outfit. It will make you comfortable, and it will be easier to take the outfit off at the end of the evening."

The light touch of the puff maddened Abby's naked skin. Her breasts tingled, her nipples crinkling into peaks, her skin racing.

Zac shifted in his chair, leaning forward to rest his elbows on his knees, his loose hair falling forward.

"The outfit, is it for a private event or a party?"

"It's for a private event."

"A de Vere's party, perhaps?"

Zac had mentioned that name while they were relaxing on a riverboat cruise along the Seine, earlier that afternoon. Abby nodded. "You are either very good at guessing, or you are psychic."

"The event is held once a month, and it's tonight, it was easy to guess." Her laughter tinkled around them. "I go to the event myself."

"You will be there tonight?"

Gabrielle nodded as she helped Abby step into the skirt and swished it up and over her hips.

Abby smiled, pleased that she would know someone else there.

"It's a very sexy time, and I get to see people enjoying my designs."

"You designed these clothes yourself?"

"Many of these outfits, yes. Some of them I have imported to suit the particular fetish of my clients."

She unfolded the corset around Abby and shifted it into place. "Bend forward and drop your breasts into the molded leather cups."

Abby did so, her head turning to watch Zac in the mirror. He was riveted.

"Oh yes, a beautiful fit." Gabrielle stroked her hand over the supple material enclosing Abby's waistline, making eye contact with her in the mirror. "This is one I designed, and it is lovely to see it on so suitable a client."

"It's truly amazing."

Gabrielle was pleased with her remark, a hint of color rising on her cheeks. "It is perfect for you. Do you have heels?"

Abby nodded.

"Good, and you must wear your hair up on the crown, spilling down."

"I should be thinner," Abby said, looking at her breasts squeezing up between the flame tips with a sense of misgiving.

Gabrielle's slim eyebrows lifted in alarm. "Oh no, a corset looks best on a woman who is shapely." She began to tug in the laces, her arms flying, her concentration fully on the job.

Abby's breath caught in her throat as the leather tightened into a vicelike grip. She breathed high and shallow, then got used to the strange tightness and breathed easier.

"You are just right," she added, as she tied the laces. "As the leather warms it will fit closer still, like a second skin. The corseting will apply pressure to your womb and to your breasts, it is very arousing, yes?"

"Yes," Abby murmured as she wavered slightly, heady from the odd but stimulating sensations the leather had on her.

Gabrielle pulled the curtain fully aside and gestured for Abby to step out. As she did, she found that everything she needed to know was written on Zac's face. Awe, desire, love, and pride.

"It was made for you," he murmured, eyes shining.

She nodded, noting the bulge in his jeans. She glanced at Gabrielle. "I've got one question."

"Yes?"

"How do I put it on, later, without you to assist me?"

Gabrielle glanced at Zac with amusement. "Your lover will be there to help you. I'm sure he can manage a few laces."

Zac smiled his wolf smile. "We may never reach the party."

Inside a heartbeat, Gabrielle responded. "That's why you must start early, and with plenty of champagne."

Zac lifted Abby's jacket from her shoulders and handed it to a hovering doorman.

"*Amusez-vous bien,*" the man said as he gestured down the hallway and into the crowded area beyond.

They emerged into a club zone, humid despite the air-conditioning. The atmosphere was charged. Energizing industrial dance music and the buzz of chattering voices filled the room. A background light show spangled the place in alternating pools of color. The dance floor was thronging with scantily clad partygoers. A mezzanine bar swept up on one side, overhanging the floor at one end, like something from a sci-fi movie.

"Oh look," said Abby, laughing, "it's a yellow brick road."

He followed her nod and saw the path paved with yellow bricks that led up to the mezzanine level. "Nice touch," he agreed. He tucked his arm around her waist, drawing her up for a kiss. The leather cinched her so perfectly, he wanted to keep his hands on her, stroke her outline through the soft yet rigid containment. "Are you ready to party?"

Her eyes sparkled, assuring him that she was indeed ready. "Yes, but tell me quickly: Who is the guy rushing this way as if to talk to you?"

Zac smiled to himself. She was so canny. "Jacques de Vere, the owner. He also owns the biggest alternative venue in Paris. I let him know that I'd be interested in working with him, maybe using the new club as an overflow or associated venue, just to get it started."

Jacques, a lean type with short spiked and bleached hair, had made his way through the crowd and put his hand on Zac's shoulder in greeting, glancing over at Abby with interest. "Zac, *bienvenu*, I'm so glad you could be here with us tonight." He was dressed in black leather jeans and a tight, transparent shirt that revealed his nipples were pierced. While he talked to them, he still moved with the dance music, at one with his party.

"*Belle, très belle*," he said when Zac introduced Abby. He lifted her hand and breathed against her inner wrist, as if scenting her out. He growled, baring his teeth.

Abby chuckled. His animalistic charm made her glow. She looked regal with her hair spilling down, her leather corset and tapered skirt outlining her figure so dramatically.

"Please, allow me to show you around the play rooms." He carved a path through the dance floor, leading them on a circuit through adjacent rooms, some smaller, some just as large. In one a bevy of half-dressed women gossiped, eyeing them as they walked through.

"The play rooms will be more active later," Jacques explained. "People like to relax first, dance, have a few drinks."

Much like any other party, Zac thought to himself.

Some rooms were well-lit; others were dark caves with walls of black, soft furnishings, and ecstatic moans emerging from the hollowed recesses. Zac tried to gauge which appealed to Abby and saw her looking with interest at a room with mirrors and oddly placed chairs. It was lit with hazy purple light.

Jacques turned to them. "We don't allow any photographers or press, so you are free to relax and enjoy the surroundings without concern."

The last space they entered was adjacent to the first and boasted a large Jacuzzi with a poolside bar, where several partygoers were swimming naked while watching the dance floor beyond.

Jacques gestured at the bar and joined them for a round of tequila slammers. He told the barman they were complimentary guests for the evening, and then left them.

"Let's dance," Abby said, as soon as he'd gone.

Zac took her close against him in the crowd, and she moved against him like a sexy cat, sidling in and out of his arms, her body so seductive in its movements.

After a while she locked her arms around his neck and nodded over to one side, to where Jacques was chatting with guests. "I can't help teasing you over this, but I thought you weren't letting business intrude on this weekend." She looked at him with a half smile and a curious glance.

"We aren't. This is for you, really. I found about his side interests when I was doing research on potential audiences. He seems willing to work with me, so I took advantage of the situation by expressing curiosity about his exclusive events."

"But the fact it's part business is fun," she replied. "It adds another dimension to the experience." When she glanced at him there was a definite mischievous look in her eyes, and it made him wonder what she was up to. "A lot of the people are watching you, Zac."

"That would be because I have the most outstanding woman in the room in my arms."

"Oh no, I think there is more to it than that. They have heard that the mysterious club owner from London is entering the scene here," she whispered with such a sense of intrigue, he couldn't help laughing. Perhaps she was right. He didn't really care. He was with her. He felt strangely contented, simply proud to have her on his arm. The place was full of exotic attendees in overtly sexual clothing, but he was happy to be with Abby.

His hands rested on her waist, and she led him into the sound again, her body nestled inside his. It was arousing, their moving so in tune, as one and yet within the crowd of dancers. As other bodies moved around them he felt only touches, not people. He was aware of the crowd, but his energies poured into the woman in his arms. He wanted her. His cock was hardening.

A voice drew him back.

"Hello, Abby." Gabrielle was looking over her shoulder, her arm around another woman who, like her, was dressed in oddly retrospective corsetry. "Oh, you look so good, both of you." She nodded approvingly at the silk shirt Zac had purchased.

"Gabrielle." Abby gathered her into a hug, the three women moving into a huddle amid the dance floor.

"This is Naomi. Look, Naomi, the flames found their home."

The second woman moved around Abby's other side to check out the outfit. She spoke in French at great speed, seemingly impressed. Both women kissed her before they danced on, and it created quite an image. Abby looked regal, a timeless queen between two handmaids, but her eyes were on him as they plied her with kisses from each side.

He got her back in his arms, and the heat of arousal was coming off her in waves.

"I thought I'd lost you to the girls."

She ran her finger up the length of his fly. "What, with this on offer?"

His cock throbbed for her, solid and locked tight inside his leather pants, eager to be out and against her instead. He clasped her flame-enclosed breasts with his hands. "Do you want to go somewhere?"

She nodded.

She took his hand and led him through the throng and around the interconnecting rooms, occasionally glancing over her shoulder as if to make a note of who watched them pass by, until they reached the one with mirrors and the oddly placed chairs.

"Sit here; this chair reminded me of your Mackintosh dining chairs." She gestured at a thronelike chair.

"We come all this way, and you want me to sit in the chair that reminds you of home?" He felt like an old married husband as he said it, but she nodded and laughed with delight. An ache of love and pride in his chest threatened to buckle him.

He sat in the chair and reached for her, eager to have her body back against his. She resisted and put her hands on his shoulders and then slowly slid down to her knees in front of him. Her hands moving inch by inch down his torso to latch over his belt.

"I thought you wanted to be watched."

"We *are* being watched."

She was right; other figures moved at the far side of the room, half making love, half watching them make love. "But I thought—" His breath and his words were ripped away when her hands undid his belt, then the zipper.

240

"I never said what I wanted to be watched doing, did I? Believe me, this is turning me on in ways you can't possibly imagine. Besides, you've a reputation to build." She winked, nodded in the mirror behind him, and freed his rock-hard cock, taking it in her hand.

Glancing up, he saw Jacques de Vere reflected in the mirrors, a leggy brunette in shiny hot pants and a bikini top clinging to him like a vine. Jacques grinned and nodded when their eyes met, then pulled his woman down onto his lap as he took a seat.

Bloody hell. She was right, and she hadn't been looking around to see who was watching her, but who was watching him. He looked down at her as she knelt between his legs, holding him, so sure, so incredibly sexy. Her cheeks were glowing, her eyes so very catlike in her arousal.

"Abby . . ."

She rode her hand up and down the length of his shaft, making him clutch at the chair to ground himself. His balls were tight and high inside his pants, his spine crawling with tension.

Her fingers lifted his balls free, stroking them. She looked at him with tenderness and affection, shot through with sexual prowess.

"Abby, you don't have to do this; this was for you."

"I'm an investment advisor; I want your business to succeed. Call it instinct." She gave a delighted laugh. "Believe me, it's giving me the thrill of my life." She lowered her head to his cock, strands of her glorious red hair spilling across his leather-covered thighs, her gaze still on his as her beautiful mouth covered his throbbing crown.

His heart hammered in his chest. He was crazy about her. He felt awed by her, incredulous.

She sucked, drawing him in, her tongue rolling against the underside. Thrills rocketed through him, burrowing deep into his groin, his mind charged with the power she gave him. His cock was fit to burst. Her tongue came out, stroked the length of his cock from base to tip and back again. Her mouth was heavenly, seductive. She looked like a siren, so sexy, so desirable.

"*I want your business to succeed.*" *Her words echoed in his head, circling like demons.*

As she took him completely, riding his cock against the roof of her mouth, he shut his eyes tight. His head fell back against the headrest, his hands gripping the arms of the chair. *Abby.* In his mind, he called her name over and over again, trying to fight the demons. *Abby. So perfect and yet potentially so unattainable.* While her mouth worked its magic, controlling him totally, drawing out the essential man in him for all to see, he felt as if his heart was being pulled from his chest.

In the early morning light, Zac stirred. Abby was asleep, and he looked at her face in the pale light. He resisted the urge to kiss her and got up. He picked up the robe that lay across the end of the bed, slipped it on, walked over to the balcony, and stepped out into the still air. In the distant sky there was a suggestion of dawn. The fountain trickled below, but he could only discern its outline vaguely.

He clutched the wrought-iron railings on the balcony. What now? Abby would be leaving in a few hours. The day after tomorrow would change everything. She'd said that she loved him, that she wanted to be with him. Would she still feel the same way?

He became aware of her presence behind him before he heard her, and turned round. She tied her robe and then swept her loose hair back over her shoulder before reaching out to touch him.

"Are you OK?" She looked concerned.

He nodded.

"The sun's coming up," she whispered.

She stared at him as he moved closer to her and took her face in his hands. He kissed her, brushing his mouth over hers, savoring the feeling of her soft warmth.

"Oh, Abby, it's been amazing, but it isn't enough for me, one weekend."

She shook her head.

"I want us to share everything." He kissed her forehead and brushed his fingers through her hair. "Think about it, but if you feel the same in a few days, would you consider moving in with me? I could do with some help finishing the apartment." He added the last part quickly, covering up his concern about pushing too fast and at the wrong moment.

She stared at him, and her expression was wary, her eyes searching his. "I can't think of anything I'd like to do more, but we need to get to know each other a little better, don't we?"

Her wariness hurt, but he couldn't blame her. "Yes," he said quietly, knowing that it might never happen after Monday but wanting to feel that their relationship would continue to develop.

His hands moved to her waist, and he untied her robe. His hand went straight to her pussy, and he slid his finger into its warm groove. She gasped, and he looked into her eyes, leaning close against her.

She rested back against the railings as he pressed himself against her. He moved his face into her neck and breathed her scent deeply and then sucked her throat as if taking her into his body, never to let her leave. He could hear the pace of her breathing, feel the tension in her.

His hand rose to her throat and circled it. "Do you trust me,

Abby?" His fingers stroked her throat. "I must know that you trust me," he whispered again.

She closed her eyes. "Yes, Zac, I think I do."

"Oh, Abby, my love," he whispered. His fingers stroked her throat. She did love him, unreservedly. He believed that. The only thing he didn't know was how she would react when she found out he hadn't been completely honest with her.

fourteen | ﬞourteen

Suzanne stood in the middle of her studio apartment and put her hands on her hips, eyes narrowed with mistrust as she glared at Nathan. "You complete and utter bastard."

"Suz, please, you're wrong. It was a mistake, yes, but it isn't as bad as it sounds."

He paused, studied her expression, and groaned. Loudly. He was sitting on the edge of her bed, naked, scrubbing his hair with the heels of his hands while he tried to explain.

"Excuse me? You came on to me because you were tracking Abby for your boss, and that doesn't sound bad—how?"

"I didn't come onto you, I . . ." *Shit.* No matter how he put it, it sounded dodgy as hell. "I met you because Zac had asked me to keep an eye on her." Desperation hit him. "She's working for him, for Christ sakes, but she lied. What would you think if you were in his shoes?"

She shook her head, staring at him with a mixture of threat and defense. "No way, no way can you get away with this. Either of you."

That last statement was definitely a threat, he thought with resignation. He wished he hadn't brought it up while she was starting to get dressed for the day. There was something totally unnerving about an irate woman wearing only a bra. Being forced to confront a bunch of escaped cons seemed somehow preferable. Her face was flushed in an angry hue, eyes smarting as she gesticulated madly, her bare pussy staring at him just as accusingly as she was. The neat blonde thatch, still glistening from their earlier oral indulgences, was like a magnet to his hungry eyes. Or maybe it was easier to look down there right now than at her accusing stare.

"Look at me when I'm talking to you," she shouted. She rolled her eyes, turned away, and bent over to snatch up her matching panties, the ones that she'd dropped in horror when he'd begun his confession.

The twin globes of her gorgeous bottom filled his vision. He ached to hold her, remembering how good those buttocks felt in his hands when he lifted her onto his cock and held her tight.

She turned around.

Eyes up, eyes up.

"Bloody men," she muttered under her breath as she pulled the scrap of lace on. She threw him another disapproving glance. "You think the world revolves around you. Well, listen here, buster." She pointed at him with a condemning finger. "Abby lied because blokes can't deal with her being cleverer than they are, and she liked Zac, so she didn't want to scare him off."

"I figured it must be something like that."

"Oh yes, right, it's easy to be wise after the event." It was as if she focused on him then, rather than the situation, because her expression changed. "You know, I really thought we had something good. I thought we were building something strong here."

"We do; this isn't about us." He looked at her, hands outstretched. "Please, Suz, try to understand. I told you because I care about you, because I didn't want you to find out by chance."

She shook her head vigorously. "Oh no, don't even try with me, Nathan, right now the important thing is I get to *my friend*," her voice had lifted several decibels, "and apologize to her for bringing this to her door."

She stomped over to the wardrobe and started rooting around, hauling things out and throwing them on the floor behind her.

Dynamite comes in small packages, he reminded himself miserably, and this one had exploded big time. The fallout could be disastrous, especially if she got to Abby before Zac told her himself.

In her kitchen, Abby ran through her plans while pouring a bowl of cereal and humming along to the morning jingle on the radio. The sun was shining, she was happy. It was going to be a momentous day. She felt calm and well-prepared.

Once she got to the office, she'd have time to look through her presentation notes again before the meeting. It was really a recap, an opener for discussion on future management with Roberson and potential growth areas for the portfolio. But she wanted it to go well. She wanted to end her time at Robertson's on a high note.

The night before, on her return from Paris, she had typed and printed her resignation. After the meeting, she would see Tom and give him her formal notice—and at the end of her day, Zac was her reward. Okay, so she had to take it slowly, get to know him. But she wanted to live dangerously! It was a new life, an exciting life. One filled with possibility. Eating her cereal absentmindedly, she counted the hours until she sealed her destiny.

While she dressed, she took a moment to enjoy her own decadent smile in the mirror. How her life had changed, how much pleasure she had encountered by following her desires and being brave. Not reckless, no, but brave. She knew that now.

She opted for a classic black dress, cut long, sleeveless and simple. She wasn't much in the mood for power dressing; her power came from within. She tied her hair in a thick plait and slung it over her shoulder. After she put on her makeup, she picked up the necklace that Zac had given her. She drew it over her lips as she smiled at it, then slid it round her throat and let it kiss her skin slowly before it nestled into place.

The office was in chaos when she arrived. There was no sign of Suzanne at her desk, which probably accounted for it. That unsettled her. Apart from being unusual, she'd planned to ask Suzanne to schedule her meeting with Tom. She strode down the corridor, avoiding Ed, who got up as if to speak to her when she passed his office.

She closed the door behind her. Within a few moments, there was a knock. She sighed. She didn't really want to speak to him until she had the meeting out of the way.

Surprisingly, it was Penny who came in and clicked her stiletto heels over to the desk. She folded her arms, her tight-fitting suit riding up, her shoulders looking like evil twin humps as she stood staring at Abby with those strange gray eyes.

Abby smiled unreservedly at the spectacle of the badly fitting suit. "I'm rather busy, Penny. What is it that you want?"

Penny's mouth twitched with annoyance. "Tom has asked Eddy and me to be at this meeting, because of our earlier work on the account. I wanted to make sure you aren't going to cause any problems for us."

Abby couldn't restrain a chuckle. "Me, cause problems for you?" She swung her chair back and forth, delighting in the other woman's fear of public reprisal. "Now, Penny, you shouldn't judge other people on your own standards. That's much more the sort of thing you'd do, not I."

Penny glared at her.

"Incidentally, you're more than welcome to have Ed. I'd finished with him anyway."

Rivets of ice formed in Penny's eyes. She didn't like being called to order; it was obviously beyond her experience to be confronted so directly about her devious ways.

"What, were you expecting me to be upset?" Abby leaned forward, looking at her earnestly. "Do you really think I'd ever let you steal anything that I wanted to keep, you silly girl?"

"It wasn't like that . . ." Penny muttered, looking flustered, her voice trailing nowhere.

"Of course it wasn't . . . but if you're still trying to steal my job . . ." Abby smiled at the other woman's frozen stare. "Well, you're welcome to go for that, too; I'm handing in my resignation later today, and then I'm out of here."

Penny did a fair impression of a fish swallowing air.

"Why don't you run along now." Abby directed her toward the door with a dismissive wave of her hand.

Penny's lips tightened to a pinch. She turned on her spiky heel and stomped out of the room, slamming the door behind her.

Abby spun her chair to the window and allowed herself a brief moment of gratification before returning to the papers on the desk.

Within a couple of minutes there was another knock, and before she had time to answer it, Ed opened the door and walked in. He looked confused, rather sheepish, and truly embarrassed.

She stood up in an effort to make him feel unwelcome.

"Abby." He walked toward her. "Penny said you're intending to leave, is it because . . ." He looked so uncomfortable that she actually felt sorry for him—momentarily.

"No, Ed. It isn't because of us, you, Penny, whatever."

He didn't look convinced.

"It's time for me to move on. I want to go freelance; I have for a while. The time's right, that's all."

It was as if her words didn't quite reach him. He looked confused. She walked to the door and opened it, urging him to go out. He stood in the doorway.

"It's OK, Ed, let's just go our separate ways. We had a very flimsy relationship, and it was over anyway, wasn't it?"

He frowned. "But I thought we . . . I thought you wanted me, that we had something special."

"Excuse me?" Abby folded her arms; she was amazed. "Let me get this straight. You want me to tell you how much I need you, after discovering you with another woman?"

"Well, I . . ." A confused frown took up residence on his forehead.

"Or perhaps what you really need is to carry the guilt of my broken heart, to make you feel more of a man?" She sighed deeply, shaking her head. "I'm sorry, Ed, I'm not going to be able to give you that particular pleasure, because it would be a downright lie."

He gave her a pleading glance, clearly confused by her words. It wasn't what he had been expecting. "You're upset, I can see that."

Christ almighty. The man only saw what he wanted to see. Outright rejection was the only thing that would get rid of him now.

"Let's face it, Ed, we had sex occasionally . . . that is all it was. It was convenient, we were fuck buddies. Let it go; I did. I'm seeing someone else now." She gave him a bright smile, grabbed the door handle, and waved the door to and fro, to scoop him out.

He shuffled a couple of steps, then stopped and turned to face her. "Who are you seeing?"

She sighed again, loudly. "Ed, I don't have time for this. I have to look over my notes and get ready for this meeting." She turned away from him, looking down the corridor to make her point.

He began to speak, but Abby didn't hear him anymore, because someone familiar had caught her eye. Tom was standing in the reception area speaking with another suited man. *Zac. What is he doing here?*

Ed's voice had gone quiet. He turned to follow her gaze. "Oh, you haven't met the Ashburn client yet, have you?"

"Ashburn client?" she repeated, her heart rate climbing, her thoughts in chaos. *It can't be.* She looked at his familiar hair. It was tied back, and he was wearing shades, but it was undeniably him.

"Tom just introduced us. He's the son, name's Zachary Bordino. Apparently he recently took over from his old lady."

She looked at him, frowning. *I've been working for Zac?*

"Don't worry, Abby, he might look a bit eccentric, but he seemed sound enough. He mentioned that he thought our work with the account was excellent."

She swallowed, looked again. "He did, did he?" Her breath was catching in her throat.

"You look worried. Concentrate on the meeting; you'll be fine." He reached for her shoulder, squeezing it. "We can talk again later."

He trailed off, but Abby barely noticed; she was still riveted to the spot watching Tom introducing Zac to Penny.

As she stared at his profile in dismay he turned toward her, looking over Tom's shoulder, as if drawn by her gaze. No thoughts seemed to form in her mind, just a rush of chaotic emotions. Fear, hope, confusion, love, and pain. The confusion was overwhelming.

After the initial moment of contact finally lapsed, Zac reached for his shades, folded them into his hand, and revealed his eyes to her. He looked at her with such intensity, it sent her heart tripping and another wave of chaos through her mind.

But he was calm. *He knew.*

She felt her hand go to her face, and her breathing flew even further out of pitch. *Why the hell hadn't he said something?* Heat flared within her.

Meanwhile, Tom gestured toward her, and Zac nodded at him and then glanced back at Abby as they walked closer.

Tom was going to introduce them. She about died. Clutching at the doorframe for support, she wished the moment away.

But no, he kept getting closer, determined, immaculately presented in a charcoal suit, a black shirt and tie beneath.

"Abigail, allow me to introduce you to Zachary Bordino, the Ashburn portfolio client."

Zac reached out his hand. "I'm very glad to meet you, Abigail. We've been impressed with your work, and I came here today specifically to acknowledge that." His expression was laden with concern.

"She's our brightest rising star," Tom interjected with a smarmy, possessive smile.

Zac threw him an irritated glance.

It was a nightmare, surely? She felt as if she was on a stage and didn't know the lines. His hand was still outstretched. Reluctantly, she took it. "I'm sorry. I was expecting someone else. Adrianna?"

"Yes, you were. I am Adrianna's son. I thought it best that I attend. I've taken over my mother's business, but I didn't want to interrupt your flow of work with this information earlier." He squeezed her hand firmly, his eyes flickering secret messages to her.

Why, why didn't you tell me? Hurt, angry hurt spilled through her. This was the obstacle that she had felt between them, the secret that he had hidden. *Why?*

"Your professionalism is unquestionable. You've got my full trust." He paused to let his message sink in. "On everything you do."

He'd well and truly prepared for this, she realized with a curious sense of irony. But then he'd had the time to do so. She bloody well hadn't. Her gaze fell to his hand, which held hers so firmly, so reassuringly.

She pulled away.

Tom glanced at his watch. "Let's get some coffee before we kick off. Abby?" He put out his arm, as if to take her under his wing.

She shook her head and stepped back into her office. "I just need to go over my presentation notes. I'll join you shortly."

Zac's brow was furrowed, but then he gave a slight shake of his head—as if the situation was beyond his control—and a hopeful half smile as he walked away from her view.

She turned back into her office. Closing the door behind her, she leaned against it. Her heart was pounding; thoughts crashed against one another in her mind. What was going on? He'd known. Not only that, but he must have known all along, because he was so calm when she'd told him in Paris that she wasn't just a receptionist. He'd looked sort of gutted, as she recalled. She'd mistaken it for disbelief or a sense of wrong that she'd lied to him, but it was more than that; it was because of this, the fact that she was working for *him*. That was obvious now. But how had he known? She paced the office, her mind ticking over frantically.

She stopped, steadying herself with one hand on the edge of the desk. Of course, he would have had the staff dossier from when they first took on the Ashburn account. It was standard company policy to supply full details of all employees to new clients. They were given as much information as possible to reassure them about allowing their millions to be handed over to complete strangers. He not only had a photo of her, but he knew her whole life story. Everything. What university she went to, her personal interests, her favorite authors, what historical figures she admired.

No wonder he hadn't asked her much about her work—after that initial bout of teasing, which made much more sense now. She'd assumed it was because he didn't want to pry into that side of her life until she was ready to discuss it with him. In reality it was because he already knew it all. She remembered her early feelings of being watched. *Watched, or watched over?* Had he been observing her at first because of her work with his money—or because he hadn't trusted her after what had happened with the woman he'd wrongly trusted in the past?

She put her head into her hands and thought back to the moment she met him. He'd been delivering documents, he'd told her later as a favor to someone. Why hadn't he said whom? Her blood ran cold as she retraced the sequence of events. *I lied.*

She put her face in her hands. After what he'd been through before, it was no surprise he was wary. She remembered him saying he wondered what she was going to say next, when she'd gone to the venue that Sunday afternoon. He'd probably had notification from Tom that she was taking over the account. She would have been very fresh in his memory when she turned up at the club. He would have questioned her motives; of course he would.

"Oh fuck." He'd been the one receiving her reports, arranging to have documents signed. That's why he knew when she would call, and he was always ready to meet when she was.

Just when she thought she was sorting her life out—now this. Chaos. What on earth was she going to do? She had a sudden desire to flee the building and hide herself somewhere. *Keep your head.* She sat down and tried to rationalize her feelings.

Seconds ticked by. She stared at her PC, letting the familiar sight of the Robertson logo scrolling on the screen saver ground her.

That's when curiosity bit her. She moved her hand to the mouse, shifted it. She took a deep breath. Pulling up Google, she typed in Zac's name. First up was a link to a press release for the current art exhibition at The Hub, but it was the second link that leapt out at her, sending her into a frenzy of embarrassment.

Ashburn heir heads up new arts venture—Zachary Bordino trades in his playboy lifestyle for the art world.

Abby shut her eyes, slumped in her chair, and massaged her temples. "How the hell has this happened to me? Why didn't I know?"

She'd been blind to the truth. She'd managed to fall in love with a man without knowing the first thing about him. *That's not true.* No, it wasn't. The voice of reason just about saved her from cracking up. She knew a lot about him, enough to fall for him, just not the key link between them. But why hadn't he told her?

There was a solid knock at the door. Her head snapped up, and she stared at it; her breath drew to a halt. *Zac?*

"Come in." She said it as loud as her voice would let her, quickly grabbing the mouse to close down the Web page on her screen.

The door opened, but it wasn't Zac; it was Caroline who came in. Abby breathed again.

Seeing her hunched over the desk, Caroline came over and stood beside her. "I heard about Penny," she said. "That dirty underhanded bitch! I knew she was up to no good, but I never thought she'd stoop so low as to seduce Ed when he was still trying for you."

Caroline looked so disgusted on her behalf that Abby gave a slightly hysterical laugh. Her day was getting more surreal by the moment.

"I just knew there was something funny going on between them." She hitched her skirt up to her knees and sat on the corner of the desk, reaching out to put a reassuring hand on Abby's arm, as if she was standing by her in the face of treachery. "I did try to warn you about her. She was always jealous of you." She rolled her eyes. "Ed should have known better. Men!" She ducked down and peered at her closely. "You need to check your mascara, sweetie, it's smudged."

"Oh, thanks." Abby snatched a pocket mirror from her top drawer and rubbed away the smudges.

"Now, are you going to be OK with them being there during this meeting?"

Abby put down the mirror and gave her a dazed smile. "Thanks, Caroline. I think I'll cope with Penny and Ed." It was then that she realized they were all going to be in this meeting together. Penny, the underhanded bitch; Ed, who wanted her to be heartbroken; Tom, the leering boss; and Zac. Zac, the man she'd been working for all this time—unknowingly—while falling desperately in love with him. What a bizarre collection of personnel it would be.

She felt light-headed, slightly drunk at the prospect of standing in front of them all, speaking about the serious business of investment and return, to a bunch of onlookers with personal investments of a different kind. The financial stakes weren't the only ones to be concerned about.

"Listen," Caroline said, "I could sit in on the meeting. Tom hasn't asked me to do so specifically, but I could be there for you, for moral support."

Why not? She could certainly do with an ally. "Yes, that would be great. Thanks, Caroline, I'd appreciate it."

"Good girl, I'll be right there for you." She squared her shoulders as she stood up.

"Could you tell them I need another couple of minutes? I just need to clear my head."

Caroline nodded. "You take all the time you need, honey. Make them wait, the backstabbing bastards." And with that tender sentiment, she headed for the door.

When she reached it, she turned back. "You'll be fine, and just wait until you get a look at the client. He'll take your mind off it." She winked. "This guy is totally gorgeous." She waved her hand in front of her face to indicate his heat level.

Abby gave a weak smile and continued to stare at the door after Caroline had gone, trying to imagine herself walking out through it herself, with true confidence. As she did so, the door sprang open again, and Suzanne ran into the office, hair awry, bag clutched in her hand, her jacket done up all wrong.

"Blimey. It's like Piccadilly Circus in here," Abby mumbled to herself in disbelief.

"Abby, oh Abby, I'm so sorry." Her eyes were puffy and red. She looked as if she'd been crying.

Abby stood up, clutching at her desk for support. "What is it?"

"Nathan, he told me everything, he confessed that he only came here and met me because he wanted to find out about you, for Zac."

Abby's eyebrows shot up. "Nathan? The guy you've been seeing is *Nathan*?" She stared at Suzanne, incredulous.

"Yes." Her cheeks flamed. She looked mortified. "He came here with papers for you last week. I asked him out for a drink and, well . . . things went from there. But he's just told me this morning that he works for the other guy, Zac." She pointed at the door behind her, as if they were all standing right outside it. "And he said that Zac was worried about you lying to him, or something." She frowned, clearly confused.

"Go on," Abby urged, swallowing down her rising urge to run away. She was freaked by what Suzanne was saying, and more than a little unnerved by the way she kept pointing at the door.

"He said it didn't mean anything bad." She ruffled her hands through her hair, her eyes squeezed shut. "Damn, I wish I'd listened properly when he was trying to explain." She looked at Abby. "I walked out on him."

Behind her, the door crashed open. Abby clutched the desk and watched in disbelief as yet another person charged in. Incredibly, Nathan himself stood in the middle of her office.

"Jesus," he declared. "This place is a maze. I thought I'd never find you." He moved toward Suzanne, who immediately folded her arms across her chest defensively and turned away, lips pursed.

Abby dropped into her chair. If one more person walked into the room, she was definitely out of here. Not one hour ago she thought her life was sorted. Now it was in total chaos.

"Baby, please," Nathan pleaded with Suzanne. "Listen to me. I'll leave the job, even though Zac's been my best friend." His voice went low, then wavered high. "He saved my life for God sakes!"

"I didn't know that," Suzanne murmured, glancing back at him.

Neither did I. Abby's curiosity was up and racing, too, but this wasn't the time to hear the story.

Seeing that he'd caught her attention, Nathan reached out for Suzanne. "I'll do anything you want." He touched her shoulder.

Suzanne shrugged him off but still cocked her head to listen.

"Please understand that I care about you; I didn't mean to do any harm. I was just supposed to find out if . . ." He glanced at Abby, as if he'd noticed her presence for the first time. "Abby." He turned to her, cleared his throat, attempted to smooth his hair down and stepped forward.

For one dreadful moment she thought he was going to ask her for Suzanne's hand in marriage.

"Abby, please forgive me, and Zac; he was confused by your motives and he . . ." He glanced at Suzanne as if he thought she was about to make a run for it and he'd have to chase after her again. "He just wanted to know . . . dammit, he wanted to know what the hell you were up to!" He looked at her, a man driven by his emotions, eyebrows raised, wild-eyed, hair standing up at cross purposes.

Abby sat back in her chair and put her face in her hands. It started small then got bigger, until her whole body shuddered with laughter, release hitting her hard. Tears ran from her eyes, and she wiped them away, mindful of her mascara. When she finally got a grip, the pair of them were staring at her in concern, clearly not sure if she was laughing or crying.

"Right, I feel a whole heap better for that."

Nathan glanced at Suzanne, who shrugged.

Abby stood up. "Sorry about that; this is all a bit surreal. And I'm sorry you two have been caught up in it. Please, Suzanne, don't blame Nathan. Nathan, please don't leave your job. This confusion was *mostly* my fault for lying about my job. I'm not happy with how Zac has handled this, not *at all*, but I'll deal with him. Now, if you don't mind, I have a meeting to attend." She gathered the documents that she'd not yet looked over and staggered to the door.

"Oh, Nathan, I can't believe you came after me," she heard Suzanne whisper as she passed the pair of them.

"Just as well I recognized the boardroom from the other night; I nearly ended up in there," came his reply, with laughter.

Abby didn't even want to think about what that meant. She shut the door behind her, leaving them to each other. The corridor was mercifully silent. She took several long, slow, deep breaths. There was only one thing to do—there was only *ever* one thing for a woman like her to do—and that was to go ahead with the meeting as planned and face any unexpected problems as they came up, which she was sure they would.

"Be professional," she whispered to herself. Breathing evenly, she walked along the corridor. She wanted to show them that she could do this. She wanted to show the lot of them. No matter how many damn obstacles they cared to throw in her path.

When she reached the door she paused again, but she knew what she needed to do to get through it. This mattered. This was her telling moment.

I dare you, Abby. I dare you.

fifteen

Abby turned the door handle and entered the room, adopting as calm an expression as she could muster.

Everyone was present and already seated, except for Zac, who was standing by the window, looking down at the street with a frown. He turned when he sensed her enter, his attention immediately focused on her.

He assumed a relaxed pose, one hand in the pocket of his trousers, the other holding a copy of the agenda and accompanying documents that she had prepared for the meeting. His face, however, told a different story. He was watching her as if he could read her every thought. She had never seen him so focused; he was razor sharp.

She became aware of a voice speaking. Tom was doing a lead-in for her. Zac put his papers down on the table, walked over to her, and pulled out her chair.

"Allow me, Ms. Douglas."

"Thank you." She gave him a wry smile, taking the seat.

Zac sat down opposite her. She tried to control her erratic breathing while Tom completed his standard introductory speech.

Zac listened, but his gaze sidled over to her. His hooded lids gave him the perfect cover for subtle spying. A smile crept up on her as the thought occurred, a smile that he caught and returned. His face was so familiar. She saw him smiling at her that way in Paris, and then remembered the concern in his eyes when he had asked her to trust him, minutes ago. A shard of hurtful pain lodged in her heart. Confusion hit her hard. Her breathing flew out of pitch.

But Tom was done.

She sat forward in her seat, went into autopilot. She could hear the tremor in her own voice. She cleared her throat and began again, focusing entirely on the paperwork in front of her in order to avoid the unsettling man who watched her so closely. Her lover.

Concentrate.

Going through her summary, she covered the work done to date—intended as a hook to bait the signature for the ongoing management of the account. She had planned to open up a discussion about continued growth with suggestions on where to go from here, to involve the client. Could she really do that now, though? She felt the need to glance up but tried to avoid eye contact with Zac at first. Instead she looked toward Ed, who'd been the team leader on this work to begin with, but he was staring sheepishly at the table. When she looked at Tom, he nodded in approval, but his expression had an unwanted intimacy that made her look away. Caroline gave her a warm, supportive smile, which was some help. She was aware of Abby's discomfort, although not the true cause.

When she glanced at Zac and her eyes met his, her voice faltered again.

He leaned forward and made a remark about the figures she had quoted, encouraging her to continue. Her fingers flickered into her hair, and then she snatched up her pen, pointing to the place on her notes where she should be. He'd been acting like that all along, she realized, subtly commenting. Teasing her. Testing her. She began to speak, and then the pen trembled. She dropped it from her hand, and her fingers went to her temple. Leaving her and asking her to meet him in Paris had been the final test. Or was this the final test? Why was he testing her at all? To find out how desperately she wanted him? Her heart pounded in her ears. Bits of their conversations from the past ten days sped through her mind. Her own words had ceased to come, and then she realized Zac was speaking. He was covering her silence for her. She looked up.

He was aiming his comments at Tom. "I certainly have no complaints about the work you have done for us, particularly the remarkably informed and well-judged decisions that have been taken in the past ten days."

Tom gave a smug smile. "Abigail has demonstrated that she has the ability to carry this account forward." He gave her a wink and a smile, both of which annoyed her. "She's a top-notch investment advisor, and your account would enjoy continuing growth under her guidance."

Zac nodded, returning his attention to her, his gaze drifting over her. "It would, I agree. I've been well aware of her skills and her potential from our daily correspondence and her talented handling of our investment portfolio."

Her face heated. *When did this meeting turn into being about me?*

"Ms. Douglas is very thorough," Zac continued. "Gifted." His eyes grew darker; he was obviously thinking of something other than work.

She wanted to slap him.

He must have sensed her change of mood, because he took on a more serious expression. "Your judgments have been excellent, and we benefited greatly from your management. It was also apparent that you might have been under a lot of pressure, assuming sole control at such short notice from your boss?"

Not surprisingly, Tom frowned at that remark.

What is his point? she wondered. Zac certainly seemed to be leading the discussion in a certain direction, but she couldn't figure out where. And she couldn't avoid his direct question.

"I haven't had any real problems . . . although I have had a few unexpected issues to deal with." She sent him a stern look. She was trying to indicate her annoyance with him, but it didn't come out that way. The remark only served to remind them both of their week burning up the sheets.

His expression warmed; his mouth curled imperceptibly. Then Penny shuffled in her chair, harrumphing loudly, and both Zac and Abby turned toward her, drawn by the noise.

Penny glared at Abby with a gray-eyed warning, a tense, tight-lipped mouth.

Oh my, she thinks I'm referring to her and Ed. Abby felt a laugh coming on and turned away, trying to quell it.

Mercifully, Zac began to speak again, directing his words at Tom. "However, despite the excellent work that has been done with the foundation's investments by Ms. Douglas, I'm not planning to renew the contract with your company." An awkward silence followed.

"Might I ask why?" Tom asked cautiously.

"Of course. My mother was forced to take early retirement due to poor health; the Ashburn Foundation was her company. She wanted to pass it to me at a time when I was busy with other commitments. We needed someone to monitor the investments in the interim." He looked at Abby, letting her know this explanation was for her benefit.

She stared at him in amazement, trying to take everything in and slot it into place.

"I want to resume control of the portfolio at this point, an option my mother had written into the contract . . . with your agreement." He paused and glanced at Abby again. "I would, however, like to offer Ms. Douglas the opportunity to continue sole responsibility for the investments that she has managed so well, but under the auspices of our own organization. I would like her to return with the portfolio to our company . . . to become part of our team." He stared at Abby openly, all his cards on the table.

Her heart fluttered to a stop. She felt weak. She remembered him pouring her champagne, the day after she had traded the domain company shares in, the very day she'd proposed the property bid. He'd been celebrating with her then and having a quiet joke about it, without her knowing.

Her stomach churned; she felt shaky. The tension in the room was so focused on her that she thought she was going to crack and make a run for it. She thought her heart had stopped beating, aware that everyone in the room had fallen quiet but unable to break eye contact with Zac. He smiled at her, making an intimate connection.

Penny let out an exasperated groan.

Ed's pen fell to the table.

"Oh really, this is absurd business practice," Penny muttered, and shuffled her papers. She was sending daggers out with her angry gray eyes, jealous to the end.

Zac's eyes twinkled. He leaned back in his chair and let his hand slide to the place on his arm where Abby knew his tattoo was. A rush of feelings took her; they were the yin and yang now, this was the bed of thorns. She smiled down at the table. She breathed.

Tom blustered into the silence, his hands flickering nervously. "Your behavior is highly inappropriate, Mr. Bordino. I can't believe you have suggested such a thing." His eyes were darting about as he tried to think of the right thing to say. His expression was the most unsettled Abby had ever seen him. It made her wonder what her own expression was showing. "This is hardly the time or the place to poach my staff." He was outraged.

Zac smiled. "I could have put this suggestion to Ms. Douglas under other circumstances." He paused a second to allow her to absorb his message. "But I thought it appropriate to mention it to her now, when she has completed her current phase of work on the account and has all the options before her." He made a sweeping gesture around the table, then he turned back to Tom.

"I would also like to suggest that as Ms. Douglas has managed the investments so very well, that she is allowed to continue to have sole control. By that I mean that if she decides to take the opportunity I am offering her, that you should allow the Ashburn Foundation to remain in her control here, while she works her notice. That is, if you insist on her working notice? If she decides to leave, I would prefer her to be able to leave immediately."

Tom stared at him, completely unnerved at his client's impudence, a red flush rising over his face. "You've got bloody cheek."

Someone laughed. It was Caroline. Everyone looked at her. She subdued her expression and cleared her throat. "From a legal point of view, it's unheard of but rather refreshing that Mr. Bordino is so open with his intentions," she said. "After all, we have 'the best interests of the client's account at heart.'" She was quoting the company doctrine and ridiculing it. She looked at Zac admiringly, and then she flashed Abby a smile.

Abby wondered if she had guessed that they were already involved. She began to feel more controlled and realized it was now up to her to make the next move. "I think we should concentrate on the subject of the meeting: the review of the account as it has been handled over the past weeks."

"Hear, hear," Tom said, still frowning heavily, his ice-cool facade completely shattered.

She looked at Zac.

His eyes were at her throat, and she realized her fingers were sliding on the necklace he had given her. She paused the movement.

"As you wish." Zac looked up with a light smile, one of inquiry. He had that invitation in his eyes that made her respond without logical thought. Her body wanted to talk to his, without words. She couldn't suppress a smile.

She glanced around the table again. Caroline was watching her with open amusement. Tom was sitting back in his chair, drumming his fingers on the table, a frustrated look on his face. Ed was looking at her with a confused frown. It occurred to her then that she knew Ed so well, yet she felt so faraway from him. She really didn't know Zac at all but felt so very close to him.

Her glance fell to Penny. She looked extremely annoyed; the green-eyed monster was eating her up from the inside. It made Abby want to laugh out loud.

She'd begun to feel empowered. There was much to be said, but for now she was back in control and ready to move on. The first thing that needed to be done was to clear the decks of clutter. She began to speak, rearranging herself in her chair to resume control of the meeting.

"As we have reached the past couple of weeks in my summary of the work we have been doing, I think it would be fair to let Ed and Penny leave now. They were not involved in the recent investment decisions, and I am quite sure they have plenty to occupy themselves with elsewhere."

Caroline's hand flew to her mouth to contain the giggle that emerged.

"Right, I've had quite enough of this farce," Penny announced and stood up with a loud casting-back of her chair, wrestling her papers off the table as if it had been her decision to leave. She stomped across the room but turned back at the door. "Eddy!" she said, in a commanding voice.

He had sat unmoving, seemingly in shock at the outcome of the meeting, but at Penny's command he shuffled to his feet. He still had a confused expression on his face, and he mumbled some polite comment as he left. He didn't look at Abby again.

"Where were we?" She flicked through the pages of her report.

"Page five, second paragraph," Zac said quietly.

She looked up at him. He was so gorgeous; she wanted to climb across the table and straddle his hips right there and then. A voice in her mind whispered, *Take the dream.* Was it his voice or her own?

"Thank you," she replied, and her eyes lingered on him before returning to the pages. She saw that the next item for discussion was the property investment she had made. "Were you happy with the Irish investment?" she asked, reducing the summary to an informal discussion immediately.

"Absolutely. In the light of current vacation trends, the sort of luxury retreat you have suggested is a very sound proposition. I look forward to seeing the results."

She smiled to herself. Did he picture them sharing the experience, exploring the romantic getaway together just as she had? A thrill of anticipation shot through her.

"I am not so sure," Tom said, annoyance at the turn of events making him touchy. "People like to get away to the sun for a break." He was preparing for a squabble.

"You can't get a suntan on the moon, but I wouldn't mind a holiday there," Zac retorted, laughing quietly. It occurred to Abby then how amusing Ed's description of Zac as "eccentric" was, and she smiled to herself.

"Anyway, the trend is increasingly away from package holidays to more varied, short weekend breaks." His words cut Tom off before he really began. "This sort of investment will function all year round, offering cozy, snow-filled winter weekends and lazy beach holidays in the summer." He was looking into Abby's eyes.

She let him in.

He lingered there.

"In a word?" he said, quietly.

"Heavenly," she murmured.

Tom mumbled something incoherent and then gave up the fight.

Zac turned back to him. "If you aren't interested in the finite details of this particular aspect of the investment portfolio, perhaps you wish to pursue something else?" He was shedding the others, taking up where she had left off.

She moved on his words immediately. "Yes. Perhaps we should go over the more detailed analysis of restoration proposals, and so on." She looked at Zac. "In my office?"

He nodded and stood up immediately, closing the meeting with his movement.

Caroline leaned back in her chair and winked at Abby, who smiled at her in appreciation. It had been nice to have the other woman's support during the meeting, and she wondered again how much of the true situation Carolyn had guessed. Tom was mumbling as he got up and stomped out of the room. Zac stood and held the door open, watching Abby as she lifted her papers and walked over to join him.

"Would you like to follow me?" Abby said, as she led him from the room.

"With pleasure," Zac replied and bowed his head close to her as she passed. He followed her down the corridor. When they got closer to her office, she could see that the door stood open, and it was empty of other people, thank God. She glanced back at him and paused at the doorway, waiting until he had stopped beside her.

She loved him, but if she paused to think about all that had happened, confusion swamped her. Could they truly have a future together?

Zac followed her in and closed the door behind them. He had seen every tiny reaction pass over her, felt her every change of mood. Each expression of shock and indignation hurt him that bit more, each hint of tenderness like a gift of hope. He waited to hear what she was going to say, giving her the chance to begin.

She folded her arms emphatically, her papers still clutched in one hand. "I should never speak to you again after what you just put me through." She glared at him defiantly and waited for his response.

"I thought you handled it very well," he replied after a moment, deadly serious.

She glanced at him with a warning glint in her eyes, but he wasn't teasing her now. He had orchestrated the morning's events. Now it was her turn. They stood motionless a moment, captured in time by their conjunction, their destiny.

"You kept your head while all around you people were losing theirs," he added.

"I'm flattered that you were listening to my ramblings." Her expression was controlled, but he could see that her arms were tense across her chest. She was mad at him, and he understood why.

"Of course I listened. I've listened to you all along."

"You deliberately misled me; you didn't trust me." She stared at him, the hurt obvious in her eyes.

"I admit that, and I'm sorry. But you soon showed me how very wrong I was."

"It was because I lied about being a receptionist, wasn't it? And because you'd been hurt before?"

He nodded. "Once I realized my error, I had to find a way out of the pit I'd dug myself into. I love you, Abby. I had to find the right way to handle this situation."

She looked poised, and yet she awaited his explanation. He wanted to take her into his arms but restrained himself.

"The best I could do for you was to show you how much I love you and let you do what you do so well. You told me how important it was for you to remain professional. I wanted to let you do that, but I was there for you, every step of the way."

"I know you were, and I appreciate that. But why didn't you tell me I was working for you?"

"At first I thought, why complicate things? Then I realized something more important, that I wanted us to negotiate our relationship on our own terms, not those forced on us by our circumstances. When I invited you to Paris, it was because I wanted us to be alone, to be ourselves."

"But you knew. You had me at a disadvantage."

He shrugged. "That was no easy thing to carry, believe me. This last week has been hell for me, trying to decide what would be best for you. I've wanted to tell you every second of every day, but once I felt I understood you, I realized how important your work is to you, and I didn't want to step in the way of your professionalism. In the end I decided to walk the line, to let you do your job and to try to show you how I felt in a way that you would remember after this strange moment in time has passed."

"When did you know? Did you already know, when you came here with the courier package?"

"No, not until after that. When I gave you my card, I didn't know. I wanted to know you, the woman; that was my only motivation. After that, things got complicated."

"You knew when I came to The Hub."

"Yes, by then I'd taken over my mother's investment portfolio. When you came to The Hub I tried really hard to resist getting involved." He shrugged. "I couldn't."

She stared at him, listening. Then she frowned. "I feel as if I should've known."

"Why, you could never have guessed. This was no one's fault; it just happened. *We* just happened. But *we* were meant to."

She nodded, silent as she took in his words.

He never tired of looking at her, eating her up with his eyes. "It doesn't matter how we met, or what our jobs are. We are meant to be together. We're perfect for one another."

"You were at the auction, at Fitzsimmons, weren't you?"

He stared at her, shocked that she'd seen him. "Yes. I'm sorry. I had to know what happened before I left for Paris. I wanted you to get the place so badly. The night before, we . . ." He remembered their passion, and he ached for her.

She nodded when his words trailed away. "I know. The castle became special. The whole time I was working on buying that property, I was thinking of you, of being there with you."

Relief hit him and hit him hard. He needed to know. "Did you mean what you said in Paris? Do you still feel the same?"

"I did. I love you, Zac, you know that. But this is a lot for me to take in. You were demanding a level of trust that might have been beyond me."

"Might have?"

"Might have." A tinge of amusement warmed her expression.

He felt the barriers between them falling away, and his chest filled with emotion. "Where do we go from here?"

She turned away from him slowly.

"Tell me about this job," she said carefully.

Hope had him firmly in its grip. She hadn't thrown him out, screamed, or accused him of all sorts of dishonest activities. But then she wouldn't, would she, logic said, she'd keep her head. God, he loved her.

She wandered farther into the office and shifted something on her desk, making room so she could sit on the edge of it.

He looked around the space, taking her other life into his consciousness. They still had so much more to learn about each other; it was going to be so very good. He began to walk in her path.

"I would want you to take full responsibility for all matters relating to the Ashburn account. You would be independent; I'm quite aware that you need that." He paused significantly and looked at her.

"You may even want to work from your own company, as a consultant for us."

Her eyes glistened softly. That meant a lot to her; he knew it would. "Go on."

He reached into his pocket to pull out some papers.

"A draft contract for your perusal." He moved closer to her. His eyes roamed her body, and he held the folded sheets out to her.

"You've taken a lot for granted." She arched her eyebrow at him, but a gentle smile lifted the corners of her beautiful mouth.

He wanted to kiss her, to take her in his arms. "No," he said, his expression serious. "But I like to have every eventually covered." He reached down to kiss her gently on the lips.

She leaned up to meet the kiss, as hungry as ever for him.

He pulled away after a moment and reached into his pocket again. "However, I have taken the liberty of booking us a flight to Ireland next weekend. I thought you might like to come and look over this property I recently acquired?"

"You've got bloody cheek, Zachary Bordino." Her eyes flashed at him, and her hand rose as if to slap him.

He stood his ground and waited for her hand to fall, but it paused before it touched him and slowed its pace to stroke across his face instead. Then it slid down to his jaw, and her thumb rested on his lips.

He was hers, and she still wanted to have him. Life was worth living.

"Zac," she whispered, calling him to her.

He smiled and covered her hand with his.

"Here, I'm right here, my love," he murmured. Then he closed on her and kissed her deeply.

She stood against him and slid her hands inside his jacket, running them over his chest and up his back.

He flexed under her touch, responding to her readily.

"What about working my notice?" Her eyes twinkled suggestively. She was thinking what he was thinking; he could tell.

"We could try to get you fired. I'm sure there's something in your contract about not having sex with the clients."

"True." Her hands moved down and closed over the taut line of his buttocks as he reached down and drew the material of her dress up with his hands.

"But maybe we should do it right here, now, just to be sure." The skirt swished up over her legs, and he slid his hand under it to stroke the back of her thigh and caress its inner softness.

She smiled, pressed her hips into him, and dropped her head back, looking into his eyes. "If I do accept the contract you're offering, I would want lots of extras with the job." Her hand embraced his erection.

"I could have it written into your contract."

Her beautiful cat's eyes were burning from the inside, her breath hot on his face. She caressed his cock through his pants, and it swelled readily against her hand. She reached up and untied his hair. "That's OK," she said, lying back on the desk and pulling him over her. "I think I can trust you."

epilogue | epilogue

SIX MONTHS LATER

Abby wiped the steam off the mirror and peered at herself. Her skin was glowing, her eyes bright. The pure Irish air had done her good, even if it was brisk and fresh to the point of icy at this time of year. The seasonal beauty was even more mesmerizing than she had dreamed, the roaring skies overhead, the smell of smoke from peat fires wisping across the rolling landscape from the distant cottages, the joy of drinking hot toddies in the local pub after a windswept walk on the shore.

She shrugged on her robe and glanced around the bathroom, smiling, as she tied it. The furnishings were superb, beyond her wildest hopes for the restoration. She noticed that the bathroom was some-what reminiscent of the hotel they stayed at in Paris, but maybe that was her subconscious intention. She had put a very personal stamp on features like this when she'd got together with the interior de-signer they hired for the project.

The suite was another fine salon in style, breathtakingly decorated in luxurious fabrics, but it was the bathroom in particular that reflected the surrounding landscape so that it was very personal to the building and its location. Large moss-colored marble titles covered the walls and floor, where an ornate bathtub was sunk beneath soft, hazy spotlights. The inset tiles around the tub were the colors of the sea where it merged into the rich, mottled greens of the land. Under the hazy light from the sunken spots, it was a treasure trove, a cave of sensuality. After a day spent walking on the shore, stepping into the shower and all this gorgeous color was perfect, a union between the land, the sea, and the house.

"They've done so well with the bathroom," she called out.

"I think we should keep this suite for ourselves," Zac replied from the bedroom.

She couldn't help chuckling. It was the only part of the restoration that was fully complete. He'd insisted on it so they could be here at this time of year, when snow was expected. "This is the show suite, and you'll never make any money if you want to keep everything for us."

"Let's have less of the investment manager advice and more about taking time for the important things in life, please!"

She heard the phone ringing and then his voice speaking as he answered it.

She shook out her hair, pulling it as straight as she could before it dried. By the time she rejoined him in the bedroom, he was nearing the end of his conversation and laughing into the phone.

He looked like the lord of the manor, so darkly handsome, dressed in a black robe and laid out on the many pillows and cushions on the big white bed, and so he should. Her dark prince.

She walked over to the window and once again admired the fabulous view, while he completed his call.

After he put the phone down, he sauntered over and joined her, standing behind her and nestling her in against his warm body. Together they looked out across the grounds at the beautiful shoreline. On the other side of the castle, the view was of rolling fields, miles and miles of lush countryside. It was so different from their vibrant city life—now divided between Paris and London, until Pharamonds was up and running—and it was such a perfect extreme. Like the ebb and flow of the tide, they tuned in to each and every difference, enjoying it together.

He kissed her ear. "Happy?" he whispered.

"Oh yes."

"That was Suzanne."

"Problems?"

"Nothing she can't handle." He chuckled softly. "She's dealing with that pretentious artist with true panache, by the sounds of it. She's a dynamo PR guru."

Abby smiled. "I'm so pleased. She loves it, too."

"She said to tell you she bumped into Caroline on the tube yesterday."

Abby turned to face him, looking up at him with curiosity, her hands linked around his neck. "Oh yes, and did she say how she is?"

Zac nodded. "Says working at Robertson's is 'doing her head in.' Now that you and Suzanne have gone, there's no one with a sense of humor anymore. I think we should try to poach her." He grinned, but she knew he was serious.

"Don't you think you've poached enough of Tom Robertson's staff already?"

"I poached enough of his staff when I got you, my love." He kissed the end of her nose. "The rest is just a bonus. It serves him right for coveting *my woman*."

She loved the way he said "my woman." She pulled him down for a kiss.

"Besides," he said as they separated. "Now that poor old George has announced his retirement, we will need someone to deal with all the legal stuff for us. He'll soon be off doing tai chi with my mother; I can just picture it."

She smiled; it was quite a picture. "If that's the case, and Caroline is unhappy, I could speak to her when we get home, let her know about the opportunity. Then it's up to her if she wants to go for it."

"That's decided then." He put his hand inside her robe, caressing her breast gently. "Now come back to bed." He attempted to move her away from the window, but she laughed and glanced over his shoulder as he spun her round in his arms.

As she did, something caught her eye. The sky was laden with thick clouds rolling in from the sea, flurries of snowflakes drifting down from it. "Zac!" She gestured at the window. "Look, it's snowing! Our snow-filled beach."

He glanced over but opened his robe, nestling in against her warm body. "The snow can wait."

She wriggled in his arms, looking out once more at the view. "But, Zac, I'm curious. I want to know what happens now. Does it melt into the sea? Does it sit on the sand?"

He dropped his robe off, pushing hers from her shoulders as well. "I love your inquisitive mind, but the snow can wait for just a little while. I've opened champagne. I want to make love to you."

She smiled affectionately; he could indeed distract her from anything, including snow on a beach.

"Besides, I've got something I need to ask you."

"What is it?"

He bent and lifted her, carrying her to the bed. Resting her down against the pillows, he climbed between her thighs, easing them open. His cock was hard against her mons, drawing her attention away from just about everything in the world, apart from him and the way they molded together so perfectly, in every way.

"Do you love me?"

She gave a breathy laugh. "Is that what you wanted to ask me?"

"No, but I wanted to hear you say it again."

"I thought you'd be bored with hearing it by now," she commented.

"Never." His eyes were filled with longing.

"I love you, Zac, always will."

He pushed his hand under the pillow and brought out a ring, which he turned between finger and thumb, catching the light with the diamonds. "In that case, will you marry me, Abigail Douglas?"

"Zac!" Her heart swelled with pleasure. She pulled his head down and kissed him, her body clinging to his.

"Hey." He pulled back, denying her the kiss. "Don't avoid the question. Will you marry me?"

She put one finger on the end of her chin and looked away with mock concentration. "Well, now, I don't know."

He growled, pinned her arms to the bed, and nudged her face with his, forcing her to look at him. "I dare you to say yes. In fact I *double dare* you."

She gave a happy sigh. "Yes, Zac. Dare or no dare. I will marry you."